'From the ominous and shocking beginning to the heart-pounding ending, *Expectant* had me in its grasp ... It was great to be back in Sam's world again ... an every-woman, witty, clever, hilarious, vulnerable and so extremely relatable ... I'm fully invested in her' Nikki Crutchley

'It is Symon's copper Sam, self-deprecating and very human, who represents the writer's real achievement' *Guardian*

'New Zealand's answer to Siobhan Clarke' *The Times*

'Atmospheric, emotional and gripping' *Foreword Reviews*

'Reads like the polished effort of a genre veteran. More, please' *Booklist*

'An absolute must-have' *Daily Express*

'A deeply involving novel and a damn good thriller' *NB Magazine*

'Real verve and personality ... Excellent storytelling from an author who goes from strength to strength' *Mystery Magazine*

'Chillingly intense with a finely honed sense of place' Craig Robertson

'Powerful, coolly assured, and an absolute belter of a read' LoveReading

'Symon's talent for creating well-rounded characters permeates throughout' *Crime Watch*

'With a twisty plot, a protagonist who shines and beautifully written observations of the cruellest things, this is crime fiction at its best' *Kiwi Crime*

'Loving this series more with every book and fans are going to just eat this one up. Welcome back Sam (and Vanda). Definitely recommended' Jen Med's Book Reviews

'I do really love this series – it's always a treat. A good, gripping crime series with excellent characters' Independent Book Reviews

Other titles by Vanda Symon available from Orenda Books:

PREY

Vanda Symon

**ORENDA
BOOKS**

Orenda Books
16 Carson Road
West Dulwich
London SE21 8HU
www.orendabooks.co.uk

First published in the United Kingdom by Orenda Books, 2024
Copyright © Vanda Symon, 2024

Quote on page 21 from 'Sunday Afternoon at Two O'clock' by Janet Frame,
© Janet Frame, 1967. Reproduced with the kind permission of
Janet Frame Literary Trust.

A catalogue record for this book is available from the British Library.

ISBN 978-1-916788-22-0
eISBN 978-1-916788-23-7

Printed and bound by Clays Ltd, Elcograf S.p.A

For sales and distribution, please contact *info@orendabooks.co.uk* or visit
www.orendabooks.co.uk.

To Louie, the coolest of cats.

PROLOGUE

The rain pelted against her coat, the sound deafening against the hood pulled down over her head. Sharp, cold needles hitting the exposed skin of her face. She pulled the hood tighter and dashed back across Harrop Street and up the first flight of steps that rose towards the entrance to the cathedral. The brooding dark skies emphasised the harshness of the grey stone, and the church, whose interior had been so warm and welcoming just minutes before, took on a menacing stance, its Gothic bulk towering over The Octagon before it. As she raised her foot to start the ascent up the next flight of stairs two figures emerged from the cathedral's doors. Something about the way they moved sent a prickle of caution up her spine, and she slipped back behind a plinth. Even in the poor evening light and wrapped in coats there had been no mistaking who they were. Memory of the conversation she'd just endured cut through her mind, the shock and distress washing back over her in a wave that left her breathless. She turned and crept back down toward the street; there was no way she was going to risk a replay. Yet curiosity began to overcome fear. She paused, took a deep breath and returned to her vantage point, edging her head around the corner just enough to get a glimpse of the scene playing out above yet remain unseen. She needn't have worried about being observed, as judging by the gestures and back and forth of words the figures above her were too engrossed in their heated debate to notice. Despite pulling the sides of her hood back behind her ears, closing her eyes and straining to hear, the voices didn't carry over the thrum of the rain. She could only imagine what was being said, but she hoped the words spoken earlier were being challenged and recriminated against, that at least someone was defending her.

She watched as the pair gradually descended the first flight of stairs to the landing, then edged over towards the side of the cathedral and the steps down to the side path. They had lost any shelter the arched entranceway afforded and were exposed to the full onslaught of the elements, but this seemed not to trouble them, as they paused at the edge of the landing, leaning towards each other, fingers pointing, accusing. One reached out to grab an arm but was angrily shaken off. Freed, the other person turned to descend the stairs, but before they could, the hand reached out again, this time to grab at their shoulder. They spun around, and this time as well as knocking away the arm, they leapt back up to the landing and delivered a blow to the stomach. The man looked down to where he had been struck, then back up into the face of his assailant, before reaching up and grabbing them by both shoulders. The pair began to spin in some twisted sort of waltz, turning and turning, *one, two, three*, until they reached the edge of the stairs. His back to the void, gravity pulling and fate pushing, the man fell, arms uselessly helicoptering, trying to halt the inevitable as he tumbled, tumbled down the flight to his oblivion.

CHAPTER 1

This red-letter day had come around way quicker than I was mentally prepared for, and for some absurd reason I felt the small flutter of butterflies in my stomach as I approached the CIB room. Thank Christ it was empty. I was relieved, because it gave me opportunity to claim my spot and settle in without fuss, but still, a little part of me would have liked a cheery welcome back and a high five or two.

Six months on maternity leave and some things hadn't changed. The carpet was still ugly and no one had managed to banish the stain where Smithy had spilled the entire contents of a bottle of Worcestershire sauce several years ago. That probably contributed to the slightly funky smell of the place, along with Otto's running shoes, which were stashed under his desk in a gym bag that pre-dated the Bee Gees and hadn't been washed since then either. Oddly, both of those things were comforting. What wasn't so comforting was the sight of my allocated desk, looking bare and forlorn, tucked into the far corner. Johnny's iconic words from *Dirty Dancing* jumped to mind, but no one was going to come jiving to my rescue and whisk me centre stage for a swan dive. And to be perfectly honest, I didn't want centre stage. I preferred the 'sidle in and try not to get noticed' option for my return to work, in the hope that no one was reminded about the rather dramatic antics around my departure six months ago, and that those memories didn't turn that swan dive into a swan song.

I dropped the repurposed box for A4 paper that housed my belongings onto the desk. Then I couldn't resist immediately playing with the electric stand/sit controller. The desk surface rose up, the desk surface dropped down – then up and down once more for good measure. That itch scratched, I pulled out of the box the ponytail palm that had survived six months at home under my care and placed it on the front-right corner, creating a definitive border to my realm, and hopefully providing a visual reminder to prevent my annoying habit of taking my hip out on the edge of the desk. I wasn't known for my gracefulness and ability to negotiate furniture. And the presence of the plant immediately made the place feel friendlier.

Next, I pulled out my *World's Most Average Mum* mug, a gift from my charming partner, and the packet of Dilmah teabags I'd purchased specially for the occasion. Call me a tea snob, but I wasn't about to drink the rubbish they provided in the kitchenette; some standards had to be maintained. I opened my drawer to tidy them away and smiled at the sight of a bag of Whittaker's Hokey Pokey mini bars greeting me, a present from Sonia, no doubt. Bless her. She understood that every girl needed an emergency chocolate supply.

The next things out of the box were my pencil case – I wasn't prepared to risk a stationery emergency, and my lunchbox. The whole lunch thing gave me a chuckle. Paul had insisted on making it for me this morning, but said I wasn't allowed to open it until I got to work. Partly because he didn't trust me not to channel my inner Hobbit and eat lunch as second breakfast, and partly because he took great delight in creating surprises for me. It was one of his more endearing qualities, and as it meant I didn't have to get anything else organised on top of myself and the kid this morning I'd been happy to indulge him. I popped open the lid on the kitsch *Frozen*-themed tin, a gift from Maggie, and clapped happily at the items before me. There was an egg sandwich, cut in half diagonally and with what looked like a ridiculously large, yet perfect egg to bread ratio. There were even bits of chive in evidence. Awesome. An obligatory apple nestled into the triangular space next to the stacked sammies. I laughed at the cupcake clearly purchased on the sly from New World. On my last day of work before maternity leave when I was looking rather rotund he'd sidled a pig cupcake into my lunchbox. This one was a cow. Cheeky bastard. That reminded me – I reached into the box and pulled out the breast pump. I hadn't quite figured out where I was going to sneak off to for some privacy to relieve the inevitable boulder boobs later in the day. Hopefully the family room would be free when the need arose. Even thinking about it caused that unsettling tingling feeling in my breasts, where I wasn't sure whether the contents would remain on the inside or whether the breast pads were going to prove their worth. The natural progression of that train of thought was wondering how the wee poppet was getting on without me. In an attempt to make the transition back to work as easy as possible for everyone concerned, Paul had taken this week off to be with Amelia before she started at daycare next week. We'd see how the whole 'Mumma isn't there' thing and the 'bottle and breast pumping' thing went, and if worst came to worst he could bring her down to the station for a feed. Part of me was hoping for the latter, because to be honest, I was missing her already, and it wasn't even 9.00am yet.

This wasn't going to be easy.

CHAPTER 2

It must have been a slow day on the crime front, which was always a good thing. The morning briefing lived up to its name for a change and was brief. All of the ongoing investigations and operations were drug related – the constant battle to keep the scourge of society that was crystal meth, or P, off the streets; dealing with outbreaks of violence between rival gangs – the kind of background crime that the majority of Dunedin's population went about their lives being oblivious to. For us it was a fine balancing act between operating under the general public's radar yet making them feel safe, while being in the faces of those that caused the problems. It made me very glad I wasn't normally involved in the day-to-day of the narcotics division.

The most gratifying thing about the briefing was the waves and smiles and hugs from people who seemed pleased to see me back. It washed away some of my anxiety about returning to work. Not all of it though. DI Johns, aka The Boss, or as I fondly referred to him, Dickhead Johns, had a penchant for singling me out for some extra-special attention. I had hoped that time would make his heart grow fonder, and it was looking promising so far. I had gone for the inconspicuous approach, positioning myself as far towards the back as possible and next to Smithy, whose bulk overshadowed mine. The Boss was winding things up and people had started to make heading-off movements, and part of me fist-pumped on the inside – I'd made it past the first hurdle.

I should have known better.

With the dramatic timing he was renowned for, DI Johns announced very loudly across the room, just as everyone was starting to move, 'Ah, Shephard. You decided to come back and join us?'

Everyone froze, including me.

Heads turned my way.
I could feel my face heating up.
'I'd like to see you in my office, now.'
I felt like a possum in the headlights.
Damn.

⁂

'It's good to see you.'
We both knew he was lying.
'It's good to be back.'
Ditto.
But then, that wasn't a total lie. Having been fully immersed in motherhood for months a part of me was desperate to reclaim my professional persona and carve out some time for myself. Jury was still out on the remaining part.
'How is the baby?'
I didn't know whether he'd just forgotten her name or hadn't bothered to learn it in the first place. I suspected the latter. I gave him some credit for asking about her welfare though.
'Amelia is doing really well and growing up fast, thank you. That six months flew by much too quickly.'
I had brought her into work on a number of occasions to introduce her to the staff and so she could get a bonus hello and cuddle with Dad. Hadn't gone out of my way to show her to The Boss though. I didn't think he'd be a 'goo and gah over a baby' kind of a guy. He probably didn't even goo and gah over his own kids. I stopped that train of thought straight away. Just because he was a grumpy, arrogant, misogynistic piece of work on the job didn't necessarily mean he was like that at home. He might have medals for being husband and dad of the year at home, although I highly doubted it.
'Well, now that you're back on board I expect you to settle straight back into your work. We can't afford for you to be less than one-hundred-percent effort, we're too stretched for staff.'

That augured well for a family-friendly work environment and easing back into the job. Sitting in a chair opposite Dickhead Johns was never a comfortable experience, even with a metre and a half of desk between us. I hadn't missed our special little tête-à-têtes at all. There must have been an actual point to all of this, though, so I pushed the conversation forward so he wouldn't have further opportunity to make me regret coming back to the job.

'What was it you wished to speak with me about?'

He drummed his fingertips together and seemed almost hesitant. Not a response I was familiar with from him.

'Everyone else on the team is tied up with ongoing operations that don't need your assistance in their current stages.' How to make a girl feel welcome. 'So I'm going to put you in charge of an investigation of your own.'

I felt my eyebrows shoot up. Wasn't expecting that. In times past The Boss had always given me the crap jobs and ensured that I was completely aware of my place in the hierarchy. His personal, and frankly obstructive, input into my career had started before I'd even moved to Dunedin, when he'd made it quite clear he didn't approve of my inclusion in the detective training programme. We hadn't got off on the right foot back in my Mataura days, probably starting when I threw up on his shoes, and ever since I'd felt I was on a hiding to nothing with this man. He certainly had never offered me a lead role before, or anything even close. There had to be a catch.

'It will help you get back into the swing of things.'

'Thank you.' The suspicion may have snuck into my voice.

He pushed a file box to the front of his desk. I hadn't seen a bona fide cardboard file box for a case in years. Documentation was digitised nowadays. Policing didn't involve as much paper as it used to, and hard copies were only used for specific purposes. I leaned forward and dragged it onto my lap. It was a hefty wee number.

'In 1999 the Reverend Mark Freeman's body was found at the

bottom of the stairs of St Paul's Cathedral in The Octagon. The postmortem revealed he had a knife wound to his abdomen, but that alone would not have been enough to kill him. Cause of death was injuries sustained from falling down the cathedral steps. He broke his neck. An exhaustive and frustrating investigation was undertaken at the time. It continued for years, but no one was arrested for his murder.'

Great, a cold case. That was the catch. I knew it was too good to be true. Cold cases were only given to those officers that people wanted to keep out of the way of investigations because they were either a pain in the arse, deemed incompetent, or an embarrassment. Or in my case, all three. But they were always pitched as a 'you'll be doing us a favour if you can figure it out – no one else has been able to crack it – we have faith in you' enterprise. At least I now knew where I stood.

'It is one of the very few unsolved murder cases in Dunedin history, and the fact it remains unresolved is a major source of frustration for me.' The way he said it suggested a personal interest. I did the maths, twenty-five years ago. Johns would have been in his late twenties. I wondered if he was hell on wheels to work with back then too or was just serving his apprenticeship in being a prick.

'You were involved in the investigation?'

'I was a detective constable at that time, so was not in charge of the investigation, but yes, I was involved in doing a lot of the leg work. As you can imagine, with a case involving a highly esteemed member of the clergy there was a lot of pressure to find out who the killer was, both politically and from the community.'

That explained the personal connection.

'The case made headlines nationally and internationally, so the fact that it remained unsolved did not sit well with those in the police hierarchy or with local government, and certainly not in the Church. And of course it grated with all of us who had been involved in the investigation. Your return is an opportunity to re-examine it with fresh eyes, get some closure, so I'm reopening the investigation.'

I didn't need to look up from the page I was glancing over to know that expectation and pressure would be written all over his face. Even worse was the dawning realisation I was probably going to have to consult back and forth with him on details or for clarification. The thought of working closely with The Boss did not appeal in any shape or form, and I was pretty sure the feeling was mutual. I wondered if he'd considered that prospect before saddling me with the one that got away? If he'd thought it through, surely he'd have realised that he was going to have to swallow some major pride if I achieved what they didn't twenty-five years ago and solved the sucker. And if I found anything lacking in the way the case had been handled, or if I found any errors on the part of the investigating officers then I could very well point the finger at him. Grim experience told me he wasn't one to take kindly to anybody questioning his abilities.

'What resources will I have?'

'Everyone else is tied up in active cases, so it will just be your time. Although, if you do require an additional pair of hands you may be able to call on the services of Detective Constable Richardson if she's available.' Sonia was good to work with and very capable, and I should have been grateful for the opportunity of her assistance, but I couldn't help but think he'd put the two young women together on purpose, that misogyny had a role to play here. Perhaps I had become too cynical when it came to questioning his motives.

'Is there anything that I need to know about this case?'

'What do you mean?'

'Is there anything in particular from your earlier experience that I need to be mindful of? Any conflicts of interest, any timing issues? And why re-open the investigation now?'

He drew his hands up to his face, palms together as in prayer, fingers resting against his lips.

'Any investigation that involves working around the Church needs careful tact and consideration.'

Implying I didn't have any.

'It's twenty-five years now that this case has been weighing on my mind. That's not the kind of anniversary you want to celebrate.'

Fair enough.

He gave a large sigh, and what was probably the closest I'd ever seen to a wave of true emotion crossed his face.

'The Reverend Mark Freeman was my wife's father.'

Fuck.

CHAPTER 3

How the hell was I going to handle this one? I plonked into my chair and cupped my head in my hands. Suddenly the thought of tracking down meth-cook scum of the earth didn't sound so bad after all.

The Boss had dropped one heck of a bombshell. A myriad of thoughts had swirled through my brain as I made the slow walk back to the office. The first had been, how on earth was I going to stop him interfering in the case that was so close to home and in which he had such a massive conflict of interest? That was going to take some extra-special tact and management on my part, and frankly I didn't know if I was up for it. The second thought had been how had he been allowed to work on the case in the first place if he'd been in a relationship with the victim's daughter? That would have been an even bigger conflict of interest and dodgy as hell. Those sorts of things weren't as frowned upon back in the day as they were now, but still. Then it had dawned on me that of course Felicity must have been his second wife. He'd referred to Mark Freeman as 'my wife's father' rather than 'father-in-law', which implied a degree of separation and that they didn't have a personal bond. He may never have even met him, other than knowing him as the deceased, a victim of a crime in a case he had worked on in his murky past. A quick chat with Smithy would be able to confirm The Boss's marital history. Detective Malcolm Smith wasn't a gossip, but he had the ability to absorb information from what might seem innocuous sources and come to light with it at the appropriate time. It was one of the skills that made him a good detective. It also meant you had to be a little careful what you divulged if you didn't want a secret or an element of your life revealed at a later date. To his credit Smithy used it only where appropriate. He'd always taught me to use your super-powers for good.

Now I was back at my desk, I opened up the file box and found the summary of the victim's family information. As I suspected, Felicity was only a teenager at the time of her father's murder, and I didn't think DI Johns would have thought a relationship between a grown man and a fifteen-year-old was in any way shape or form appropriate, not to mention illegal. Despite often not seeing eye to eye with the man, I credited him with at least some morals.

The order of the day would be to sit and read through the material in the box, then form a plan of attack. Couldn't help but shake my head in disbelief. Me, in charge of an investigation. In a way it took me back to my Mataura days, when I was the sole charge police officer in the town and got to call the shots. This was the same concept, but the shots were a lot grander and the stakes much higher. Having felt slightly miffed that The Boss had fobbed me off with a cold case, I was now getting over myself and was excited by the challenge, and by the knowledge that if I did this well then it could potentially help advance my career. I doubted DI Johns would have thought about that when he put me in charge. Advancing my career didn't seem to be high on his priority list.

I thrummed my fingers on the desk and looked around the office. The place was devoid of life as everyone was out and about, doing their thing in the field, which was good, because there wouldn't be any distractions. But to be honest I would have welcomed some. Part of the allure of coming back to work was for the grown-up company – being able to talk with folk who generally didn't reply with goos, gaas, giggles and raspberries – so it was a bit of a bummer that company was otherwise engaged.

I didn't need the clock to tell me a few hours had passed and it must be getting close to lunch time. Boulder boobs were go. They weren't quite at the 'it hurts to have my own arms touching them – must hold 'em out like the chicken dance' stage, but they were getting there. It was the downside to producing enough milk to feed a small town. When Amelia was born and I first started the breast-feeding it took forever for my milk to come in, and I had been tempted to give it up, for her hungry sake and mine. But when it did kick in, crikey, I was a bona fide Jersey cow. I gave the breast pump plonked next to me on the desk the side-eye. The family room next door was free, and it was all part of our return-to-work plan, but still a part of me couldn't quite bring myself to express at work. Instead, I picked up the phone.

'Hey.'

'Hey yourself. How's your day going?'

I didn't know if Paul realised the complexity of that question.

'Well, it's been interesting.' I could hear little cooing chatty noises in the background, and my heart gave a wee wrench.

'Interesting? Going to elaborate?'

'Gawd, have you got an hour? It's not quite the conversation to have over the phone. It's more an in-person job.'

'Which is code for...?'

Damn, that man could always see right through me.

'It would be great to see you and Amelia.'

A soft chuckle drifted down the phone. 'In time for her lunch I take it?'

'That would be nice if you can manage it.'

'I'm sure it can be arranged. I'll just change her and we'll head on down.'

I was so relieved, but a little part of me felt like a big fat failure. How on earth was I going to adjust to this working-mum gig if I couldn't even hack the first day back on the job?

Paul must have caught the minute quiver in my voice and, bless him, realised the battle raging in my heart, because he uttered, 'If it's any consolation, I think a little someone here would love to see you too.'

CHAPTER 4

A volley of knocks at the door startled two of the people in the room. The third didn't so much as flinch as she was completely engaged with the task at hand: guzzling lunch.

The door eased open a fraction and Smithy's head poked around it.

'Oh good, it is you two. Otto said you'd be in here.' Before either of us could comment, he waltzed in, shut the door behind him and plonked himself down on the adjacent sofa.

I didn't bother correcting him on the head count, and I didn't recall inviting anyone else to the lunch date. Paul looked as surprised by the arrival as I was, especially as Smithy appeared completely unfazed by the fact that his work colleague was busy breast-feeding and was exposing far more skin than he'd have seen from her before. He also seemed completely oblivious to the idea that maybe we were in here with the door closed because we wanted some privacy and that maybe his intrusion wasn't entirely appropriate or welcome.

He boxed on regardless. 'Look, The Boss just had a word and told me that he'd put you in charge of the Freeman cold case.'

That got my curiosity up. 'He has. What did he say about it, exactly?'

Smithy was well aware of the unfortunate dynamic between The Boss and me, and between The Boss and everyone, to be fair. Being male and large, he didn't tend to be on the receiving end of the extra-special one-on-one treatment I was subjected to over the years, but he was self-aware enough to recognise his privilege.

'Just that he was reopening the case and he was putting you in charge of it.'

'And did he mention whether there's any particular significance about the timing of this?' I paused to look at Paul. 'And why me?'

I had only just begun filling Paul in on the details of my mission and on what I had gleaned from the morning's reading, so his curiosity was piqued just as much as mine.

'It does seem a little odd after all this time,' Paul said. 'And even odder that he gave it to Sam.'

'Well, as to the why you, I don't know the motivation there. I was a little surprised, to be honest, given the history between you two. All I know is that he's asked me to keep a quiet eye on you.'

'Ha, so naturally you're here telling me.'

'Yup.'

'And he would have asked you to do that to make sure I don't stuff it up?'

'Oh, I'm sure he has total confidence in you.' The line was delivered deadpan, but he then followed up with a chuckle.

Amelia had unlatched with a schlock sound and come up for air, so I sat her up, ready to pop her onto my shoulder to deal with any gas. Paul, bless him, reached over to grab her and do the honours, so I fumbled around, doing up the maternity-bra trap door, and rearranged my clothes into some semblance of order so Smithy didn't have to cop a complete eyeful. Not that he seemed to care. He did have children of his own with his ex-wife, so must have been used to it. Having initially been annoyed by his arrival into this space I began to feel a sliver of gratitude that he didn't make feeding feel awkward. Maybe the logistics of this wouldn't be so bad after all.

'I can't help but think any gift from him comes with hidden barbs, so please excuse me if I'm not overcome with joy at the prospect of dealing with this one,' I said.

'Wise to think there may be another agenda, but to be honest I can't think what that would be. If you're successful it's a win on all fronts; if you're unsuccessful, then he could perhaps use that as ammunition against you, but considering he was on the team that couldn't solve the case twenty-five years ago, everyone would recognise the hypocrisy in that.'

The air was punctuated by a hearty belch from my right that provoked a snigger from Smithy.

'She's definitely your daughter,' he said.

Given my tendency to windiness I couldn't refute it. I only hoped the belch didn't have any follow-through. Mind you, given the general state of the sofas in here, a little milk spillage wouldn't be noticed.

'So I gather The Boss told you about the personal significance of this case?'

'He did indeed, although I already knew about the connection between him and the victim.'

Smithy had been around for as long as DI Johns, so I wasn't surprised he already had some knowledge of Reverend Freeman's murder. I worded my next question carefully.

'And you're confident the connection wasn't there when the case was being investigated?'

His left eyebrow rose a smidgeon. 'At the time of the investigation The Boss was married to Michelle, his first wife. That relationship fell apart a number of years later. So no, there wasn't anything untoward with respect to Felicity Freeman, if that's what you were asking. I'd say that relationship didn't start until well over a decade after.'

'I thought so, but you know I had to check.'

'Fair enough. He's a prick, but he's not that kind of a prick.'

I reached over with a spill cloth and wiped the line of milky dribble that was heading from Amelia's mouth towards Paul's shoulder. The action was met with a smile from the kid and some vigorous pumping of her legs. Paul didn't seem to mind becoming a human trampoline.

'What about the timing? Why would he want to reopen the investigation now?' Paul asked.

'He'd mentioned it was twenty-five or so years,' replied Smithy, 'so maybe it's just a numbers thing.'

'He mentioned that to me too,' I said.

'Maybe it's like an anniversary gift to his wife, finding out who killed her father after all this time. I suppose you could see it as a romantic kind of a gesture.' If Smithy saw that as a romantic kind of a gesture it explained a lot about his lack of success with women.

'I believe most people give something pretty and silver for that one, not an invasive police investigation to stir up all of your worst memories and retrigger your trauma.'

'Now that you put it that way I can see why—'

Smithy didn't get to finish his sentence as it was interrupted by a very long, wet and gurgling fart that emanated from Amelia's butt.

'Oh shit,' Smithy said.

Amelia had stopped bouncing and I could see the look of concentration on her face.

'Bags not, that one's yours,' I said as I whipped my thumb up to my forehead.

Another stomach-churning *shloop* came from the business end of our daughter, followed by a satisfied little grunt from the other.

'Oh, holy shit,' Paul echoed.

CHAPTER 5

The Cathedral of St Paul the Apostle, or St Paul's, as Dunedinites affectionately called it, stood proudly at the head of The Octagon and was one of those magnificent Dunedin buildings you passed by all the time but didn't really appreciate. Like many Dunedinites, I was guilty of taking for granted the magnificent architecture we had here, tributes to grandiose dreams, or the gold-rush times when the city was prosperous and the buildings reflected its status and grandeur as a major centre of trade. The city would be nothing without landmarks like the gloriously ornate railway station, the imposing First Church, the university clocktower building, to name but a few. Nowadays the city wasn't quite so prosperous, and many of the once-proud structures had a hint of mankiness to them. Not that I was against mankiness. In my mind that only made the city more interesting, but then, having come here from a two-horse rural town, my point of comparison wasn't exactly first-class. In my mind Dunedin was still the Big Smoke and a major upgrade from what I was used to.

I approached St Paul's from Lower Stuart Street, wanting to experience the full impact of its dominance over the heart of the city. It didn't disappoint. At this time of year the plane trees had shed their leaves, the twists and angles of their naked branches providing an eerie filter to the view. The traffic on the lower Octagon was pretty non-existent so there was no need to take my life in my hands to cross it. The three seagulls in the middle of the road squabbling over a paper bag with what looked like scrags of hot chips didn't seem concerned either. I walked across the plaza and noted that in terms of, for want of a better word, menace, St Paul's outshone the neighbouring and rather ornate Municipal Chambers. The cathedral had that pointy and angular Gothic look to it, and the closer I got the more imposing it felt. I crossed the central carriageway, narrowly avoiding getting taken out by a bearded guy in a three-piece suit on a rental scooter – should have known the footpath would be more dangerous than the road – crossed the grass and climbed the stairs up and around to the Robbie Burns statue. I glanced up at the poet. I always found it a bit odd that the centre of our city celebrated a poet from the other side of the world. Mind you, our city did try to replicate the street names of a certain Scottish metropolis. We weren't called the Edinburgh of the South for nothing.

'What did you see on that dark and stormy night, young Robbie? Got anything you can tell me?' Chances were he didn't see a hell of a lot. His back was to the cathedral for a start. Today his head was sporting a jaunty orange traffic cone. It probably made a nice change from the bird shit.

A lady who'd been hidden out of sight on the other side of the plinth looked at me like I was a few sammies short of a picnic and walked away rather quicker than was called for. I was pretty sure I wasn't the only one who had chats with the bard when needed, although, unlike the Saturday-night drunks, I wasn't waiting for a reply. Back in 1999 Robbie's eyes were the only ones looking over The Octagon and its surrounds. The abundance of CCTV cameras that now kept sentinel didn't start making an appearance until 2010. So, alas, for this case there wasn't convenient footage of the deadly deed taking place, and there certainly was no facial-recognition software to tell us exactly who was responsible. DI Johns and the police of the day had to rely on good old leg work and extensive interviews to conduct their investigation. They hadn't been able to collect any DNA evidence from the victim or the scene due to the atrocious weather conditions, which had ob-literated any trace. That must have been gutting, as DNA testing was in its infancy back then, the latest, shiny-new crime-busting thing. Unfortunately for them the latest thing was a wash-out, and the good old leg work didn't result in a conviction. Hence, here I was today, chasing ghosts from a case that was stone-cold dead. Robbie here showed more signs of life.

The wind funnelled down the hill from Stuart Street. I leaned into it and pulled the zipper high up on my jacket to fend off the chill. There was an octagonal bronze writer's plaque set flush into the brick pavers in front of me, so I carefully stepped around it. In my mind standing on Janet Frame's plaque would have been akin to walking on her gravestone, which was a hard nope. My caution was a bit ridiculous really, considering the plaque was embedded into the footpath, but I wondered if everyone else felt it rude and did a sidle around them too. The quote on the plaque elicited a smile, firstly because of its perfect placement in front of the cathedral. Whoever chose that had a good sense of humour. And secondly as it seemed so appropriate to the job I had been tasked with.

Having been to church the people are good, quiet,
with sober drops at the end of their cold Dunedin noses,
with polite old-fashioned sentences like Pass the Cruet,
and, later, attentive glorifying in each other's roses.

Hmmm, had the people been good? The bit about the drops on the end of the nose resonated as well. The only thing missing was the roses.

According to the case files, the night of the Reverend Mark Freeman's death had been as wet and wild a one as Dunedin could throw. It was in stark contrast to today, which was sunny and bright, but which only went some way to counteract the bitter cold. And it certainly did nothing to counteract my growing unease.

Reading the case notes about the scene of the crime and studying the photos was all well and good, but I needed to get a real-world sense of the place – gain a feel for the space, the angles, the scale, and overlay the scene in my mind onto it all. Standing here by the verdigris-coloured iron gate posts and looking up, the cathedral's looming presence made my senses take a vertiginous shift. The great marble steps stretched up to the church's arched maw like a stairway to heaven – or hell, depending on your mindset. My mindset must have been in more Hades territory, as the two towers jutting into the sky on either side resembled a set of fangs. Probably not the effect the architect had aspired to.

I had only set foot inside St Paul's once before, and that was for a funeral. At that time the emotional load and sense of occasion had meant I didn't really pay much attention to the physical space. Instead, my memory was one of ceremony, grief and the smothering weight of a family's overwhelming loss. And it wasn't even my family. I was in attendance that day as part of my job, as a sign of respect to the victim of a heinous crime. Churches and funerals in particular seemed to have a disproportionately large negative effect on my psyche. I avoided them like the plague.

The crime that had destroyed any sense of the cathedral as a place of refuge and safety and shocked its parishioners twenty-five years ago took place on a wintery night on the third of July, sometime between 8.30pm and 9.00pm. Sunday choral evensong had finished around 8.00pm, and the attendees had all departed by half past, leaving the Reverend Freeman to turn off the lights and close up. His wife, Yvonne, and their two teenaged children had already left him to it and returned home, but when he hadn't arrived at the vicarage by 9.00pm and didn't reply to her message, Yvonne had sent Callum back to the church to check if Dad was okay. As it turned out, Dad was far from okay. The unfortunate seventeen-year-old had found himself in the awful position of discovering the body of his father. Not the kind of thing you wished on anyone, let alone a kid.

I made my way up the first grand flight of stairs and across the mid-way landing before pausing and turning back to take in the surrounds from this vantage point. The purpose of the steps' scalloped shape seemed to be to gather people in before the next flight funnelled them directly up between the two giant, square, carved-stone pedestals. They were an oddity. Squat and flat-topped, they were built like something substantial was meant to be installed up there, but then never was. Perhaps some other grand statuary or edifice had been intended, but they ran out of funds, or couldn't agree on what to erect. The only things in occupancy now were a couple of seagulls and some persistent weeds. My curiosity was piqued. I'd have to look up the history. It certainly felt like unfinished business. I walked past them up to the next landing and turned around to face The Octagon.

At this landing, two other, narrower, sets of steps rose from either side and connected with the central staircase. One came up from Stuart Street and the other came up from the Harrop Street side. This was the set that drew my attention, as it was at the base of these stairs that the body of Reverend Mark Freeman had come to rest. The theory was that after a struggle, during which he was stabbed, he had fallen, or been pushed, and tumbled to his death. From where I now stood the steps fell away steeply, and I could see how he would have broken his neck in the plummet. Standing here also answered another of my questions. When reading the case notes I had wondered how, even with the poor weather, nobody had witnessed the events leading up to the Reverend's fall, or the fall itself, when the cathedral was so visible from a usually bustling Octagon. Surely there would have been people around. But standing here now, the large pedestal base obscured the line of sight from The Octagon, and the stairs themselves had solid stone banisters, and the retaining wall at the bottom prevented any perspective from Harrop Street. The only place with a grandstand view of the scene would have been the top floors of the ten-storey Forsyth Barr House, which towered over everything from the far side of Stuart Street, but according to the case files it was deserted late on that Sunday night. There hadn't been any sad individuals working overtime there on their weekend.

I negotiated my way down the deadly side stairs, taking note of any potential vantage points, but there were no clearly exposed areas, and with the foul weather on the night in question what few people may have been in the vicinity of The Octagon would have been more intent on staying dry and getting from point A to point B rather than admiring the view. From the bottom of the stairs a path wound its way from my left past the cathedral-office door, around the side of the building and up to the carpark at the rear. I didn't even know that was there. It was bordered by a rose bed along the Harrop Street retaining wall. Surely not the roses Janet referred to? Kind of cool if they were though. The concrete kerbing defining the rose garden was studded with small bronze plaques. I moved closer to examine the engravings and saw they were memorials to parishioners past. I wondered if they were simply plaques, or if the dearly departed's ashes had been scattered through the roses? I cringed at the thought. Given the number of memorials that would be a lot of remains over the years. The roses looked healthy though, so maybe they liked them. Kind of doubted they'd be good for them though. I knew the staff at the Dunedin Botanic Gardens were forever reminding people not to scatter their loved ones in the rose gardens. Was there a plaque for the dearly departed Reverend? I worked my way along, and sure enough, on the end of the row closest to his final resting place a simple bronze memorial stated: *Revd Canon Dr Richard Mark Freeman 14.8.49 – 3.7.99*. He didn't quite make it to fifty, just pipped at the post. Interesting that he used Mark as his given name, not Richard, and I also noted he was Dr Freeman. What was his doctorate in? I assumed something theological. Something to look into.

I moved over to where the Reverend Freeman's body had lain and scanned around, turning a slow three-sixty. It was a perfect little pocket of invisibility in what was mostly an exposed and busy site. Was that planned, or had someone just got lucky?

Even on this sunny day, my body gave an involuntary shudder that couldn't be entirely attributed to the cold. I was overcome with a sense of dread and I didn't want to be here anymore. Standing here, at the spot where his body was discovered, there was something about the sheer weight of the cathedral's looming presence, the cold indifference of those precipitous marble steps, and the mind-twisting incongruity of a murder taking place at a house of sanctuary and worship that made me realise this case was not going to be easy, on many levels.

CHAPTER 6

There was still another hour of my working day to go, and quite frankly I was knackered. It was a different knackered to running-around-after-a-baby knackered, but I was knackered all the same. My brain didn't have the capacity to concentrate on anything too gritty this far past lunch and caffeine, but still, I didn't want to squander the available time. What could I do to fill the hour? Who could I use these minutes to talk with? After a little mental dredging around a name came to mind, and I reached for the phone.

It didn't go straight to voicemail, which was encouraging as I loathed leaving messages, and then, sure enough, a few rings later a familiar *basso profundo* voice graced my ear.

'Sam.' The way he drew out the 'am' always made me smile.

'Alistair,' I elongated the 'air' just to mock him. Even after all these years I couldn't help myself.

Alistair was a pathologist at Dunedin hospital, and I had frequently called upon his expertise when it came to postmortem results and any medical nitty gritty I needed clarification on. We went way back to our school days. He used to come stay on the farm with my family during the holidays, his professional parents being far too busy to cater for the daily needs of a vacationing teenage boy, but far too untrusting to leave him home alone. He was in the same class as one of my older brothers, and it said something about the environment he came from that he viewed being around the, let's say 'special', kind of love and attention only my mother could give as an improvement on his own situation. We were respite care, despite the care.

'How's parenthood treating you?' he asked.

'Pretty good so far. Can't complain.'

'You know you missed an opportunity hooking up with that man. We could have made beautiful babies together.'

I tried not to snort down the phone. He was joking of course, but also not joking. He'd been a try-hard from the age it was seemly to do so, and had even kindly offered to burst my cherry when I reached the age of consent. But I had graciously declined, and he had graciously accepted the rejection. It wasn't that I had anything in particular against him – he did have some charms, but he was like a bonus annoying brother, so yuck and nope all round. It hadn't stopped him from re-extending the invitation over the years though. Nowadays, given my domestic situation, this little game of cat and mouse had gone from being an irritant to becoming a fun bit of ritual, but even by his standards, that statement was a pearler.

'Of course we would have, Alistair: beautiful, intelligent, but very short.'

'True,' came the reply, mirth colouring his voice. 'Talk about break a guy's heart. Now you only ring when you want something. So what can I help you with?'

Sprung.

'I guess it's pointless to deny it. It's my first day back at work, maternity leave's over...'

'Should I offer congratulations or commiserations?'

'Jury's still out on that one.'

I heard him rattling around with something so guessed he was at his desk.

'And you're calling in a favour already?'

It took a considerable amount of self-control not to make a smart-Alec comment. It was in my best interests to massage his ego, especially when I wanted something.

'Of course. You're my first port of call. I need your expertise.'

'Ha ha. You don't fool me. Nice greasing up. What do you need?'

This was why I loved talking to him.

'The Boss has put me in charge of a cold case, to, in his words, "ease me back into the job".'

'Congratulations. I'm sure he did that to be considerate and caring, and with your best interests at heart.'

'That's the one.' Alistair was familiar with The Boss's charming, generous nature and sunny disposition. 'I don't know if you will remember it from when we were kids – it's well before your time professionally – but back in 1999 a priest was murdered at St Paul's Cathedral.'

'That rings a bell.'

This time I couldn't suppress the groan.

He seemed happy with the response. 'Actually, I do remember it. That was pre-high school days when we were still living in Dunedin, not long before Alison and Bryce moved to Gore for work and shipped me off to Southland Boys.' I never could get used to Alistair referring to his parents by their first names. My mother might be a battle-axe, but she would always be Mum. The formality and degree of separation suggested by his use of their names spoke volumes about his relationship with them. Mind you, I would have felt bitter too if I was shipped off to boarding school in Invercargill when there was a perfectly serviceable local one. Gore High School had a reasonable reputation, and had done a decent job with a number of my friends, including my former flatmate Maggie. They all survived to tell the tale, and even reported enjoying it there. But Alistair's dad had been a Southland Boys old boy, as had his father before him, so as far as Bryce was concerned what was good enough for the father was good enough for the son, and no argument would be entered into.

'The murder must have made an impression on you then.'

'It made an impression on the whole family. The olds went to church at St Paul's, so it was very close to home.'

My eyebrows shot up towards my hairline and not just because of my surprise at his parents being churchgoers.

'Were they there the night of his death then? Did you know the Reverend?' I knew Dunedin could feel like a small town, but seriously, what were the odds?

'Not really and no. We weren't dedicated churchgoers. My parents are more "going through the motions" people. It was all about appearances for them – we had to be seen to be good Christians.' He put a hoity toity voice on the 'good Christians' bit. 'But we didn't attend every week. When I did go to St Paul's, not willingly I might add, I went to the Sunday school and didn't really pay attention to the ministers, so I don't remember anything about him at all. And we tended to go to morning services rather than evensong, so fortunately, we weren't there the night he died.'

Of course it would have been way too convenient for me to stumble across someone I knew who was there on the night in question, I was never that lucky. But still, Alistair's parents would be worth contacting as they might be able to provide some insider information on the Reverend, and on the parish as a whole. I was certain the congregation would have been spouting their own theories on the whos and whys of his death.

'Do you think your parents knew him well? They might be useful for me to interview. Do you know if they were talked to during the initial enquiry?'

'I have no idea if they were or not. But I'm sure they would be happy to talk. They're still living in Gore. I can send you their contact details.'

'That would be great, thanks.'

'So what did you actually call for, again?'

'Oh yes, that.' The serendipitous discovery of Alistair's family's closeness to the case had distracted me from my original mission. 'I was wondering if you would be able to have a look through the post-mortem report for Reverend Freeman and let me know what you think. I haven't found it in my files yet. I just have the summary information that mentioned a stab wound but that the cause of death was a broken neck as the result of a fall. If you could cast your discerning eye over the full report, that would be appreciated.'

'How appreciated?' he asked.

There was always a price to pay with Alistair. I happened to be aware of one of his favourite currencies though – well, one I was prepared to trade in.

'I could find a way to acquire some of Mum's world-famous Louise cake.' Back in the day, a batch of Louise cake seldom lasted the afternoon, much to Mum's annoyance.

He paused to consider the proposal. I hoped he hadn't suddenly decided to get healthy, or had gone all faddy and sugar-free.

'It's a deal. You drive a hard bargain. Send through the case number.'

CHAPTER 7

'You do realise this has been your first day back at work, and you're talking shop already.'

We were curled up side by side on the sofa taking care of a cup of tea while figuratively keeping our fingers crossed that young Madam Amelia had finally drifted off to sleep. She'd grizzled for a bit, the way she did when she couldn't quite make up her mind if she was going to go full bellow, or couldn't be bothered and would give in to the tiredness, but all had been silent for at least five minutes so it was looking hopeful. Given how tired I was after my first day back on the beat, I carried a slight pang of anxiety that she'd reconsider her position and need another round of settling. It would definitely be Paul's turn if that was the case. She preferred his singing of the bedtime song to mine anyway. I didn't blame her. I suspected his version of 'Ten in the Bed' was more comical as well as more tuneful.

'Sorry. God, didn't take long to fall into the old habit, did it? Do you want me to talk about something else? The Roman Empire? *The Godfather*? Fly fishing?'

'No. I'm just yanking your chain. You know damned well I'm curious about your case. It's a lot more interesting than the one I'm on.'

I noted some fuzzy white movement out the corner of my eye and before we knew it Tori had jumped onto the sofa and was busy wiggling into a spot in the middle, where she could be touching both of us at the same time. Like all well-trained cat owners, we moved to accommodate her demands.

'There's not much to report after one day. Mostly reading through the case notes and trying to figure out a plan of attack. I did go get some fresh air after lunch and take a look around the cathedral and the murder scene. But other than that, it was just that interesting phone call I had with Alistair I was telling you about.'

'Pretty solid effort for a first day.'

'Thank you. Not bad, eh? Oh, and thank you for the cow cupcake – I appreciated the sentiment.' I gave Paul a thump on the arm.

He gave me a kiss on the cheek. 'Pleasure,' he said. 'So what's your plan for tomorrow?'

'Start arranging some interviews with any of the key witnesses who are still in Dunedin. It will take a bit of hunting to find out where people are living now and to get contact details. Hopefully most of them are still in town. I thought I'd start with Felicity Johns. Being legally attached to The Boss, at least I know for sure she's here in Dunedin, unless there's something he's not telling us.'

'Low-hanging fruit approach?' The comment was followed by an attack on a Toffee Pop biscuit.

'You betcha. Nothing wrong with that. It will make me feel like I've moving forward with this investigation. It will also signal to the Grand Poobah that I'm taking the task seriously. Can't help but feel there's a lot riding on this. He's going to be breathing down my neck on this one.'

'And it's going to be a minefield of conflicts of interest and who's in charge of what. Have you set the boundaries with him on that yet?'

'Not exactly,' I said. Meaning not at all. 'He's not the easiest of people to have those kinds of conversations with.'

'Don't put it off. Last thing you want is a dust-up.'

Somehow I had the feeling no matter how clear I made things, The Boss would take offence and find a way to make a scene.

After a series of nudges Tori gave my elbow a wicked head butt, which almost made me spill my tea, so I swapped hands and started obediently scritching behind her ears.

'I'm still curious as to his motivation – why reopen the case now and why give it to you?' Paul said. 'No disrespect to your sleuthing powers, which are impressive, but you're not exactly his class pet.'

'I'm asking myself the same questions. If anyone I thought he'd have Smithy on the job. The Boss doesn't feel threatened by him, even though he's the first one to call out his bullshit. I can never figure that one out.'

'It's cos he's a guy,' Paul said simply. 'He's the same with me too.'

I tickled under Tori's chin and addressed my comment to her. 'God, it must be nice having a penis sometimes.'

She purred. Paul chuckled.

'But seriously,' I went on, 'I reckon The Boss would always help advance Smithy's career. So call me suspicious, but part of me thinks he's put me in charge of this case instead because he wants me to fail.'

'Valid suspicion. But then the whole exercise would be pointless and would just reopen old wounds for his wife and her family. He's an arsehole, but I don't think he'd sacrifice his family's wellbeing just to score points against you.'

Paul was right. No one could be that heartless, not even The Boss. And if I was honest with myself, I probably didn't rate highly enough in his world that he would make the effort to set me up to fail. I was just another annoying bug for Dickhead Johns to swat. But I was a bug that got results. My methods in the past may not have been textbook, but they got answers and had helped solve crimes. He couldn't deny that. So was putting me in charge a grudging acknowledgement of my skills?

'Maybe he thinks I'm the best one for the job.'

Paul turned and gave me a look that was part pity and part 'get real, lady'. 'Sure, you keep thinking that.'

CHAPTER 8

The Johns' family home wasn't quite what I'd expected. In my mind I'd assumed a high-powered man with the degree of privilege and entitlement Johns exuded would own a swanky home in one of the posher suburbs, like Roslyn or Māori Hill, so I was a tad surprised when the address I was given was for the not-so-swanky Musselburgh. But when I pulled up outside it became clear their house wasn't quite as humble as others in the street. One of the welcome quirks of Dunedin was the way you could have a million-dollar new-build next to a student hovel next to a grand villa next to a seventies brick eyesore. La Casa Johns was a sizeable two-storey red-brick Edwardian dwelling surrounded by an established and well-tended garden. Despite its size, it sat comfortably with its bungalow neighbours. The front porch was softened by a jasmine vine that had woven itself erratically between the trios of pillars set on plinths that surrounded the portico. A set of shaggy and in-need-of-a-haircut ball topiaries bordered the footpath. It was a grand entrance that exuded warmth and charm. Unlike its owner.

I tugged my top down and brushed my pants flat before reaching up to press the doorbell. Despite being the one whose finger hit the buzzer, I was still startled by the clamour of its ring. It was symptomatic of my nervousness about having to interview The Boss's wife. I had seen her from afar on the odd occasion when she'd come into the station, but had never been formally introduced. Considering the rather fraught working relationship I had with her husband, I couldn't help but wonder if he had moaned to her about me as much as I had whinged to Paul about him. Or to anyone else who would listen for that matter. If so, I wasn't exactly sure what kind of a reception I'd get.

An approaching silhouette appeared in the frosted-glass door panel, slowly expanding to fill the pane. The ghostly figure was accompanied by the tell-tale yapping of a small dog. The door began to swing inward, and a white, furry Westie bullet-shot out before it had a chance to finish opening. The yapping bullet circled around my legs a few times before shooting back inside and taking position at the feet of its owner.

'Oh, take no mind of Gemma. She gets a little excitable with visitors, but you don't need to worry, she's very old and very sweet, and is more likely to lick you to death than nip you.'

'She certainly is very cute,' I said. I'd always envisaged DI Johns as a big-dog kind of a guy – German Shepherd, Rottweiler, mastiff, something of that ilk – not a yappy ankle biter. 'You must be Felicity Johns. I'm Detective Sam Shephard. Thank you for agreeing to meet with me at such short notice, and the invitation to talk at your home.'

'That's quite okay, Detective,' she said as she extended her hand. I reached out and took it and was pleased to encounter a warm and firm shake. There was nothing worse than a limp fish. 'I have seen you before at the station, but I don't believe we've had the opportunity to be properly introduced.'

Felicity Johns was a striking-looking woman with a set of cheekbones that stood out like small apples. She had closely cropped brown hair, and with her bright-blue eyes the effect was like looking at a pixie. She was tall for a pixie though, towering over me by close to a foot. Not that it was hard, considering I scraped in at just over five foot. Her rich, contralto voice also contrasted with the elfin effect. She was comfortably dressed in jeans and a hoodie, albeit a designer one. Overall, Felicity Johns came across as relaxed and not the tightly wound, prim and proper wife of a superior arsehole that I'd pictured. The butterflies that had been dancing a small fandango in my stomach started to settle down. Even from this brief doorstep encounter I could sense no animosity or guardedness. Maybe she was oblivious to the workplace tension and The Boss hadn't slagged me off as I had imagined.

'I thought we would be a lot more comfortable here than down at the station. That place isn't exactly welcoming. Come in, and don't worry about taking your shoes off.'

She was right, in more ways than one. The station was impersonal at best, and the thought of having DI Johns hovering around us like a blowfly at a barbecue did not appeal.

I stepped into the wide entranceway and pushed the door closed behind me before Gemma could make a bolt for freedom.

'We'll go through to the kitchen,' she said, and led me along a passageway that judging by the glimpse of greenery down the end, extended the length of the house. It felt peculiar knowing I was in The Boss's lair, his inner sanctum. Part of me felt it was intrusive and I shouldn't be here, but the other part was dying to be nosey and see what his life away from the job looked like. So far it was not what I had imagined. The home might have been grand in scale, but it was in dire need of some TLC. To my right an impressive wooden staircase with ornate balustrades swept up and around to the floor above. In contrast, underfoot a threadbare Axminster carpet looked like it had time warped in from the seventies. Its browns and oranges didn't quite go with the butter yellow of the walls below the picture rail, the effect just discordant enough to make my eye twitch. Felicity must have read my mind as she piped in, almost apologetic, 'We're working our way through the house with renovations. The entrance and hallway are next on the hit list. I don't know what the previous owners were thinking.'

As we approached the back of the house, it became apparent where the money had been spent. The entire space had been opened up and modernised like those kitchen-diners I drooled over when watching *Location, Location, Location* or *Grand Designs*. It had large French doors opening onto a patio big enough to hold an impressive outdoor table and chairs before it transitioned into the garden. A pyramid skylight in what must have been an extension bathed the room in sunlight. Sometimes those modern additions jarred and felt out of place, but in this instance the Johns had managed to retain the charm and warmth of the era yet still create a kitchen to die for. I was suffering major envy.

'Can I make you a cup of tea?'

It was very kind of her to offer, and when people did I seldom declined. It was amazing how the simple act of polite acceptance and chatting over a cup of tea could break down some of the apprehensions people might have when talking with the police. Tea was the great leveller.

'That would be lovely, thanks.'

While she filled the kettle I hiked myself up onto a pedestal bar stool on the opposite side of the marble-topped island. The moulded shape of the black vinyl top brought back memories of the rather less comfortable tractor seat from the farm. I couldn't help but swivel on it a few times to settle in. The kettle was one of those space-agey, stainless-steel designer-looking things with a bird whistle that I'd lusted after in design stores but whose price was way out of my league.

She got straight to the point as she set about getting the mugs ready. 'So I understand you're reopening my father's case?' No need for me to find an opening, then.

'Yes, that's right. As I said when I rang earlier, I've been asked to look into the case to see if we can make some progress on it and find out what happened. To try and give your family some answers after all this time.'

She gave a small sigh and reached over to rearrange some vibrant-coloured gerberas artfully homed in a jug to the side of the countertop. 'Greg told me he'd asked you to do that.'

The way she worded that sentence implied that she had been informed rather than consulted.

'So it wasn't your family wanting to reopen the case? It was DI Johns' initiative?' I couldn't bring myself to call him Greg, even to his wife, but still it felt a little awkward referring to him by his professional title.

'It was. I was really quite surprised when he told me.' There was a slight undertone to her voice that I wasn't quite sure how to interpret.

'So it wasn't a good surprise?' I asked with a hint of hesitancy.

She laughed lightly and looked at me with a surprising openness. 'Yes and no. Don't get me wrong, we would all dearly love to know who killed my father and get some justice for him, but it's been twenty-five years. It's taken a long time to come to terms with what happened and find some kind of peace with it. I worry that it's going to open up all of that trauma, all of that grief, especially for my mum. And what if there's still no outcome?'

I felt a real pang for her then. This was the first time I had been involved in a historical case, and in her shoes I'd be worried too about the emotional toll examining the past would take on myself and my loved ones. Dealing with grief was hard enough under what we'd consider normal circumstances – illness, accident, old age. Layer over that the knowledge someone had murdered your loved one, and the intrusiveness of an investigation and its effects could be devastating.

'It's perfectly understandable for you to be worried, and unfortunately it's inevitable in a situation like this that it will bring back old hurts. But we've got support services available if you need to talk with someone, and I really encourage you to make use of them.'

The whistle bird started to warble before working its way up to full song. Felicity lifted the kettle off the hob, plucked out the bird and poured the water over the teabags in the mugs.

'And we will be as sensitive as we can,' I went on. 'We understand it's going to be difficult on you all.'

'Thank you, I appreciate that,' she said. She pulled open the refrigerator door. 'Milk?'

'Yes, please.'

She finished making the teas and brought them around to my side of the island.

'Come sit over here where it's more comfortable.' I followed her over to a pair of bold geometric-print armchairs, nestled into a corner. Along with a small circular coffee table sporting a 'string of turtles' pot plant, they created a cosy wee nook. Gemma took up her station, almost disappearing into a white, fuzzy and very comfortable-looking dog cushion. It was the perfect camouflage for her.

'Do you mind if I ask: why do you think DI Johns decided to reopen the case at this particular point in time? Why now rather than, say, ten years ago?'

'He didn't say, but I suspect it was because my mother has recently been diagnosed with cancer. Unfortunately, it's quite advanced and the prognosis isn't very good.'

'I'm so sorry to hear that,' I said. 'I hope she's comfortable and they're keeping on top of any pain.'

'She's doing alright, considering, thanks. Greg adores her – they get on like a house on fire – so I think this is his way of trying to do something when we all feel so helpless.'

I could certainly relate to that sense of helplessness. My mind couldn't help but drift to thoughts of my dad. I looked down to the floor to prevent her from seeing my eyes welling up.

The portrait being painted of The Boss as loving son-in-law was in stark contrast to the malevolent force that haunted the corridors of our institution. I was pretty confident my work colleagues would be struggling to get their heads around it too. By Felicity's description our workplace bully was a pussy cat at home, displaying an empathy we sure as hell had never seen. You'd think having worked in law enforcement for so long I would have learned people could be two-faced, but my encounters had always been along 'nice to your face but awful behind your back' lines, rather than the vice-versa situation I was seeing here.

'Is your mother aware that we're going to reinvestigate the case?'

'I don't think so. Not at the moment, no. But I will talk with her about it, because I'm sure you'll be wanting to interview her as well.'

'Yes, it would be very helpful if you could give her some warning. Especially as it's likely to upset her.'

I wanted to ask Felicity about the night her father was killed, but where was the best place to start? What would be the most comfortable way into the conversation? I went for an opener that didn't require any thought.

'How old were you when your father was killed?'

'I was young, only fifteen years old at the time, and my brother Callum was seventeen. I can tell you it was a tough age to lose your dad, especially in such a dreadful, dreadful way. And it wasn't just about getting my head around the fact he was gone, that I'd never see him ever again. We had to come to grips with the knowledge he'd been murdered and deal with everything that went with that. There was so much attention. From the police, from the media, people wanting to know what happened, the church, kids at school. It was everywhere. There was no way to escape from it.' Teenage years were turbulent enough at the best of times. Mine were a time of brilliant highs and not-so brilliant lows, a time for figuring out who I was and where I fit in the world, all the while dealing with the weirdness of the physical changes involved in growing up and the hormones that drove them. Most of the time I was trying to avoid attention. It must have been horrific for Felicity to find herself at the centre of a case like that.

'That must have been so hard for you all. That level of scrutiny is difficult. And as I said earlier, I am sorry to make you revisit an awful time. But hopefully this time we will see justice served for your father.'

I took a sip of tea before pressing on and taking her back to that fateful day.

'No doubt we'll have a few conversations in the weeks ahead, but for now it would be helpful for me if you could talk through the day he died. Had anything out of the ordinary happened?'

She shook her head. 'No, it was a stock-standard Sunday. We went along as a family to the ten o'clock choral mass. One of the other priests took the earlier eucharist, so it was a later start for us. After church, we had the Nicholson family for lunch.'

'Did you often have guests?' I asked.

'Reasonably often. Mum enjoyed entertaining, and opening up our home to others was part and parcel of being a priest's family. We'd have people around for lunch or dinner at least once a week. On that day it was the Nicholsons. They had kids of a similar age to us so I liked it when they visited, I could escape with Becky to another room after eating rather than endure the long-winded adult conversations. Dad did like talking.'

That seemed a universal trait, along with bad jokes. In my family it was farm talk. My father could wax lyrical about soil composition or the intestinal parasites of sheep and cattle all day, and I could imagine church talk was just as stimulating for a long-suffering teenager.

'And that meal was all friendly with the Nicholsons? You weren't aware of any issues there?'

'No, not at all. It was all relaxed and good. They left mid-afternoon. Dad went back into his study to prepare for the evening service like he usually did. It was a very wet day so we all stayed at home, didn't go out to do anything special. We had early dinner so we'd be ready for church at seven. It was all very normal.'

'So what time would you have left the house to go to the service?'

'The vicarage was very close to the cathedral, literally up the hill and around the corner on Smith Street. We walked down together in the rain that night. Dad would never let us drive that distance. It didn't matter how filthy the weather was – rain, hail, snow. He and Mum disagreed on that front.'

'She sounded the more sensible of the two,' I said.

That elicited a smile. I would normally never have quipped like that on a first interview, but there was something about Felicity that put me at ease, and fortunately she didn't take offence.

'And the service. Did anything eventful happen? Anyone unexpected there?'

'No, just the usual. It was a choral evensong, and they are lovely, one of my favourite services. The numbers were perhaps a bit lower than usual, probably because the weather was so awful.' She sipped on her tea before returning to the second half of my question. 'There may well have been visitors there. Being the cathedral and right on The Octagon, tourists or out-of-towners would often attend. But to be honest, I didn't pay that much attention to who came and went each week.'

The next question was a little more sensitive.

'Were you aware of anyone who had anything against your father, who may have had a dispute with him or any reason to want to cause him harm?'

She shook her head and reached down to give Gemma a scritch on her now-exposed belly.

'No, I wasn't aware of anything like that. Like I said, I was only fifteen at the time, and to be honest, I think if there had been any issues like that going on in the background, Mum and Dad would have been careful not to talk about them in front of us. They liked to cotton-wool us in a way. I think the term nowadays would be "helicopter parents"?' She said the words with a hint of eye-roll.

'Was that something you resented?'

'Yes and no. In some ways I think it was good not to know everything that was going on. But on the other hand, being brought up in the Church like we were, I think we had a pretty strict, black-and-white upbringing, yet also had a rose-tinted view of the world, so when harsh reality hit, like when Dad was killed, we weren't that well equipped to cope with it.'

Would I fall into that trap as a parent? Be so busy trying to protect my child from the harshness of the world that they didn't learn to negotiate it safely and on their own terms. I had always scoffed at helicopter parents, especially having had my family upbringing, where we were basically left to our own devices on the farm and if we hurt ourselves it was our own damned fault. Dishing out sympathy was not one of my mother's strong points. Criticism yes, sympathy no. However, now I had a baby of my own, I could understand the temptation to overprotect because it broke my heart to hear Amelia cry from a minor scrape, let alone a major catastrophe. And catastrophising was something my brain had been very guilty of. I wondered if Felicity had also experienced that insight when she had children?

'What about after the service was over? How long did you stay on?'

'I didn't stay that long. People left pretty quickly because the weather was appalling and they wanted to get home. Mum had left pretty much straight away because she wasn't feeling well. She had migraine zigzags and wanted to get home and take something before the headache kicked in. There were a few others around. Mel Smythe, the youth leader, some other regular congregation people Dad was talking with. I didn't pay that much attention to be honest.'

'Was your brother still there then?'

'He left just before me.'

'He didn't wait so you could walk together, considering it was dark?'

'No, he was in a hurry to get home to some game on his PlayStation. He was a bit obsessed. Let's just say he was a typical teenage boy and wasn't too good at thinking of things like that. I didn't mind walking by myself though. Home was close and there were lots of street lights along the way. I felt safe.'

Well, she did at that point. I bet that changed overnight.

'And you didn't wait to walk home with your father?'

A frown creased her face then, her lips pursed and I detected a quiver in her chin.

'No, I didn't. He told me to go ahead.' When she continued her voice carried that thickness of someone trying to hold it together. 'I've wondered every day since then whether, if I had stayed, if I'd waited, things would have been different...'

❧

Although it hadn't offered any revelations into the death of the Reverend Mark Freeman, talking with his daughter had been valuable.

It had given me a sense of connection to the victim and his family, and to why we were doing this in the first place. The pain was still deep and would probably never go away. I felt sad for the woman I'd just talked with, and ached for fifteen-year-old Felicity, who after all these years still harboured guilt. The murder of her father would have effectively robbed her of her childhood.

It was good to feel that, yes, things were under way though. Often the hardest thing about a new case or project was starting, setting out, overcoming that inertia and not being daunted by the enormity of the task ahead. Today's progress was good, but I had to remind myself to remain impartial and not be influenced by how I connected with people. Because there was something between Felicity Johns and me that had simply clicked. I knew I would have to be careful, because as I walked back down the path, reviewing our conversation in my head, something was bugging me, and when I opened the car door and took a final look back towards the house it dawned on me what it was. The question that had been floating around in the back of my brain from the moment I met Felicity Johns.

How could someone so nice be married to such an arsehole?

CHAPTER 9

'Shephard.'

That tone didn't bode well. Judging by the way other heads in the office whipped around, I wasn't the only one who recognised trouble when I heard it. The fact trouble had made the effort to come to me rather than summon me to its lair further drove home the imminent danger. Normally the sight of The Boss striding down the room to confront me on whatever his grievance du jour was provoked a spike in my heart rate and danger in my bowels, but not today. Was I finally becoming immune? Or was I just tired, hangry and couldn't give a shit right now? I suspected it was the latter. Immunity was never going to happen. There was no vaccine for that.

He came to a halt half a metre more into my personal space than was necessary. It meant from my seated position at the desk I had to crane my neck somewhat to look up at him. At least his nostrils were tidy, if somewhat flaring.

'What did you think you were you doing interviewing my wife without informing me? I did not appreciate finding out from her that you had been to visit.'

I should have known this was coming. If I didn't deal with this kind of expectation right now then trying to undertake the case in any meaningful way without his ongoing interference was going to be impossible. I noted the wary faces of Smithy and Sonia watching proceedings. It was good to have witnesses present, ones who would hopefully have my back. I could have stood up, but that wouldn't have made a significant difference in the height disparity, and oddly I felt I had more power pretending to be nonchalant from down here.

'I wasn't aware it was a requirement for us to inform the husbands of any women we interview in the course of an investigation. Are we supposed to ask their permission now?'

The pressure wave through the room almost made my ears pop. The silence was only broken by his massive inhalation of breath.

'Don't you get smart with me, Detective. I don't care who you think you are, but in future if you are going to have any discussions with members of my family, you come through me first. Do I make myself clear?'

Oh, he'd made himself perfectly clear, and I wasn't having a bar of it.

I swivelled around on the chair so that I was facing him directly and slowly rose to my feet, closing the distance between us even more, so we were now uncomfortably close. I may have only been level with his chest, but I made a point of slowly lifting my head to meet his rather frosty gaze. I wasn't about to be intimidated by this arsehole.

'Then let me make myself clear. If I am to undertake this case, which is at your request, I might add, then I have to be able to operate without any interference from you. It is precisely because of your close relationship with the case that we have to be seen to be completely impartial. Any interference on your part would be seen by potential defence lawyers as members of the police having special treatment, or even worse, as impeding the case. We would get laughed out of court and any hope you might have of finding closure, of finding justice for Felicity for the death of her father would go flying out the window.' By now my voice had gone from what I had planned as measured indignation to semi-rant and my index finger had risen to pointy height. 'I assume that you actually want to find his killer, that that is the purpose of this exercise? If that *is* the case, then you need to back off and let me do my fucking job.'

I hadn't intended the F-bomb either, that just snuck out. It seemed to do the trick though, as he took a small, but in my mind significant, step back. Although, again, judging by the intake of breath, he wasn't done. I braced myself for the next volley.

'She's right,' a craggy bass voice interjected. I had been so focussed on dealing with the mountain of angry man-flesh directly in front of me, I hadn't noticed that Smithy had moved down to this end of the room. 'You have to back off and let the investigation take its course.'

There was nothing quite like an even bigger mountain of man-flesh wading into an argument, although this one did it with a tone of authoritative calm. It seemed to have the desired effect of diffusing the situation though, as The Boss took another small step away from me and turned towards Smithy. I felt safe to let my pointy finger drop to my side.

'Look, Greg,' Smithy said, 'we know this will be difficult for you, because it is directly affecting you and your family and has had a massive impact on their lives, but as Sam has pointed out, with this case it's more important than ever that proper processes are followed and we're seen to be impartial and fair.'

A small silence ensued, and you could see the struggle on The Boss's face as he realised that we were right and for once he wasn't going to be able to bully his way in, or micromanage the case on any level. He looked back at me, and I wondered how he was going to negotiate this one without losing face and making it look like he was making a concession.

'Well, I still expect a full report on progress each day.' The tone was defiant. Pride meant he couldn't possibly admit his approach was wrong, but it had a hint of defeat to it.

'I'm sorry, but that can't happen either,' I said.

'What do you mean that can't happen? I'm the senior officer and I'll need to know what's going on.' The edge had returned.

'We are going to need to change who is higher up on the chain of command on this one. You have a direct conflict of interest. Even reporting to you could be seen as giving inside information to parties involved.'

'Are you implying my wife or her family had anything to do with this?'

'Of course I'm not, but again, when we find out who committed this crime, we can't give defence lawyers any possible room to claim interference or unfair advantage or protecting their own self-interest. They would take any opportunity to discredit the veracity of our case to defend their client. That is their job. So think about it: how would you feel if we finally found out who did this, but then because of your actions, we couldn't bring them to justice? Could you live with that?'

You could see from the defeated expression that the answer was a resounding 'no'.

CHAPTER 10

The boulder boobs were starting to make their presence felt, and with that, the realisation I hadn't had enough to drink today, or eat for that matter. Something I would have to keep an eye on. With a slight sense of dread I opened the drawer and pulled out the breast pump. Pride meant I couldn't admit defeat and ask Paul to bring Amelia down to the station for a feed two days in a row. He'd messaged earlier to give me a progress report on how their day was going, and apparently she'd been as happy and settled as a clam. So I couldn't even use the excuse that she needed her mother. There was nothing for it, I had to work up the courage and give it a shot. Expressing at home wasn't an issue at all, it was just doing it here at the station that felt somehow wrong. Pump in one hand, water bottle in the other and protein bar in pocket, I made my way out of the office and headed towards the family room. Of course, Murphy's Law stated I was going to bump into someone in the hallway. Fortunately, it was Smithy. Given his indifference to my feeding Amelia yesterday, I didn't think he'd be phased by the logistical realities of the working mum. He took one look at the implements I was carrying and slowly arched an eyebrow. On his craggy face the effect was comical rather than quizzical.

'Going alright there, Sam?' he asked.

'Fine,' I said. My reply may have been a little curt, but I was borderline hangry and just wanted to get the job done.

'Anything I can help you with?'

I felt my eyes widen and before I could filter it, the words 'fuck off' spat out of my mouth. My arms crossed defensively over my chest.

A look of utter horror passed over Smithy's face. 'No, no, no, I don't mean with that,' he said waving wildly at the breast pump. 'I meant with the case – do you need any help with the case?'

Was it mean of me to get immense satisfaction at seeing him squirm?

'Well, I'm glad you cleared that up, because do you have any idea how creepy that sounded?'

He backed away a step, hands raised. 'Not intended, believe me.'

'Good, and no, I don't need any help at this exact moment in time, but I'll be sure to call on you if I do.' And with that we both hastily beat a retreat in our respective directions.

⁂

The muesli bar had taken the edge off the hunger pangs, and I was washing it down with some water when my phone rang. I looked at the name on the screen and decided, yes, this was one call I would take.

'Alistair.'

'Sam.'

There was a pause.

'What on earth's that strange noise in the background?'

I looked down at the electric pump doing its business. 'Milking machine.'

Another pause.

'Right.'

I smiled. 'You've had a chance to look through the postmortem report?'

'Yes. It was very thorough. The pathologist who performed the autopsy taught me back in the day. He was a great teacher and highly esteemed, so I have a lot of faith in the veracity of his findings.' For Alistair to say that was a grand endorsement as he wasn't shy about giving his opinions on people's abilities, or lack thereof.

'So, what are the salient points?'

'As you mentioned in your summary reports there was a stab wound to his abdomen.'

'Was there only one?'

'Yes. The shape indicated it was from a blade, so some form of knife. The cut was clean, so it was reasonably sharp, and the skin patterning and bruising indicated it had been stabbed to its hilt with some force.'

'One hard thrust.'

'It would appear so.'

'Were they able to identify the type of a blade?'

'Straight edge, not serrated, and it went in to a depth of ten centimetres and was only around one and a half centimetres wide. The Reverend Freeman was a lean man with not much abdominal fat to speak of so we can say that the blade would have been around nine to ten centimetres long – there wouldn't have been any travel.'

I wondered what he meant by that, and then it dawned on me that if he'd been overweight the depth would have been longer as the abdominal fat would have given way a bit like when you poked something spongy with your finger and it sank in, rather than when you poked something hard.

'So that's quite short for a blade then.'

'Yes. It's pocket-knife territory rather than boning- or hunting-knife territory.'

'Good to know. Would the wound have been fatal?'

'No, not where he was stabbed in the abdomen. It missed any major blood vessels and his liver. It did perforate his bowel, but that would not have been fatal if he received medical attention quickly.'

'Can you hang on a tick?' I said. It was time to swap sides. Last thing I wanted was uneven boobs. 'Just got to do some juggling.'

I got myself sorted and returned to the conversation.

'So what was the cause of death then?'

'He had a cervical fracture that severely damaged his spinal cord at C2 level – broken neck, essentially. That would have been as a result of the fall down the steps. In addition to the fracture, he had head injuries consistent with coming into contact with stone steps.'

My body gave an involuntary shudder at the mental image my mind had concocted of the Reverend tumbling down those steep stairs. It fed me the moment emphatically, in slow, excruciating motion.

'Would that have killed him instantly?' I asked. Hollywood often portrayed people who broke their necks when falling down stairs after being pushed by some villain as being dead before they hit the bottom. Oddly enough, I didn't trust Hollywood's take so much. I also didn't want to think the Reverend suffered in any way, had lain there at the bottom of those stairs, conscious of the fact his life was drifting away.

'In some instances, yes, almost instantaneous, as at that level of the spinal cord the nerves are tied to your ability to breathe. And given his head injuries, it's likely he was unconscious before he hit the bottom, if that's what you're asking.'

Alistair, bless him, was well aware that I was a bit of a bleeding heart and couldn't bear to see animals of any kind, including humans, suffer. His reassurance did make me feel a little better, given the circumstances.

'Was there anything else of note? The Reverend didn't have any old injuries or scars that were of concern?'

'No. The only significant scarring he had was from a surgical procedure for a compound arm break documented as a sporting injury. Rugby.'

The good old national game.

'Thanks for that, Alistair. I appreciate it.'

'No problem. Feel free to get back to me if you have any further queries. And say hi to your mum from me.'

'Will do.'

I hit disconnect on the phone and hit disconnect on the boob.

The fall down the steps was pretty self-explanatory. A push or a struggle. The knife raised a number of thoughts though. If it was a pocket knife or something of that ilk, something you might carry as a matter of course, was this planned or was it opportunistic – or reactive? If planned, you'd think the perpetrator would have brought along a weapon that had the potential to do more damage than a ten-centimetre blade could, that would kill someone more efficiently. There would be less chance of a struggle and things going wrong. And if it were me I would have chosen a spot somewhere a little less exposed than the centre of a city at a major landmark. If it was opportunistic, then was something stolen? I didn't recall from the case notes anything mentioned as being missing, but I would go back and have a closer look. Did they take a collection at the evening service? If so was the cash left on the premises and stored in a safe, or was it taken off site, and by whom? Was the Reverend's wallet taken or any other valuables? If the stabbing was reactive, what could have provoked such an attack? An attack against a man of God on the steps of a cathedral on an ungodly winter's night.

There were so many questions.

CHAPTER 11

Two of the mundane but very necessary tasks for the afternoon was compiling a list of those people I needed to interview over the coming weeks and tracking down their current whereabouts. People shifted about so much nowadays and difficult as it was for me to believe, not everyone was so bewitched by Dunedin's charms that they wanted to live here forever. Being a university city made it even more of an issue. An endless merry-go-round of students came, graduated and left, as did academics and teaching staff. Circumstances changed, jobs and career opportunities arose, the lure of family could entice people away. Staying put for twenty-five years was a rarity. Of course, one line of questioning might be about why they left Dunedin in the first place, although I suspected no one would come right out and say 'I had to leave town because I killed a man'.

Once I had this information I could figure out the logistics of how and when to interview those who no longer lived in the city. Given my circumstances I didn't relish the idea of travelling away from home and Amelia for any period of time. In fact, if push came to shove, I'd delegate that job and send Detective Constable Richardson, or someone else who wasn't lactating.

I created a new spreadsheet on the computer and started recording the names and details of people who had been interviewed during the initial investigation. There was a sizeable list of witnesses, most of whom were parishioners. There were also some witnesses from nearby offices and businesses, as well as staff from the Hoyts movie theatre, who first alerted the police on the night in question. There were also a couple of 'of no fixed abode' individuals, who were known for hanging out in the central city area and who might have seen something. Alas, the list of identified suspects was nowhere near as comprehensive as the witness list.

I would start with the family, friends and witnesses side of the ledger first, but I would prioritise who I would follow up with. There was no need for me to talk to every person who had been in the church that night. That approach hadn't borne any fruit twenty-five years ago, so it was hardly likely to now. I would distil the list down to those I deemed key players.

Reverend Freeman's wife, Yvonne, still lived in Dunedin, as did their son, Callum. Felicity had been kind enough to give me their contact details this morning. Yvonne Freeman had never remarried and lived by herself in a council flat near Callum and his family in Caversham. They would be the first on my list of people to talk to. Firstly, because of convenience – I knew where they were located so they were easy pickings, so I'd make the most of that. Secondly, I needed to get a sense of the stakes here, forge a connection with the case and those most affected by the crime. I needed to hear their stories for myself – not least to find out why they had been pretty much eliminated as potential suspects straight away. I didn't want to make assumptions there, wanted to come to my own conclusions after examining the evidence and testimony. But I also wanted to feel what Reverend Freeman's death meant for them, in tangible terms. Knowing that would help drive me forward when the case got tough, and I was pretty certain it would, when the very cold leads froze up altogether, when I felt there was no progress.

A phone call earlier to the St Paul's office manager had confirmed the current situations of the cathedral staff from that time. The then Dean of the Diocese, The Very Reverend Dr Donald Donaldson, had unfortunately passed away three years ago at the veritable age of eighty-five, but one of the other priests, the Reverend Jesse James, now retired, was still in the city and an active member of the church. The original groundsman was still working for the church, even though he was fairly antique by now, which was the office manager's description of him, not mine. She was also able to provide details for the youth leader, Mel Smythe, who, though no longer involved with the diocese, still lived in Dunedin. The way she talked about her with almost a note of distaste made me curious as to the situation there. Office managers were up there with medical receptionists and hairdressers when it came to having a pretty good handle on people and what was afoot in any given community. They tended to be the fonts of all knowledge, the gatekeepers to information, and knew, figuratively speaking, where the bodies were buried. I was curious as to the cause of her disdain. I made a mental note to ask her about it when I went to the church. Delia O'Brien had been in the role for the last ten years, so was not around at the time of the murder, and didn't even live in the city back then, but she could clearly remember the shock it caused around the country. It wasn't every day a priest was killed on the steps of his church, and it made her, along with the rest of Kiwi Joe Public, feel that nowhere was sacred, nowhere was safe.

The list of serious suspects or persons of interest barely warranted the title of list. Over a period of months in the initial investigation, those closest to the victim – his family, church colleagues and friends – had been eliminated. That left only a couple of leads to pursue. And pursue them they had. One of the people brought in for questioning on multiple occasions was Aaron Cox, a man then described as of no current address and who, according to the case files, Reverend Freeman had befriended and was helping to try and get back on his feet. He had a chequered history of addiction and gang violence, and had spent time in the hospitality of the justice system, but apparently he had found God and seen the error of his ways. The Reverend had been advocating on Cox's behalf with the various welfare agencies and community organisations as part of his rehabilitation into polite society. The story gave me the impression that Reverend Freeman was a man who fought for the underdog. But judging by the case notes, there were members of the police who were certain the underdog had bit the hand that fed him. But they had failed to find any evidence of this, despite subjecting the man to several gruelling interviews and poking around into every facet of his life. Cox had been present at the service the night Reverend Freeman was killed, but couldn't provide an alibi for the time afterward, stating that he was sleeping rough then because he was no longer eligible to stay at the night shelter. That awful night he claimed to have found a dry spot hidden in the Moray Place car-parking building. He had been in his late thirties then, and would be knocking sixty-five now. I wondered if the trajectory of his life had improved, or if being the focus of a police investigation had ultimately made it worse. He certainly seemed to have been the centre of a lot of attention. It might take some digging to find out if he was still living in the city, and if so where. Was he even still alive? He was high on my must-see list.

The only other person, or persons, on the suspect list had never been identified. At the time there appeared to have someone, or ones, waging a campaign of nuisance against St Paul's. It had started with tagging and petty vandalism in the cathedral grounds. Spray paint on the wooden doors, but, interestingly, not on the stone-work, which would have been hell to scrub off. Apparently even the nuisances had a sense of what was a minor irritation and what was a serious pain in the neck. Well, to start with, anyway. Over a period of months the vandalism had escalated to broken windows and bomb threats. On three occasions worship services had been disrupted due to anonymous calls to emergency services. The result was everyone having to be evacuated from the building and the hassle of the police having to do a sweep of the premises. Even with this escalation, though, it was a big leap from petty inconveniences and a bit of property damage to outright murder. None of it had been directed at any one person so speculation at the time was that it was bored or aggrieved teenagers. The incidences ended abruptly after the death of Reverend Freeman. That could be interpreted in two ways: firstly, that the perpetrator or perpetrators had indeed been responsible for the murder, so job done. Or more likely, they were scared off by the prospect of being blamed and punished for killing a priest when they had nothing to do with it and all they had intended was some puerile entertainment and to piss people off.

The name I reluctantly added to the 'must talk to' list was Detective Inspector Greg Johns. I did place a question mark next to his name, though. Part of me thought it could be valuable to talk with a member of the investigating team from the time. Reading past reports was well and good, and they included the concrete evidence and what people deemed necessary to put on record. But what they didn't include was the talk around the water cooler, the left-field ideas people may have had when the logical had been exhausted, the inklings and gut feelings. The stuff that wasn't followed through with, was given a light touch or couldn't be corroborated and therefore was not put in writing.

The question mark was there not only because The Boss was too close to the subject matter, but also because part of me didn't want to be biased or swayed by mass opinion, and by those very hunches and gut feelings that meant the likes of Aaron Cox were hauled back time and time again, even in the face of a lack of hard evidence. Many miscarriages of justice had started exactly that way. In fact, one of the greatest detectives of all time, even if fictional, had warned of the danger of twisting the facts to fit the theories instead of the theories to fit the facts.

Maybe I'd get advice from wiser heads as to whether or not to interview The Boss. Sherlock Holmes was unavailable, so Smithy would have to do.

CHAPTER 12

Now I understood where Felicity Johns' cheekbones came from. That was a very shallow observation to make about a woman. I'm sure there was a lot more to Yvonne Freeman than incredible bone structure, but my excuse was there wasn't a lot of sleep had last night, courtesy of a little person teething, and to be honest, this going-back-to-work lark was a lot harder than I'd anticipated. Intellectually I knew it would take a while to get used to the physical aspects – the amount of time away from home, on the job, the breast-feeding logistics. Not to mention the mental load – the amount of concentration it required to focus on a task and problem-solve, when the most I'd had to concentrate on at home for the last six months was entertaining a mini human being, and doing the occasional cryptic crossword. What I hadn't factored in, though, was the emotional toll it took. The wrench of being away from Amelia when I loved every second of being in her company. The regret about going back to work and putting her into childcare, which felt like paying for someone else to bring up my child. And the guilt over the immense sense of relief I felt at getting away from her and from the relentless demands and responsibility of looking after a baby. At times I felt like a walking contradiction. They didn't tell you about this in the manuals.

Yvonne Freeman was an older and more elegant version of Felicity Johns. She wore her greying hair a little longer – in a bob rather than a pixie cut – and she bore the badges of honour that came with ageing with style and grace. If I were Felicity I would look at my mother and think, yes, if that's my future, I'm all good. When I looked at my own mother I thought, oh dear.

Yvonne was seated across from me at her dining-room table, well not really dining room per se as her flat was compact, with the kitchen, dining and living room all in one space. But the way she had arranged her furniture and rugs created well-defined zones, which maximised what little space there was and created a cosy and very comfortable home. There was an awful lot packed in here, with shelves laden with books, knick-knacks and pot plants. I cringed a bit at the pot plants so close to the books, but they had large saucers under them and she was probably better at judging the watering levels than I was. She'd even managed to fit a piano in here without it dominating the space. It too was graced with a pot plant. A tabby cat curled into a tight ball on the sofa completed the cosy vibe.

'Thank you for inviting me to your house to talk, and thank you for the tea.'

Yvonne had served tea the proper way, with a pot, bone-china cups and saucers, and biscuits. At this stage in the day I was especially happy to see the biscuits.

'That's okay,' she said. 'If we're talking about all this again, I'd rather do it here in comfort.' It wasn't said with any resentment, more a statement of fact.

'I'm sorry that reopening the investigation into your husband's death is going to bring back memories of a difficult time. And I know it's not going to be easy, but we are hoping that we will finally be able to bring some justice for you and your family.'

'Thank you. In some ways it's hard to believe it was so long ago. So much of it feels like yesterday, but then, I look in the mirror and have to face the fact a lot of time has passed and that it's been twenty-five years since I lost him.'

'I'm sorry you had to go through that, and that you've had to wait all that time without knowing who did it to him. I assure you we'll be working hard to try and finally get you some answers.'

'You know, we lost everything that day,' she said, looking down into her cup of tea. 'People could understand the horror and grief of me losing my husband, the children their dad, but I don't think they had any idea how hard it was being a part of the investigation. How intrusive and how relentless it was, when all we wanted to do was hide away and mourn. People had no idea of the long-term effects.'

'What kind of effects?'

'Most of them didn't realise that Mark being killed meant we lost our home.'

I could imagine a host of long-term effects but that wasn't something I had considered. 'You lost your home? That would have been dreadful for you. How did that happen?'

'Mark was the priest and we were living in the vicarage at the time. We couldn't just stay on there indefinitely after he was murdered. When they employed a priest to replace him, she needed to move in with her family. Don't get me wrong, we weren't turfed out onto the streets or anything like that. The governing body went out of their way to help us find somewhere else to live, to start again, but the reality was we had always lived in vicarages, so had never owned a home of our own. Mark had been the breadwinner. I had been giving my time to the kids and to the Church, being a good minister's wife, so suddenly I was in a position where I had no real assets and had to go and find a job to support my family. I didn't have any formal qualifications, so picked up work at the supermarket at the start. It meant things were very tight and we could only afford to rent somewhere very modest. Most people thought we moved by choice. We moved because we had to.'

'I'm sorry to hear that. That's awful you had to cope with all that on top of losing your husband.'

'At first, people were great in coming forward with offers to help out how they could. But after a while the offers stopped and everyone went back to their lives, when ours had changed forever.'

I could relate to that. I had the same feeling after Dad had died. People offered their condolences and supported you at the time, but it wasn't long after the funeral that they stopped checking in and asking how I was. The bugger was those check-ins stopped at the exact moment that I needed them more than ever, when the urgency of dealing with funerals and the bureaucracy of death had waned and the grief had the time and space to hit, and hit hard. Thank heavens for Maggie and Paul, who walked alongside me all through that. I knew Mum experienced the same and likewise was grateful to some stalwart friends who propped her up.

'And how was the investigation for you?' I asked.

'Not easy. It felt like it dragged on forever. There were so many questions to answer, police coming back constantly to check another detail, ask another question, or the same question again and again. And of course the awful and humiliating feeling of having our family examined, in case one of us were to blame.' She looked me straight in the eye again then. 'We understood they were just doing their job, and in a way we would have been concerned if they didn't look at everyone, because that would mean they weren't doing a thorough job, weren't looking hard enough. But still, it did hurt.'

Yvonne surprised me with how straight to the point she was with her concerns. If she was going to be that direct, then there was no point in me sugar-coating anything that was about to happen.

'I can only imagine how difficult that would have been for you all. Unfortunately, reopening the investigation does mean that those questions will be asked again, so please don't take it personally, against yourself or your children, when we have to ask them. As you understand, we have to eliminate all possibilities. I know the police at the time were truly disappointed not to be able to solve the case for you back then. We want to get it right this time.'

'I know you do, and Greg too. Felicity told me he initiated the request.'

'Yes, he did.'

She paused then, before saying quietly, 'Frankly, I wish he hadn't.'

'Why?' I tried not to sound too surprised.

'I suspect he wanted to do it for me, because ... I don't know if you know, but I have cancer; terminal cancer. I'm on borrowed time, months, maybe weeks. I know his heart is in the right place and he doesn't want me to go to my grave without finding out who did this.

But I'm not going to be around forever, and I don't want what limited time I have left consumed by a police investigation. I want to spend my days relaxing with my kids and my grandkids, doing things that bring me happiness and make good memories for them, not things that will bring me pain.'

She gave a sad and tired-sounding sigh.

'And I don't want to get my hopes up only to have them dashed again.'

CHAPTER 13

Callum Freeman's home was a far cry from the oasis of calm inhabited by his mother. Walking from the front door, through the dining area and into the lounge was like passing through a domestic war zone where three schoolbags had detonated and their contents had exploded across the floor, spreading into the most strategically inconvenient places. In particular, the colour-coordinated effort of high-vis-orange ring binder hanging out of a matching orange backpack placed in the middle of a doorway got a ten out of ten from me. I stepped over it and the lunchbox situated a foot away from the epicentre. Callum saw me hurdling the carnage, came around and nudged them out of the way slightly with his foot.

'I'm sorry about the mess,' he said as he discreetly tried to move a hockey stick towards its bag. 'It's usually tidier than this by the time I get home, but...' He let the sentence drift off.

On any normal day he would have still been at his job as a financial analyst with one of the largest accountancy firms in town, but after a bit of to and fro, negotiating a time that suited us both, he'd offered to come home early so we could talk during my work hours. It was most appreciated. The time was creeping towards four o'clock and I was keen to call it a day. The family beckoned.

'I'm sure my mother would say all this havoc was just God getting back at me for being an obnoxious teenager.'

'Were you that bad?' I asked.

'I was certainly guilty of being messy, and probably guilty of being a bit full of myself in those days.' He gestured over towards the headphone-clad, laptop-clutching, beanbag-inhabiting sixteen-year-old boy in the corner of the room. 'I did the sullen thing a bit too. Mum's getting the last laugh, I assure you. Karma.'

'Do you want to come through to my office. We're less likely to be disturbed down there.'

As we walked past the kitchen, I noted another teenager raiding the pantry. He looked at his dad, puzzled and then looked at me, extra puzzled.

'You're home early,' he said with a voice much deeper than his gangliness would have indicated. 'Who is that?' he asked pointing in my general direction with a box of crackers. It was said with curiosity, rather than rudeness, although the differentiation there was quite thin.

'She's with the police,' his dad said. 'Detective Shephard, this is my son Zac.'

The boy's eyes widened, and then he blushed and looked decidedly squirmy.

'Come this way, Detective,' said Callum.

We walked along a dim hallway and into a decent-sized room that, judging by the two desks, was a shared office space.

As I entered Callum turned to me, a large grin on his face. 'Zac has some friends who have recently been in trouble with the law, and by association he has come under some scrutiny himself. He probably thinks we're in here talking about him.'

That explained the guilty face.

'Will you inform him otherwise?'

'A little later maybe. For now I think it will be good for him to think he could be in some trouble. It might make him reflect on who he hangs out with.'

Objectivity lesson of the day.

He gestured to an armchair in the corner of the room and pulled over another, which was currently home to a pile of papers. He'd left the door open, and I wondered if young Zac would be trying to listen in. As if reading my mind, Callum said, 'Don't worry, I'll be able to hear if anyone tries to spy on us. The floorboards are quite creaky along here. It's a handy advance-warning system.'

The office walls were decorated with the usual wall planners and whiteboards. One whiteboard was very orderly, with to-do lists that included neat little hand-drawn check boxes, to be filled when each item was complete. Two thirds of these were coloured in with a bright blue. A productive to-do list. It was affixed to the wall next to an orderly desk. In contrast the other whiteboard was covered with a hodge podge of Post-it Notes, pieces of paper attached with magnets and some fairly illegible scrawlings. It was no surprise that the associated desk was just as disorderly.

On the wall above where I was seated was a family portrait of the awkwardly posed variety on a park bench in front of a large tree. Zac and his brother looked like they were around ten and twelve years old, and between them on the seat was a younger sister, all of them dressed in their Sunday best. Callum Freeman and his wife, Penny, were standing behind their children, inner arms around each other, outer hands resting on the far shoulders of their offspring. All very symmetrical, all very formal. The parents looked perfectly happy. The kids looked like they wanted to be anywhere else but there. Alongside that unnatural monstrosity I was pleased to see another multi-picture frame with a range of photos that reflected the spontaneous and happy side of family life.

'You've got a nice set-up here. Do you and your wife work from home often?'

'I don't that much, but Penny is a freelance writer. She's employed writing content for a web company in town two days a week, but the rest of the time she's based in here doing commissioned work and short-term contract stuff.'

Callum had finally managed to find a spot for the pile of material from the armchair and sat down. Once he had settled in I got to the point.

'As you are aware I'm looking into the case of your father's death.'

'Yes, Felicity spoke to our mother and me about this when Greg first mentioned he was going to reopen the case. So we've been expecting your call.'

This saved me a lot of explaining.

'I've read through your statements and interview transcripts from the time,' I went on. 'And I realise it was an incredibly awful moment for you, but I'd like to hear you tell your story of the events of that night.'

He sat back, hands slowly rubbing together, looking up at the ceiling, like he was playing the memories out on a screen.

'Cor, it's been a long time since I've talked with anyone about it. No one asks anymore. It's hard to believe it's been twenty-five years; it still feels like yesterday. It's like everyone else has forgotten about it, but for our family it's still front and foremost in our minds.'

Given it had been that long, there were probably a lot of people in their circles, newer friends and work colleagues, who wouldn't even know about it. That had to be strange to contemplate.

'How about you talk me through that evening, from when you first went to church?'

'Well, it was a horrible, wet evening. We all walked down to the church together, and quite early, seeing as my father was taking the service. We always went together, but usually came home at different times, as Dad was often held up with people wanting to talk, or he had things to organise. We got there around quarter to seven.'

'Was the cathedral already open then or did you open up?'

'It was already open. The choir had been having a practice beforehand so there were already quite a few people there by the time we arrived.'

'And was there anything about the service that seemed different from normal?'

'No, it was your regular, run-of-the-mill Sunday evensong. It wasn't a special celebration service, or communion or anything like that. Dad gave the sermon, which ironically was based on the Bible verses from Matthew about forgiveness. Along the lines of, if you forgive things people have done to you, then God will forgive you. But if you don't forgive people, then God won't forgive your sins.'

'You can remember the sermon?'

He looked at me then, and gave a tight smile. 'I wasn't paying that much attention at the time, to be honest. I'd listened to a lot of Dad's sermons over the years, so tended to tune out. Don't get me wrong, he was a great speaker, kept it lively, didn't drone on or anything. But that one I remembered. Sermons at evensong were short, and given the events afterwards, that one will always be etched into my brain.'

Trauma would do that to you, I guessed. It was strange what stuck in your mind. Years of listening to witnesses who had all seen the same event had taught me how different we all were when it came to assessing what was important and what we remembered. Brains could be weird.

My mind went back to his choice of wording earlier. 'Why did you find it ironic?'

He looked puzzled.

'You said you found his choice of sermon ironic.'

'Ha, yeah, I did. Because as it turned out, he was preaching what we would ultimately have to do. We'd have to forgive whoever did this to him, whoever committed this crime. It felt kind of prescient.'

'Do you think he knew something, or was trying to make a statement about something?'

'I've thought about that a lot over the years, but I don't know ... Don't know what to think.'

'He hadn't mentioned being concerned about anything to you, wasn't worried about his safety?'

'No. And he wouldn't have. I was seventeen, and if I'm honest, I could be a bit of an ass. If he had confided in anyone about any concerns it would have been an adult, one of his friends or the other priests.'

'Your mother?'

'Maybe, although he tried to protect her from anything harsh or unpleasant, just like he did us kids. If he was seeking advice or guidance on something, it more likely would have been from one of the menfolk.'

The old boys' club.

'Can you talk me through what happened when the service was over?'

'As usual, we stayed for a little bit to chat with people, I guess ten to fifteen minutes. Part of that was probably reluctance to go out into that weather. Mum headed home first.'

'You didn't walk back together?'

'Not that time. We often did, but it depended on who got stuck talking, and if Felicity or I had schoolwork due we would head back straight away. Dad was always last one home because he often locked up.'

'So your mum walked home first. When did you leave, and your sister?'

'Mum had been feeling unwell, a migraine or something, so left pretty much straight away. I saw Felicity leave shortly after Mum. I got caught up talking with the youth-group leader for a little bit.'

'Mel Smythe?'

'Yeah. She liked to talk.'

'It was the middle of winter – the family didn't have any concerns about Felicity walking home by herself in the dark?'

'No, she was fifteen and quite tall for her age. It was only a few blocks, and Stuart Street is a busy road and well lit, so we were never really concerned about her safety. Anyway, she would have complained about being babied if anyone insisted on her having a bodyguard.' He paused a little then. 'Although that all changed, of course.'

It certainly did. I imagined none of them ever felt safe again.

'So when did you leave?'

'Not long after Felicity. Five minutes or so, I guess.'

'Was there anyone else still in the church when you left?'

'There were only a few people. The organist I think, the youth leader and a couple of parishioners. At the time I didn't really pay any attention, so I wasn't much help to the police there.'

'And were there any people you didn't know, people who weren't regulars?'

'There were at the service – visitors to the city, I guess. There often were, especially at the evensong, because it was always so lovely. But when I left, there would have only been a few people from the church remaining. That was all. So I didn't think Dad would be that far behind me.'

'So the three of you were all back at home. At what point did you start to wonder about how long it was taking your father to return?'

'The service finished around 8.00pm. We would have all been home by twenty past, twenty-five past. Mum started to get really worried when Dad wasn't home by nine. If he was going to be late for a specific reason he'd let her know, like if he had planned a quick meeting with someone after the service, something like that. But he hadn't said anything, so when it hit nine o'clock and he still wasn't back, that's when she asked me to run down to the church to see if he was okay.'

'Had she tried to call him?'

'Yes, but he didn't reply. He usually had his phone on silent for the service, so she wasn't really expecting him to pick up.'

Now we were starting to get into difficult territory.

'So she sent you back to the cathedral. What happened then?'

Callum took in a deep breath and leaned forward, elbows on his knees, hands clasped together.

'I could see from a distance that there weren't any lights on in the cathedral, so I thought Dad must have just locked up and I'd bump into him any second now on his way up the road. It was hosing down, so I took cover from the rain in the Stuart Street side entrance – the Robinson Porch – and waited to see if he would appear from around the back. That door was locked. After a few minutes he hadn't turned up, so I walked on down Stuart Street and up the side steps to check the front doors. They were locked too.'

'Did you see any other people around at that point?'

'No. The church carpark was empty, and there weren't any other pedestrians around. It was quite late by then and pouring down. I didn't notice anyone in The Octagon, but then I wasn't looking and

I can't remember if any cars drove past. I was keeping an eye out for my father and trying to keep my head down and stay as dry as I could.'

'And when did you finally discover him, Callum?'

'There's also an entrance down on the other side, into the cathedral office and the rooms underneath the church, so I walked across the top landing and when I went to go down the steps, that's when I saw him, sprawled out at the bottom. He wasn't moving and...' he paused to take a breath '...and I could tell by the way he was lying it wasn't going to be good.'

It was hard to see him struggling with describing the scene, but I kept quiet, gave him the space to tell the story in his own time.

'I raced down those stairs as fast as I could. I could see he was soaking wet and ... well, he was ... he looked unconscious. He was lying on his front so I tried to roll him over onto his back, but it was hard, he was bigger than me, but I finally got him over and I tried to feel his neck for a pulse, but there was nothing, so I started CPR. I was yelling out for help, hoping someone might be walking nearby, anyone, but no one heard me, nobody came.'

I could see his eyes welling with tears, and he noticed me noticing.

'I'm sorry,' he said, wiping his eyes. 'I don't normally do this. It's been so long, you'd think I'd be able to talk about it without crying.'

'It's okay. It's been a huge part of your life, and having us open everything up again will be hard on you and your family. And you were only seventeen at the time. You found your dad. No kid should ever have to do that. Don't underestimate the effect it had on you.'

He nodded. 'Yeah, I know. You're right. Sorry.'

'And how did you get help? Did you call someone? Police? Ambulance?'

'I didn't have my own phone back then. Mum and Dad wouldn't let us have them, so I couldn't just ring someone. And I didn't think to try and find Dad's. I was panicking. I kept doing CPR for what felt like ages, but nothing was happening, it didn't make any difference. I knew he was gone, there was nothing I could do. All I could think of was to go get help. There were restaurants in The Octagon and I tried those, but they had all closed, so the only thing I could think of was to go to the Hoyts movie theatre – it was the only place that was open. It felt awful leaving him lying there, it felt like I was conceding defeat and leaving him to die, but I had to go get help.'

His voice had cracked, but I could see he was trying hard to hold it together. The witness statements from the movie-theatre staff had talked of a distraught and very wet young man running up to the counter. They called the police once they'd figured out he wasn't just some drunk or tripped-out student, had managed to calm him down and worked out what he was trying to say. From then on it was all go, with police being dispatched to the cathedral and to the theatre to pick up the boy. From that moment the Freemans' lives had changed forever.

'It sounds like you did all the right things. You had no choice but to go for help.'

'But did I? Did I do it right? You know when they said that he'd died of a broken neck, I did wonder if I'd actually, like, finally killed him when I rolled him over to do CPR. They say you should never move someone if you think they've injured their neck or spine, and I could see from the angle of his head that there was something wrong, but all I could think about was checking his pulse, giving him mouth-to-mouth, trying to make him live.'

'His neck would have broken in the fall – the pathologist said that, and I'm sure other people would have told you that too. You should believe them. You did the right thing.'

He still didn't look that convinced. It would probably be one of those questions he'd ask himself for the rest of his life. I tried to steer him away from the self-recriminations.

'Can you think of anyone that may have had reason to do something like this. Anyone who had an issue with your father?'

'No, not really.'

'Not really?' An interesting choice of words. 'Was there someone you had concerns about?'

'My father was a good man, who always tried to do his best for people. He helped people when others wouldn't. Some of those people weren't exactly squeaky clean, had dubious pasts, but he believed in giving second chances.'

'Is there someone in particular you have in mind?'

'There was a guy – his name was Aaron. I don't know his last name. He'd been homeless, but my dad was trying to get him sorted with accommodation in a hostel and was trying to help him out with finding work, and other things as well. He'd started coming along to services and was one of the people still at the church when I left.'

'Did you mention this to police at the time?'

'Yes. They'd wanted the names of everyone I'd left behind when I'd gone. I wasn't entirely certain of the others, but I was certain about him. I assume the police spoke to him.'

I'd seen many interviews with Aaron when flicking through the truckload of transcripts on file. I hadn't read them all in detail, as I was prioritising the family and colleagues, but I'd go back and look at them thoroughly now.

'Is there any particular reason he came up on your radar?'

'I don't know. Not really. He was strange. I just didn't like being around him and I didn't trust him.'

It might have just been a case of Callum being a judgemental teenager, afraid of what he didn't understand. But over the years I'd learned to trust people's radars – more often than not they were right.

CHAPTER 14

'How's it going, then?'

'Are you referring to the case or the being-back-at-work thing?'

'Both.'

It had been going reasonably well – mostly. But four days in I had reached the point where I was in need of some serious Maggie therapy. Maggie had been my best friend, flatmate, confidante and reality check for years before being usurped by a bloke and a kid. To be honest, there were days where I would seriously consider a swap back. The venue for the therapy session was The Perc café; reason for choosing the venue was in the process of finding its way into my mouth. I was rather fond of their cheese rolls. Mind you, I was rather fond of everyone's cheese rolls, or 'southern sushi' as they were known down this way. Cheesy goodness rolled up in thin white bread and toasted till all melty and crispy. Extra butter on top was mandatory. I considered myself a bit of a connoisseur. Lunch with Maggs was a reward after a frustrating morning, which had ended with the glory of milking the girls. I was getting better at the whole process, but still approached it with some dread. A few refinements had been needed though. After a little confusion amongst the team as to what in the kitchenette fridge was work milk and what most definitely was not, Paul had gone out and bought a small chiller bag to store the product of my efforts in, with milkshake fabric, of course.

'This working business is taking a bit of getting used to,' I said, trying to get a long string of melted cheese under control. 'Not going to lie, I miss being at home with Amelia.'

'Well I'd be a bit concerned if you weren't.'

'True.'

Maggie was getting her laughing gear around a cheese scone that looked bigger than her head. She was being even more liberal with the butter than I was, which was saying something.

'And how's Paul going being home on Dad duty?'

'Ha, I think he's having way too much fun with Amelia this week. I suspect our cunning plan to ease her into daycare and get used to Mum not being around all the time is going to backfire, because next week there will be two of us moping and wildly missing the wee poppet.'

'Seemed like a good idea at the time?'

'Sure did.' I drained the last of my large flat white and seriously contemplated another. Much as I was tempted, I knew I'd regret it, so just reached for the water. Last thing I needed was a twitchy, over-caffeinated bubba.

'And what about my favourite goddaughter? How's she liking the new arrangements? She missing you?' Although Maggie was about as heathen as they came, she had still been delighted to be asked to be Amelia's godmother. She saw the role more along the lines of fairy godmother and chief spoiler – well, deputy spoiler, after my mum – rather than spiritual guide. Unless that spirituality was based around Gaia and a touch of white witchery. I had mental images of them having a blast dancing naked round the garden and planting garlic on the winter solstice.

'I wish. She's living her best life. She gets to hang out with her dad. They've been going to the pool and the park, and it pains me to say it, but I don't think she's missing me at all.'

'I'll bet you she is.'

'I dunno,' I said. 'Mind you, she was a bit clingy this morning, so maybe I'm not totally redundant.'

'Not at home, nor at work.' Maggs was struggling with the sheer size of the scone and offered me a buttery segment. Who was I to say no? 'Your cold case sounds intriguing. You going to do what The Boss and his pals couldn't manage twenty-five years ago and solve that thing?'

I'd popped the scone straight into my cakehole, so we had to wait a moment while I dealt with it enough to be able to speak. I loved Maggie too much to subject her to the sight of me talking with my mouth full.

'I bloody well hope so. And if I do it would please him and irritate him in equal measure, I think.'

'That would be new for you, getting on his good side and his bad side all in one go. It would be quite the achievement.' We both had a giggle. Maggs was well aware of the fraught relationship I had with The Boss and had been on the receiving end of my venting on many an occasion. But that's what friends were for. 'How's it going? Making any headway?'

'If by making headway you mean making people cry? Then sure, going great. This case just seems to be one interview after another where I'm upsetting folk.'

'What are you doing to upset them? Are you being mean and horrible, Sam?' The voice she put on made full mock of my complete inability to be nasty.

'I'm not doing anything to them. It's mostly the man's family I've interviewed so far.'

'Ah, I'm guessing they're finding the reopening of the case a bit of a challenge?'

'Yeah. I'm feeling bad about dredging up the past and picking the scabs off the old hurts for them.'

'Charming metaphor there, especially while eating. But you know, Sam, it is your job to do that, to pick the scabs. In fact, you have to do it whether they want it or not. I know you're a bit of a bleeding heart, and you don't like to hurt people's feelings and worry too much that people might think ill of you. But sometimes you've just got to put your big-girl panties on and do your job. That's why they pay you the big bucks. Simple as that.'

'The bucks aren't that big.'

'Okay, the mediocre bucks.'

'I'll take that.'

We'd scored a table in the front window and both paused to

admire a very pretty Weimaraner taking its owner for a walk down the street.

'You know, it's pretty cool that you're in charge of the whole case.'

'Yeah, that part of it is great, although I still can't help being suspicious of The Boss's motives in assigning it to me.'

'Even if they were dodgy, which is highly likely, it's still a fabulous opportunity to play him at his own game, and win.'

'I guess so.'

'That's the ultimate revenge against an arsehole boss.'

'You make it sound like a vendetta.'

'Well it is, sort of, isn't it?'

'I wouldn't call it a vendetta, more a grudge match.'

'Semantics. Either way, you solve the case and it's a win-win. You get one over on The Boss for doing what they couldn't manage quarter of a century ago, you get in his good books for finally giving his family some closure, and solving a case like this is sure to give your career prospects a boost.'

'That's a win-win-win.'

'Again, semantics.'

I laughed. This woman was my biggest cheerleader, and the dose of Maggie therapy was just the tonic I needed.

'Go on,' she said. 'You've got a case to solve. Get out there and do your job.'

CHAPTER 15

Entering through the cathedral office's small, nondescript side door was like opening a door to Narnia or some unknown magical world. I had no idea there was so much hidden away beneath the cathedral. After a small entry lobby, the parquet flooring led into a large gallery space with a number of offices and meeting rooms leading off it. The walls were adorned with an array of photos and portraits, and my eyes were drawn to a colourful trio of robes hanging in the boardroom window. On my left an impressive set of marble steps swept up into the church itself. I worked my way around the room, taking in the array of framed faces, and paused at a series of photos of the cathedral under construction. But what caught my attention the most was a wonderful, wooden scale model of the church, sitting on a table in the middle of the space, protected under a perspex case. It must have been made when they were preparing to build the new chancel and sanctuary back in the early 1970s. I always loved me a good model.

'Can I help you?'

The woman's voice made me near wet my pants. Until that moment I hadn't realised quite how on edge I was. A legacy of churches past.

'Hi, I'm Detective Sam Shephard. I have an appointment with Reverend James.'

'Oh yes, hello Detective, I'm Delia. We spoke when you first rang about looking into Reverend Freeman's case.'

Now the voice was familiar, and I relaxed a little. 'Nice to meet you in person, Delia, and thank you for being so helpful with everything the other day. Sometimes when we start making enquiries with people they can be a bit cautious, so I really appreciated that you were able to give me so much information straight away.'

'Oh, you're most welcome.' She looked well pleased by the compliment. 'Honestly, I think everyone here will be helpful. The Reverend's murder had a huge impact on the church, and the fact that no one was ever charged has weighed heavily on everyone's minds. So if there's anything we can do to help find the culprit, we will try as best we can.'

My mind turned back to our previous conversation, and her less-than-enthusiastic attitude towards the youth leader. She seemed a very open person, so I didn't think she'd mind me asking for some more background. 'Before I talk to Reverend James can I just ask you a quick question about Mel Smythe?'

'Of course, what did you want to—?'

Before she had a chance to finish her sentence the outside door flew open and the equivalent of a human hurricane breezed into the gallery.

'Delia, Detective, you must be the detective, Shephard, isn't it? Like the Lord is my shepherd? Priest humour there, even worse than dad jokes. I'm so sorry I'm late, but the roadworks were crazy and I took the wrong route. It was the right route yesterday, but they've moved everything around again, so traffic-cone mayhem, you know what it's like right now. And it's started raining out there, did you know it had started raining?'

The man I assumed was the Reverend Jesse James filled the space with a presence that was a little overwhelming, but in a loud and cheerful way. He reminded me of one of those characters off *Father Ted*, but without the Irish accent or the booze. He walked straight up to me and reached out his hand. I cautiously extended mine and tried not to look too alarmed when he vigorously pumped it.

'You know I was very happy, delighted even, when Delia told me that the police were reopening Mark's murder case. It's been far too long having that unfinished business hanging over our heads. That poor family need some justice, to get some closure so they can all move on. It's a pity it's taken – what? – twenty-five years for it to happen. But better late than never, eh?' He finally dropped my hand

and set off in the direction of one of the offices. 'Come this way, Detective. I'll see if someone can organise us a cup of tea and we can have a talk.'

I turned to look at Delia, and she gave a small shrug of her shoulders and a wry smile. 'I should have warned you, the Reverend is very chatty ... Very...' she whispered. 'I'll bring you a cup of tea. You'll need it.'

'Thanks,' I replied, mirroring her smile, and headed off after the Reverend.

We passed through a dreary office with a number of desks and printers, and into a small room at the rear. On the way through I noted an iron door embedded in the wall – probably leading to what looked like a rather large vault. It was a bit over the top for holding the daily offerings, so I wondered if the church had some valuable treasures that only got trotted out for special occasions, like the crown jewels. It did perhaps answer my question as to whether they might have kept any cash offerings on site.

'Take a seat, take a seat,' Reverend James said, pointing to the opposite side of the table as he busily hung up his coat.

'Thanks,' I said.

'This is great news, you know. I meant it when I said I was very happy you were reopening the case. I can't tell you how much of a toll it took on everyone around here. Our own dear Reverend murdered on the very steps of our church. I'll never forget that night. I got a call from Yvonne saying the police were here and something dreadful had happened, and could I come around, which of course I did. The dean was away at a national synod at the time, so I was left in command of the ship, as it were. As you can imagine, it was pretty much bedlam. No one really knew what was happening. They'd taken Callum back home. He was a mess, poor boy. You know it was me who went down to formally identify the body? That's something you never want to have to do for a friend and a colleague.'

It was like someone had pulled the rip cord on the man and he was going to talk and talk and talk until it was time to wind it up again. It was as if he'd been holding it all in for years, and now there was an opportunity, his story came gushing out, unchecked. I didn't even have to ask any questions.

'But of course you'll want to know what happened before then, at the evening service itself. Even though it wasn't my turn to preach, I always came along to evensong. I found them more relaxed, a good time to chat with people, and I always loved a good hymn or two. The night Mark died I was already here when the Freemans arrived – they always came down together. As for the service itself, he preached a good sermon – he always did, a gifted orator, that man. He preached from Matthew six, verses fourteen and fifteen: "For if you forgive others their trespasses, your Heavenly Father will also forgive you, but if you do not forgive others, neither will your Father forgive your trespasses."'

I always admired people who could quote chapter and verse, but then, he was a priest, it was his job.

He continued on without any prompting: 'The service went smoothly, no disruptions or anything like that, just another day at the office. Afterwards people milled around for a little bit, but I think because it was such a grotty night, most people left pretty quickly.'

'Did you think there was anything significant about why he chose to preach about forgiveness?'

'No, I didn't read anything into that. Forgiveness is our stock in trade. We like to remind our flock regularly about the importance of showing mercy, compassion and understanding. Mind you, given the dreadful events that unfolded afterwards, we have all had to try and show some forgiveness to whoever committed that terrible act.'

I hoped that I'd be able to give them the identity of the person to forgive. Would it be easier or harder when they had a real person, an individual to have to exercise that forgiveness upon, or was it easier to forgive a phantom?

'Had Reverend Freeman voiced any concerns to you – worries

he may have had about anything? Mentioned anyone who was causing him problems, or if he was concerned about his safety?'

'No. When we talked he had the same kind of worries as most of us: making ends meet, looking after his family, meeting our responsibilities to the Church. He never mentioned feeling unsafe in any way, or that he was having problems with anyone. And I hadn't heard from anyone else that they were worried about him – not from parishioners nor other priests.'

'So you all got on here – felt you could discuss anything, supported each other?'

'Yes, and not just the ministry team based at the cathedral, but across the diocese. Everyone got along pretty well.'

I had the impression that Reverend James would have been the social glue that kept an eye on people's welfare and wellbeing. I could imagine him being like a mother hen in a cassock.

'What time did you leave the cathedral that night?' I asked.

'Gosh, it would have been quarter past eight or so, I suppose. There weren't that many people here by then. I know Yvonne had already left, and Felicity, because I'd been chatting with both of them and said goodbye. When I went there would only have been five or six people here.'

'And none of those people gave you any cause for concern?'

'Are you asking did I think any of those people could have murdered Mark? No, not at all. They were all regulars, all salt-of-the-earth people. The only newish person was a man called Aaron. He was a bit of a rough diamond that one. Mark had taken him under his wing, but still, I don't think he would have hurt a fly.'

'Do you happen to know if he's still around? Still lives in Dunedin?'

'No, I don't. He stopped coming to church after that, which isn't surprising, seeing as Mark was the one doing all of the work with him. I know the police interviewed him a few times, but nothing came of that so they must have been satisfied he had nothing to do with it.'

'Was Callum still here when you left?'

'No, he would have gone a few minutes before me. Anyway, when I said goodnight and headed out to the car, Mark was talking with Aaron.'

'And that conversation appeared normal? No sign of any problem or tension there?'

'Not that I can recall – it just seemed like normal chit-chat. You know, I've had many a year to think about it, but I honestly couldn't think of anyone who would have had a reason to do that, to kill Mark. He wasn't all talk and no show, he was a man who walked the walk, a man of the people. There are some who take the cloth who are all show and ceremony, go in for all the trappings, want to earn the badges, as it were, get the gold trim on the robes, that kind of thing, and people like that have their place in the Church, I'm not going to judge them, but Mark was different. He lived by the values of Christ himself.'

I heard footsteps approaching and fervently hoped it was the refreshments.

It was. Delia arrived with a tray sporting a teapot, milk, sugar, a couple of mugs and some bikkies. 'Excuse me a moment, here you go,' she said.

I was glad of the break. I had very much warmed to the Reverend – he seemed a genuine and caring man – but he was also very loud and very verbose, and in this small and echoey space my ears were starting to ring. Delia gave me a wink as she retreated from the room.

'I'll play Mum,' he said, and set about pouring the tea. 'You take milk?' he asked even as he was already pouring some into my mug.

'Yes, thank you.'

I cupped my hands around the mug and took a cautious sip in case it was too hot. It was just right.

'Do you believe in God, Detective?'

I just about spat out my tea. It wasn't a question I'd been expecting.

He noted my reaction and I saw a smile cross his face. 'I'm sorry, that was quite nosey of me, wasn't it? But do you?'

I wasn't entirely sure how to answer that one. 'It's a complicated question.' I would have told most people to mind their own bloody business, but that response didn't feel appropriate, considering I was sitting in the bowels of this man's church. And besides, there was something about the Reverend James that almost made me want to answer. Was that his superpower? To make people comfortable enough that they wanted to confess all of their sins? Expose their souls? Handy skill for a priest.

'Well, do you believe in fate?' he asked next.

'Also complicated.'

He smiled at my fudging. 'When Mark was killed – no, murdered, I will say murdered, although it feels like such an ugly, confronting word to use – there were many in the congregation, myself included, who questioned how the Lord could have allowed such a thing to happen. How could this have been God's plan, what possible purpose could it have served? It did shake the faith of many of us. But I have to believe that things happen for a reason.'

He took a sip of his tea, and then made a couple of false starts to what he wanted to say next. It was clear he was choosing his words carefully, which in a man with the gift of the gab, who seemed to have no difficulty whatsoever in talking, made me suddenly wary.

'See, I believe the good Lord brings people into our lives at times when we need them. And I believe he has brought you here for a reason. I think the time has come for the mystery of Mark's *murder*' – he emphasised the word 'murder' – 'to be solved, and that revelation may finally lead us to see God's purpose, to understand.'

That put a lot of pressure on me to get to the bottom of this and do what my colleagues past had failed to. But I was up to the challenge. Talking with the Reverend Freeman's family, and now his church colleagues had provided that impetus, that drive to get to the bottom of this, for them.

Reverend James pointed at me then, as much as you could point when you were holding a mug of tea. 'I also think that life is a two-way street and you are not only here to solve this crime, but that God has something in store for you, some other reason to bring you to this church.'

Oh, Christ almighty. If the Reverend thought the Lord's plan was that I would find my way back into the fold, then he was going to be sorely disappointed. I suspected the Lord's plans and my plans were a little different.

CHAPTER 16

I'd managed to extricate myself from the chatty clutches of the Reverend James. It hadn't been all bad, though. After dropping his little mission-from-God bombshell on me he'd talked extensively about what kind of a man the Reverend Mark Freeman was. It was clear that there was a lot of love and respect there. He painted a picture of someone who was liked by everyone he worked with, who led by example and who would bend over backward to help people. In many ways he sounded too good to be true. When I intimated as much, the Reverend James was quick to say the Reverend Freeman was no saint, but he had no reason to suspect him of anything untoward that could have led to his death, hadn't got wind of any rumours or bad talk about him and couldn't think of any reason why someone would hold a grudge worth killing over. All of which left me no further ahead in the case than before. I did have one more thing to follow up on while I was here, though. I hung my head around the office manager's door.

'Can I have a quick word?'

'Sure, what can I help you with, Detective?' Delia asked. Judging from the half-pulled-on coat and handbag on the desk she was about to go out.

'Have I caught you at a bad time?'

'No, no. I was just heading down to Woolworths Supermarket to buy some more milk and biscuits for the office. It can wait.'

'It's on my way back to work. How about we walk down together?'

'Sounds good.' She shrugged the other arm into her coat and grabbed a couple of reusable grocery bags from down the side of the desk.

When she opened the door and we emerged outside we were hit

by a wall of crisp, cold air. It had stopped raining, thank heavens, and after the distinctive fug of old building I'd been breathing in for the last hour, the petrichor smell and damp grass was refreshing. Oddly enough, the wound-up and jumpy feeling I'd had from the moment I'd stepped through the door started to abate now I was out of the confines of the building. There was something about going into churches nowadays that made me uneasy. Perhaps something inside me was waiting to be struck down by lightning once I'd crossed the threshold. Not that lightning could strike indoors, in fact I was probably more at risk of it now. My eyes tracked upward and noted the brooding black clouds that still lingered after the rain shower. We walked around the side path and down onto The Octagon. The place was quite a bustle of excitable school kids released from their day's study, herding together in little groups, oblivious to any other pedestrians who had the misfortune to be out and about at this time. We had to wait for a large flock of Trinity girls to pass before we could step out onto the sidewalk.

'I hope this doesn't sound like a strange question, but when I rang the other day and we were talking about Mel Smythe, I got the feeling that there was something you weren't telling me.' We stopped at the intersection with George Street, and I reached out and pressed the crossing button. 'Did you have concerns about her? Was there an issue there?'

Now we were out of the shelter of the buildings, the brunt of the wind cut through us.

Delia pulled the collar up on her coat, trying to ward off the chill. 'Mel is an interesting woman. I can't speak to what she was like back when Reverend Freeman was killed, but in the time I've worked at the office, my dealings with her have been...' she searched for the right word '...challenging.'

The green man appeared on the traffic signal opposite with the accompanying clamour and countdown clock, so we headed across the road.

'What do you mean by challenging?'

'Well, she's no longer an active member of the Church. When I first started here she'd come along to services once or twice a month, but that dropped off over time and she hasn't been to worship here for years. But it's like she thinks the church owes her something, so every time she's in contact she's wanting something. I've come to dread her visits.'

'Do you know what caused her to drift away?'

'From what I've heard from others, it started shortly after the Reverend's death. Like many people, she was really shaken by it. Being the youth leader, she had a lot of contact with him and worked with him regularly, so it really rocked her. And of course she had a lot to do with his children and got to see the devastating effects his death had on them. People react to things in different ways, so I suppose her coping mechanism was to distance herself from it all. Reverend James would be able to tell you more about that, but I'm guessing you might need a few days to recover before talking with him again.'

I couldn't help but laugh at the very cheeky expression on her face. She wasn't wrong.

'So why did she visit if she wasn't a regular at the church anymore? What sort of things has she been coming to see you about?'

'It's safe to say she has fallen on hard times. Between health issues and employment issues, she has found herself in a difficult position. She's currently living in a boarding house and struggling with money, has done so for a while. So she's come to the church a few times to try and get some financial assistance.'

'Do you get that often – people asking for the church for help, for money?'

'No. Well not from people who aren't members of the congregation. We have had some people in the church who have exhausted all of the social services available, been to food banks, got special work and income assistance, been to budget advisory services and are still struggling. Times are tough and the aftermath of Covid hit people hard.

You can't budget your way out of poverty. And we've helped out with things like providing firewood, grocery vouchers, small things that can make a difference and take the pressure off their finances. But those people have been regulars at services, part of our community. Mel is no longer any of those things, but it's almost like she feels we're obliged to help her. It's like she feels entitled, that she thinks we owe her.'

'But she is in a tough spot?'

'Yes, and I know this sounds bad, the fact that she is so, well, nasty about it makes us inclined to say no, regardless.' So the tone I had initially heard in her voice that day on the phone was one of disapproval rather than suspicion of involvement in Freeman's death.

We'd woven our way around the outdoor tables and restaurant signage on the Lower Octagon and were now walking down Stuart Street. The Perc was still open and had a reasonable number of patrons getting in that last hit of caffeine before they closed.

'So in your conversations with others about her, no one has ever voiced any suspicion that she had some involvement in Reverend Freeman's death?'

'No, not to me they haven't. But those sorts of conversations would have been had years before I got here, so again, the best person to talk to would be Reverend James. Or the groundsman, George McKenzie. He was around then too. I'm sure there would have been all sorts of speculation back then as to why it happened and who might have committed the crime. But to be honest, no one really talks about it anymore. It's that strange mix – it's ancient history that we don't bring up, but also something that still hangs over us like a dark cloud.'

'Unfinished business.'

'Indeed.'

By this stage we'd crossed the road and wandered along Moray Place to the carpark side entrance to the supermarket. We paused on the footpath to finish the conversation, keeping out of the way of the passengers who were hanging around to catch the Intercity bus and dodging our way around their multitudes of bags.

'I do hope you find out who did this, Detective. Everyone would love to see the culprit brought to justice and finally put it all to rest,' Delia said.

'Yes, and I know the police would love to have this case solved. Our failure to do so back in the day has hung over our heads too.' Some more so than others. The Boss had more at stake than most. 'I will need to interview Mel, so thank you for that background information on her, I really appreciate it.'

'Well, I can tell you now, she's a prickly customer. I don't think she's going to appreciate you asking questions and dragging up the ghosts of the past. So good luck with that.'

CHAPTER 17

As much as I liked Reverend James, I think being around him for any length of time would have driven me to homicidal thoughts. Sometimes I marvelled at the weird way my brain worked. You'd think by my age I would have been used to it, but I still chuckled to myself on occasion when a trail of random or out-there thoughts that would have baffled the most left-field thinker led to something that was really quite sensible. In this instance, Reverend James's inability to shut the hell up went to 'what would I have done to get a word in edgewise?', to the iconic scene of Dr Evil telling Scotty to zip it in *Austin Powers*, to 'Scotch tape', to 'duct tape would have come in handy', to 'would anyone get so desperate to get some peace and quiet that they would actually kill someone to make them shut up?', to 'did someone kill the Reverend to shut him up?', to 'shut up *which* Reverend?', to 'did they kill the right Reverend, not the Right Reverend?', and finally to 'was it mistaken identity?'

The last one was the sensible question. We couldn't assume that Reverend Freeman was the intended victim. The night he was killed on the front steps of the cathedral it was dark, hosing down with rain, windy, wild and woolly, and according to the case notes he was wearing a raincoat with the hood drawn down over his head. You'd have had to be right up there in his face to know exactly who it was. Sure, you could take cues from his height and build, but given the weather, it would have been easy to mistake him for someone else.

From what I had read in the notes from 1999, no one had considered that perhaps Reverend Freeman wasn't the target of the killer. That maybe he'd been the poor numpty in the wrong place at the wrong time. Lord knows, history was littered with the bodies of the unlucky. But if he wasn't the target, then who was? Some other member of the clergy? And why would you kill someone from the Church? A minister in particular? One obvious thought came to mind. History was also littered with the unfortunate victims of abuse in various forms perpetrated by men of the cloth, by those society trusted the most. Was that the case here? Either Reverend Freeman himself, or another member of the ministry was guilty of such abuse? But surely if that was the root cause, the motive behind the murder, it would have been uncovered in the initial investigation. If people had previously had any suspicion of impropriety but kept quiet about it, wouldn't something as appalling as a murder bring them out of the woodwork?

I had noted from the church's website that it, like many faith and community-based organisations that dealt with vulnerable groups, had a safeguarding officer, someone whose job it was to protect and look out for anyone potentially at risk. I believed it was time to make an appointment with that person and have a little chat.

CHAPTER 18

It felt so good to step through the door into the magical warmth of home and the smell of dinner cooking. Fortunately for me, Paul was the kind of guy who found cooking a form of relaxation and took great pleasure in it, whereas I found cooking a chore, something I had to do in order to get fed. I was not inclined to create a three-course meal, something gourmet or channel my inner Nigella. Although I did share her immense joy of eating. On this occasion the waft that met me was from a hearty beef casserole, with maybe an undertone of overdone nappy.

'You timed that well,' he said as he handed me a smiling bundle of joy. 'You just missed a DEFCON five.'

'That will explain the big grin and very satisfied look on her face then.' I gave her a *boop* on the nose, and she responded with her signature chuckle. 'Good work, little lady.'

I looked at the clock. I really needed to wait another hour to feed Amelia and put her to bed, but my breasts were telling me they would prefer relief right now. I resisted the temptation though, for the sanity of us all.

'How was your day?' I asked.

'Pretty good. Her ladyship here was more settled. I think that tooth must have cut through now so is not giving her as much grief.' Paul headed back in the direction of the kitchen so I tagged along. 'We went for a run. I don't care how much people say those buggies are designed for running with, trying to avoid kicking the tray thing is still a nightmare. But it was fresh air and exercise, and it sent her to sleep.'

Going for a run was going to be my reward later on tonight, after the wee monster had been fed and my boobs were emptied out. I'd learned the hard way that full breasts and running were not a good combination. There was no sports bra in the world that had the structural fortitude to counteract that kind of bounce.

'How was your day?' he asked.

'It was okay. Most of it was spent talking with Church folk at St Paul's. I had no idea there was such a rabbit warren of offices and rooms under the cathedral. Can't believe I hadn't noticed that before.'

'You set foot in a church?'

'Well, technically it was under the church, not in it.'

'Still,' he said and stepped in towards me. He reached his hand up – to cup my cheek, I thought, all romantic like. Instead, his fingers dropped to my neck.

'What the heck are you doing?' I asked. I couldn't bat him away because my hands were full with a wriggly poppet.

'Just checking for your pulse, because I recall a conversation where you told me about your aversion to the places; I believe the comment you made about going back into a church included the words "over my dead body."'

'Oh, ha bloody ha.'

He looked all-too pleased with himself. 'Well, you survived to tell the tale. How did the conversations with the Church folk go?'

'Useful but not useful. Got a bit more background and I'm getting a feel for the case. The office manager was particularly helpful. She was able to let me know who was still around, who was still alive, so I've got some more people to follow up. But it all still seems horribly slow. I don't feel like I'm making any progress.'

'Don't be so hard on yourself. No one will be expecting you to crack it in a week.'

'I dunno. I think DI Johns is expecting miracles.'

'Well, in this instance he can expect all he likes, it's not going to happen. Remember, it's just you trying to achieve what a huge team of officers couldn't manage twenty-five years ago, when the trail was hot. He's essentially put one person on the job when the trail is stone-cold dead, and so are some of the witnesses.'

CHAPTER 19

There was something about Mel Smythe that I found inherently distasteful. I hated having to admit this because I prided myself in not being judgemental about people who were disadvantaged and who had clearly fallen on hard times. My mother, the queen of the judgy-judgy and the uber-critical, was everything I railed against and had vowed not to become. Yet here I was: with the best will in the world I couldn't help but feel a little put-off by Ms Smythe.

We were sitting side by side on the bottom steps of the external fire escape at the boarding house she was living in. It meant we had a bit of privacy – we were off the street, tucked around the corner from the main entrance. It also meant we were sheltered from the breeze and caught some sun. Mel hadn't invited me up to her room, which was a relief. The thought of being in an enclosed space with her for any length of time did not appeal. I was trying hard to concentrate on the expansive view out across the central city, but despite my best endeavours, my eyes insisted on homing in on her feet, or more specifically, the toenails. Even on this rather chill day she was wearing sandals, and I hoped it was by choice rather than because she didn't own shoes. They were those sporting type ones with Velcro fastenings, but they were a little too small, as her toes protruded beyond the end of the soles. Her left foot was quite deformed by a severe bunion, so much so the toe next to her big toe overlapped and sat on top of it. The right foot was only marginally better. It was those nails though. They were ridged, yellowed, thickened, long and jagged, and three of them were afflicted by a rather nasty-looking fungal infection. The way they hung over the edge of her shoes was reminiscent of a bird's claws curling around a perch. There was also a lot of crud under them. I peeled my eyes away again and prayed to God she hadn't noticed my train-wreck fascination.

Oops, she'd been talking. 'Sorry, what were you saying? I missed that last bit.' Actually, I'd missed all of it.

'I can't understand why you're dragging all this up again now. It's in the past, and you should all leave it the fuck alone.'

My eyes found her face. Everyone else I'd interviewed so far had cautiously welcomed the investigation, had hoped that someone would finally be held to account for the murder of the Reverend Mark Freeman. Yet here we had a woman who wanted to let sleeping dogs lie. I guess I had been warned, Delia was right about that.

'What's the point?' she asked.

The gaps where some of her teeth should have been were a distraction too.

'The point is the case was never solved and it's time it was.'

'But what if the person who did it is already dead?'

It was a strange comment for her to make and one that couldn't be left unchallenged. 'Do you have reason to believe whoever did this crime is no longer alive?' There was no time for wiffle-waffle – I seriously needed to get away from this woman.

'What if I did?' She was doing that chin jutting out, looking down her nose at me, border-line defiant thing. It was bad enough seeing it on a teenager, but on a grown woman it was as irritating as hell.

'Well, in that case I'd appreciate any information you could give me on who you are referring to and the basis of your suspicions.'

Now she added a flick of her head. 'What if I didn't want to give you any information?'

I wasn't sure whether she was doing it to be contrary, or if it was that she was just a shit person, but I had the feeling this chat was going to descend into the realms of farce very quickly if I didn't nip this attitude in the bud. Delia had warned me that Mel Smythe was a difficult number. She was not wrong. It was time to channel my inner Smithy and go straight to bad-cop mode, but without the good-cop foil.

'Well, if that was the case, then we'd have to have this conversation down at the station in one of our formal interview rooms, as I would interpret your refusal as you obstructing the course of justice. And if that didn't encourage you to speak then an appearance in front of a judge would be in order. And that could lead to some time in our very comfortable cells.' The sarcasm couldn't help but seep in and the consequences stated were a bit of an exaggeration. Not my most professional moment, but needs must. 'Do you have a lawyer, Ms Smythe?' Two could play at the escalation game.

The mention of the 'L' word caused her to straighten up. 'Hurmmph,' was the reply.

'Shall I take that as a no? Then, how about we start this conversation again?'

The hunch returned to her shoulders and she appeared to have pulled her head in, literally and figuratively. Was she ready to play the game? Because I was tiring of this conversation real fast.

'So, as I asked before, do you have reason to believe whoever did this crime is no longer alive?'

'No, no, I don't.'

'Is that because you know who they are and that they are still alive?'

'No,' she said, and started picking at the crud under her fingernails. They were in better condition than her toenails … just.

'Then why did you make the comment?'

'Because you're the police.'

I guess that was as good an explanation as I was going to get. Most rational people didn't try to wind us up on purpose.

'The way you said it implied you had an idea or a theory about who killed Reverend Freeman. Do you?'

'Everyone had their theories,' she said. 'Everyone had an opinion, but nothing came of them, did they? The police were useless and couldn't come up with anyone.'

The police had been unsuccessful, but I wouldn't have said they had been useless. Everything I'd read so far on the case had been thorough and logical. But I supposed results counted, and they didn't get any. She hadn't answered my question and still hadn't come to light with her ideas, so I changed tack slightly.

'What sort of things were other people saying?'

'There were some pretty wild theories.'

'Such as?'

'Drug deal gone wrong, that was a good one. They clearly didn't know the Reverend. He was so straight-laced. He didn't drink, didn't even smoke, let alone take drugs.' She said that with a laugh that implied she saw it as a character flaw rather than a good thing. She pulled a vape out of her pocket and took a drag. I guessed being immersed in a cloud of apple haze was better than cigarette smoke, but it still left me a little nauseated.

'What else did you hear?'

'That it was a wronged woman who killed him – his wife or his mistress.'

That one got my eyebrows into my hairline. 'He had a mistress?'

'Fuck no.' She laughed and took another drag. Blew the mist out the side of her mouth away from me this time. An act of consideration, I supposed. 'Didn't I just say he was straight-laced? He would never have had a mistress. He was totally in love with that wife of his. He wouldn't even look at anyone else, let alone touch.' Did I detect a hint of jealousy there? Had she had a bit of a flirt with him in the past but not been appreciated? Mel had clearly lived a hard life, and between the lank, greying hair, missing teeth and coarse complexion she looked a lot older than the fifty-three years stated in her files. But with a bit of imagination you could see that back in the day and in better times she would have been a striking young woman. 'And the missus was a bit of a do-gooder, so I couldn't imagine her having a bit on the side either.'

It wasn't something I had considered in my thinking on the case so far. I tucked the idea in the back of my mind. Matters of the heart had been the root cause of many a murder. Couldn't be ruled out here.

'Okay, those were some pretty wild ideas. What about the less far-fetched ones? Were there any people within the congregation who aroused more suspicion than others?' I figured from the level of bitterness towards the Church I detected, if anyone was going to happily point fingers, it would be her.

'There was a man named Aaron Cox who probably got more attention than he deserved from the police at the time, and from the congregation, for that matter.'

'But you didn't have any suspicions about him?'

'Oh yes, I had my suspicions. He'd been a hard man in his day, involved with gangs and drugs. He'd done time. But he'd seen the light and been "saved".' She said the word 'saved' with *ra ra* hand gestures. 'Mark was close with the man. A little too close, if you ask me.'

That comment could be interpreted in many ways. My brain went straight to the most extreme one.

'When you say "close", do you mean in-a-relationship close?' Maybe the wronged-woman theory was actually wronged-man.

'Nah, I don't think Aaron was the type to screw a man.'

'But the Reverend was?'

'No, straight as. He'd think he would burn in the fires of hell for it.'

'He was anti-gay?'

'He didn't state it, not overtly, but I don't think he was as progressive as he made out.'

My understanding was that the Anglican Church had been one of the first churches to recognise and accept LGBTQI+ people, and even allowed them to become priests. But I guessed that was a directive of the Church. It couldn't dictate what an individual thought.

'Tell me more about Aaron, then.'

After our initial rough start Mel seemed more than happy to talk now, so I'd take advantage of her co-operation while it lasted.

'Like I said, he'd been saved and seen the light, so he was trying to get involved in the church. Mark had been wanting him to do some talks to the youth group and community groups. Make him the shining example of turning your life around. To show that no one was beyond the love of God, bring all the sinners to me, *yada yada*.' I was guessing from that comment Mel had drifted well away from her faith.

'And Aaron was happy with this?'

'Oh yes, he wanted people to see how saved he was.' Now it was her turn to lay on the sarcasm. 'He loved the attention.'

'I take it you didn't like him.'

'No, not one bit. He was trying to push his way into people's trust, and I didn't trust him. I don't care what people say, you can't make a leopard change its spots.'

'Did others think the same way as you?'

'No, they were all blinded by his story, fell for it hook, line and sinker. They wanted to believe in him. They hoped spreading his story would help them save others too.'

'Do you think he could have murdered Reverend Freeman?'

She brushed at some hair that had drifted across her eyes. 'Oh, I think he could have. He'd been put away for assault and was a nasty piece of work before he converted to the good side. So, yes, he would have been quite capable of it.'

'But?'

'But I don't know. They seemed to be friends. I don't know...'

She'd reached back into her pocket to pull out the vape, and I braced myself for another assault of fruit waft. It felt like she'd put a full stop to the Aaron conversation, though, and there was only one other area I really wanted to ask her about today.

'You were the youth leader at that time. There weren't any disaffected youth who may have had a grievance with the clergy?'

'Oh, there were disaffected youth, alright. There always are. But I don't know that any were disaffected enough to do anything that drastic. Most of them were too square and squeaky clean.'

'But not all of them?'

'No, definitely not. But the Church doesn't like anyone to think their young folk might be merrily sinning.'

'Were there any of them in particular you were concerned about?'

'I always kept an eye on the Freeman kids.'

'Why?'

'It's a shit job being a minister's kid. People hold them to a higher standard than they might other kids. People were always watching. I just tried to make sure they didn't get up to too much mischief, but got up to enough to be interesting. Not sure that it worked though.'

I was curious as to what Mel rated as too much mischief.

'Were there issues?'

'Nothing that couldn't be sorted out with a bit of kindness and common sense. They weren't brats, they were good kids.'

Mel was being positively garrulous now so I decided to lob in a shock bomb.

'And you didn't have anything to do with the Reverend's death?'

She sputtered and almost fell off the step. 'Are you fucking kidding me? Of course I didn't. Killing him would have been the absolute worst thing for me to do. In fact, his murder is part of the reason I'm in this mess today. How do you think I got here? You think I live like this by choice? Thank God I'll get out of this shithole soon.' She threw her arms out wide. 'My life went to crap after he died.'

'How so?'

'Everything was fucked-up in the church after that. Everyone went a bit mental. People were finger-pointing about all sorts of things. I lost my role as the youth leader and was basically forced out.'

That seemed extraordinary. I would have thought during a crisis like that the church would have been wanting as much stability as possible, that they would have drawn together to provide as much support for everyone as they could rather than make things worse. Unless, of course, they all thought she had done it and were administering their own form of pious vigilante justice, considering the police couldn't provide the official sort.

'Why? Why would you lose the role?' She must have had her theories.

'Because Mark was the one that put me in it in the first place. He was the one who supported me. I suspect I was another of his pet projects. There were others in the congregation who weren't as keen to see me there. They felt I was a bad influence on their precious youth.'

'And why was that?'

'Firstly, I was the resident feminist. The Anglicans might be all *rah rah rah* about equality for women, women priests and all, but in reality it was still a man's world. The womenfolk were always the ones asked to be in the kitchen, do the cleaning, do all of the running around, whereas the men were given the leadership roles. I sometimes think the only reason I was the youth leader was because no guy put their hand up. Some members of the congregation didn't like it when I challenged them about the double standards, and liked it even less when some of the girls, and the boys for that matter, started asking questions too. Made them uncomfortable, upset the order of things. But weirdly, it was the women who had it in for me more than the men.'

That didn't surprise me at all. You only had to spend any time on social media to see how many women put the boot in to other women. Not everyone was about uplifting the sisterhood.

'You said "firstly". There was something else?'

'Yeah. Some of them didn't like the fact I preferred women. I think they were worried I was going to seduce them and turn their daughters into raging lesbians. They flattered themselves. Wouldn't go near those bitches with a barge pole.' I think it was the first time in our entire conversation that I was tempted to smile.

'I thought you said Reverend Freeman wasn't that supportive of gay people?'

'Like I said. Pet project. Maybe he thought God could save me from my gayness. Then he could parade me and Aaron as the sinners who saw the light. Double points in heaven.' Her laugh had an edge of bitterness to it. 'Anyway, after Mark died it all turned into a fucking witch hunt. So much for all them good Christians. They drove me out. Bastards.'

CHAPTER 20

Monday mornings carried a sense of menace at the best of times, but here it was, the Monday of all Mondays, the morning we had all been dreading. Today was day one of the great 'both back at work and the kid in childcare' experiment. It could go well, or it could go horribly wrong. So far so good, though. Amelia had only woken up once in the night so I didn't feel entirely like death warmed up. We'd remembered to set the alarm. We didn't sleep through the alarm. Amelia's bag was packed and ready to go, the fruits of my expressing labour were clearly labelled with her name and in the chiller bag – no confusing this Jersey cow's milk with others. Between us, the washing was on, our lunches were made, and I'd even got something out of the freezer for dinner. Talk about nailing it. We both agreed we could feel proud if we managed our A game on the first day. After that it didn't really matter, as long as we managed it once. The plan was today we'd both drop her in to daycare – strength in numbers and all that, then we could have a quiet cheer, or cry in the car together and tootle on down to work.

Amelia was looking intolerably cute in the wee outfit I'd chosen for her first official day. I'd gone for an olivey-green pair of dungarees over the top of a cream, long-sleeved body suit, topped off with one of Mum's hand-knitted peach-and-yellow stripy cardies. She was lying on our bed, and I was playing tootsies with her while Paul brushed his teeth.

'Just to confirm, so we're not those parents who think the other one is picking up the kid, and then no one picks up the kid,' Paul said, garbled around a toothbrush, 'you are going to pick her up today?'

'Roger that,' I said. 'I suspect we'll both be well and truly ready for it by then.'

'Well, she'll be fine. We both know you're the one with the separation-anxiety issues.'

I *booped* Amelia on the nose and she responded with a giggle and snow-angel arm-waving. 'Your dad is being mean to me. He thinks I'm a sook.'

'I know you're a sook,' was the response from the wings.

The arm-waving stopped, Amelia's face went very still, and then proceeded to go very red. I could see her little body tense up and my immediate thought was nothing good could come of this. It was either going to be sobs or shit. At this stage in the 'we have to get out of the house on time' game, was it bad to be hoping for sobs?

Next minute a gurgling akin to water-cooler-bubble bloops, at death-metal concert volume, emanated from her nether regions – liquid and chonky-enough sounding to make my toes curl.

'Jesus Christ, I could hear that from in here,' came the call from the bathroom.

After a repeat performance punctuated by a final explosive fart, the little body relaxed, the smile returned and then the arms and legs started pumping like someone was very proud of herself.

Shit.

And I meant shit.

The smell of it hit like a blast wave. It would have been fine if it was just the smell. But no. I don't know what angle she shot that load out of her butt, but somehow it had escaped out the top of her nappy, travelled right up her back and into her hair. I didn't think it was physically possible to shit so hard it got in your hair. Then it dawned on me: if it was in her hair, it was all over the duvet cover. And if it was all over the duvet cover, it was going to get all over everything.

Great.

That was a DEFCON five performance. No amount of baby wipes was going to dent that mess. It was a full-on bath poonami.

'Bags not!' I yelled.

So much for our A game.

CHAPTER 21

My wrist was buzzing. Bloody smartwatches. Even though it was supposedly silent it felt like everyone in a five-metre radius could hear it. I did a quick, surreptitious glance down at the notification to see who was calling. Mel Smythe. Curious. What did she want? The glance wasn't surreptitious enough though.

'Was there something you were wanting to share, Detective Shephard?'

Every bloody time. Sometimes I wondered if The Boss kept an eye specifically on me in these morning briefings just so he could have the pleasure of calling me out if my attention wavered for a second. 'You were late in this morning. Is there a problem?'

I noted he didn't call Paul out on being late, but I suppose Paul was exempt because humans with dicks and balls seemed to have special privileges as far as The Boss was concerned.

'No. I was expecting a call from one of the witnesses in the Freeman case later on and they just rang earlier than arranged.' It was a slight embellishment of the truth. Okay, there was only one accurate piece of information in that statement, but it seemed to do the trick. He harrumphed and moved on. He could hardly complain about my advancing the case he'd given to me to handle alone. My eyes found Paul's across the room and he gave me a wink.

🦑

It was another half-hour before we got out of the briefing. I always thought, by definition, briefings were supposed to be brief. He who liked the sound of his own voice put paid to any hope of that. I slid my desktop down to sitting level and dialled up voicemail. Judging by the 'oh,' the hesitation and the ahhhing, Mel Smythe wasn't expecting to have to leave a message. After listening to a few more mumblings I thought she might give up and end the call, but she eventually got down to business.

'Um, Detective Shephard? Mel Smythe here. I need to talk. It's about Mark, about his, you know, case.' Well, I didn't think she'd be ringing for a social chit-chat. 'Can you call me? My number is...' At this point I heard her muttering to herself: '...Shit, what's my number again?' Then 'fuck' then back at speaking-to-me volume: 'Well, you know my number. Can you give me a ring?'

We'd all been there.

The smooth automated voice emanating from my phone offered a 'to reply to this message press one' option. I took it. The number rang, and rang and rang, and after what felt like an eternity flicked over to leave-a-message mode. I knew from experience most people who were struggling financially didn't ever listen to voicemail because they were charged extra for the privilege, but given how tense Mel had sounded, I'd leave one anyway. I hated playing phone tag. My eyes flicked up to the calendar on my computer screen. I had an appointment in half an hour with the safeguarding officer at St Paul's that would take up the rest of the morning, and I had to factor in time for lunch and milking the sisters. They were already starting to feel tight. I also hated leaving messages. Actually, I just hated talking on the phone full stop. I was never destined for call-centre work. That would be my idea of living hell. Face-to-face conversations were much better. Although, the thought of being face-to-face with Mel Smythe again didn't appeal, so hopefully what she had to say was useful and not just another rant.

Mel didn't have a personalised recorded message, just the regulation weird, artificial voice with an indistinguishable accent giving obvious instructions for what to do after the tone.

'Hi, Mel, Detective Shephard here. I got your message, thanks. Are you free after lunch? One o'clock? If I don't hear from you I'll assume that time is okay, and I'll come and visit you at home.

Thanks. Bye.' Ugh. No matter how I rehearsed a message in my head, they always ended up sounding rushed and garbled.

I grabbed my coat and headed for the door. It wouldn't take long to walk to the cathedral, but due to my pathologic need to be early I wanted to leave with plenty of time to spare. Sonia flagged me down as I passed her desk. I was of the mind that Sonia Richardson was going to make a damn fine detective – hopefully soon. She had the support of everyone in the room, but like me seemed to have to work harder than most to impress The Boss. He didn't have it in for her personally like he did me, but I'd seen his subtle sabotage of overlooking her or giving her roles that wouldn't challenge her and help advance her career. The pattern was familiar, so I did the best I could within my rather limited powers to prevent it. Oddly enough, calling The Boss out on a few things had made me even less popular.

'Got some results for you. I've tracked down Aaron Cox,' she said.

'Brilliant, thank you. Where's he hiding?'

One of the first hurdles in a cold case was finding out where people were living in the current day, or, if in fact they were still alive. There were a few people from the first round of the investigation who had shuffled off this mortal coil. I hoped Aaron Cox wasn't residing in the cemetery.

'The good news is he's still alive.' Sometimes I wondered if that woman was a mind reader.

'Fab. And the bad news?'

'No bad news really. He is currently living in the Dunedin area, but he is going under a different name.'

'Really? That's interesting.'

'I know, right,' she said. 'That's why it took me a little longer than I'd hoped to track him down. He had moved away in 2002, after all of the hoo-ha of the Freeman case. Looks like he went back to Auckland, where his family lived, but returned here two years ago and has been living out the back of Waitati under the name Andrew

Cotton. He's been living off-grid, effectively. No interactions with social services, or IRD, just quietly flying under the radar.'

If you were wanting to live a little out of sight, then Waitati was certainly a place to do it. It was an eclectic community. But no interactions with Work & Income or IRD implied someone living off cash jobs and trying to avoid any attention. No one ever managed to entirely avoid Inland Revenue. Even your bank accounts were tied in to IRD.

'It takes quite a lot of effort to do that,' I said.

'Which begs the question: why go to all of that trouble?'

'Exactly. I guess I'll find out when I talk to him.'

'Happy to tag along if you need company.'

Maybe I was finally learning in my old age. Or maybe now I had a baby and people I was responsible for, I was reconsidering some of the risks I would have blithely taken in the past. And given the screeds of material I had read about Aaron Cox, his history and the way he had been pursued by the past investigation, I imagined he wasn't that fond of the police and wouldn't be that keen to talk with us again, so I said: 'I might just take you up on that offer, thanks.'

CHAPTER 22

Jesus Christ, just as well I'd been religious about doing my pelvic-floor exercises because I hadn't heard anyone approach and damn near pissed my pants when a 'hello' issued from just behind my left ear. My hyper-sensitive reaction to people sneaking up on me was getting to be a habit around here.

Instinct kicked in enough for me to step back and bring my fists up to guard, but fortunately not enough to swing around and lash out. The face in front of me looked as startled as mine, and the man was clutching a rake defensively across his chest like he thought he was the one at risk in this scenario. The next thing I noted was that the man was at my eye level. Considering I just snuck in over five foot, that put us both at the pip-squeak end of the height spectrum, a long way from the statuesque. He was also pretty antique.

I eyeballed him, and he eyeballed me, and by unspoken consensus we both slowly lowered our weapons.

'Sorry, I didn't mean to give you a fright,' he said, and broke into an embarrassed smile.

That was one way of putting it. Normally I wasn't that flighty, but there was something about being anywhere in the proximity of St Paul's Cathedral that really set me on edge. It didn't help that I'd been absorbed in reading the names of the dearly departed along the kerbing around the rose beds.

'That's okay, I didn't hear you come up,' I replied. 'I'm Detective Sam Shephard, and you are...?'

'Oh, you're the one that everyone's been talking about. The one reopening Reverend Freeman's murder case.'

One of the things I'd noticed while interviewing people connected to the investigation was they fell into two categories: those that could bring themselves to say the m-word, and those that could not. Those that couldn't skirted around it by saying he died or was killed, like they couldn't quite acknowledge the fact it was murder. I wasn't sure whether this was because they thought it was some weird kind of incident in which he was accidentally stabbed and then accidentally fell down a flight of steps, or because they couldn't believe that someone could purposefully kill a priest, a man of God. It was quite refreshing to hear someone just come out and say he was murdered.

'You've created quite a stir,' he went on.

'A good stir or a bad stir?' I asked.

'A shit stir,' he said with what could only be called a wicked glint in his eye. It was the kind of quick humour my dad used to come out with, and I couldn't help but think if he kept that up I was going to get on well with the man. 'George McKenzie. I'm the caretaker around here.'

'Nice to meet you, George.' Considering the size of the man – and the age of the man – I wondered at his ability to care take anything. The most robust thing about him was his eyebrows, which were positively owl-like. But the grounds were in pristine order and the garden beds clearly well tended, so he must have been sprightlier than he looked.

'I'm curious now – what have people been saying about the case?'

'Lots saying it's about time. Lots saying you should leave it alone because it will only drag up the hurt from the past. Pretty much everyone wondering what on earth you could hope to find now that the cops twenty-odd years ago didn't. And we all know it will be even harder now because people will have forgotten things.'

'Sounds like maybe I should give up then?' I said.

'Nah. I say someone killed him, and that someone needs to pay. They've got away with it scot-free all this time, while the poor man's family has had to live with the consequences. It would be nice for them to get some closure.'

If everyone was talking about it again then I needed to up the pace of my interviewing. I wanted to hear people's individual memories, particularly if they may be faded, not collective memory dredged up and reinforced by committee.

'A bubba at home?' he asked.

'Pardon?' Not a question I was expecting. 'But yes. How did you know?'

'You're leaking,' he said matter-of-factly, pointing to my chest.

Fuck. I thought the dampness I was feeling was contained by the breast pads, but apparently not.

'Sorry,' I said, pulling my jacket across my chest and doing up the buttons. I wondered how long before it soaked through that too. Then I realised it was a dry-clean-only jacket, so thought *stuff that* and unbuttoned it again. They would have to stay that way until I could dash home and change, but now I felt conspicuous.

'Not to worry. I've had children. Got grandchildren, actually great-grandchildren now, so I've seen plenty of that over the years,' he said. 'You're a good mum.' The way he just casually dropped the last line in brought an unexpected sting of tears to my eyes. It made me realise how desperately I had needed to hear those words, and that no one had ever said them up until now. Yeah, when I thought about it, that was right: no one. And when I finally heard them it was from an old geezer who I'd only just met. He noticed the sudden welling in my eyes and reached out and patted me on the arm.

'First I gave you a fright, and now I've made you cry. I'm doing a great job today. You'll be sticking a big red flag next to my name in your notebook.'

'I'm sorry,' I said. 'I'm just tired. This being-a-mum business is hard work.' I seemed to be apologising a lot today. I hunched my shoulders forward and pulled the fabric of my shirt away from my bra. Maybe it would dry a little. The effort was futile as it stuck straight back as soon as I unhunched.

I gave up.

As far as I could recall there was no transcript of an interview with George McKenzie back in 1999. That seemed odd considering he was an active part of the organisation.

'Did the police talk with you back during the original investigation?' I asked.

'No, I was never interviewed at the time. I was just the groundsman, and I wasn't at the service the night he was murdered, so I guess they didn't think I'd have anything to add that they hadn't heard before. Had a couple of chats with some of the police in the garden when they were passing through, but no formal statement or anything like that.'

That was an omission as far as I was concerned. Caretakers were up there with receptionists as people who quietly knew what was going on with everyone and observed who came and went, and when.

'What was your impression of the investigation overall?'

'Other than they didn't catch anyone? I guess it was okay. I'm not a cop so couldn't tell you really. They were getting a lot of heat from the newspapers and the mayor and the like. Lots of criticism about how long it was taking, and then, of course, lots of criticism that they didn't catch the culprit.' Some things hadn't changed, then. We all loved media pressure and political heat. 'I did think they got a little too obsessed with Aaron Cox. They gave him a real hard time.'

There was certainly a lot of paperwork dedicated to him, transcripts, reports.

'Were you a friend of his?'

'No, couldn't stand the guy. Steered clear. He gave me the creeps.'

'In what way?'

'Well...' He looked a little abashed. 'He was a really big guy, like tall and solid. And he had a lot of tats. And he'd done time for violence. I found him quite intimidating.' Given George's stature, or lack of it, I could relate to his not being exactly comfortable around big units – especially big units with a known criminal history.

'But despite that, you didn't suspect him of killing Reverend Freeman?'

'No.'

'Why not?'

'Well, it's hard to explain, but he felt too genuine for that. Does that make sense?'

Not really, so I didn't reply, hoping he'd elaborate.

'He was an ex-thug and down-and-out who found God. Yes, he made me and plenty of others, for that matter, feel uncomfortable, but he was kind of real. He didn't buy into all the fakery and pretence that you see in a church, people trying to look the part. He was unapologetically him. I think that's probably why he and the Reverend seemed to get along so well. And, you know, he even offered to help me out with the garden, get his hands dirty.'

That did sound like the actions of someone pretty genuine.

'So you think the police targeted him because of his past.'

'Yeah, he was an easy target. No offence, Detective, but in some ways they were a bit lazy. They homed in on the outsider and it turned into a bit of a witch hunt. And it kept the newspapers happy and the public off their backs for a bit.' It looked like a trip to the *Otago Daily Times* archives would be in order to see exactly what had been reported at the time. 'Same sort of thing happened with the youth leader, Mel Smythe. People turned against her too.'

'Why did you think that happened?'

'Because she was a lesbian.'

Blunt.

'That's a pretty weak reason to target her as a potential murderer. Were they implying all lesbians were murderers?'

He laughed. 'We'd all be in a shit load of trouble if they were. No, I think some people used it as an excuse to drive her away. They didn't like the influence she was having on the young fry.'

'And what were your thoughts on the matter?' He seemed a fairly open chap, so I was curious to see his response.

'Oh, I'm not proud to say that back in the day I was one of those who disapproved of what I thought was her lifestyle choice.'

'And you have a different viewpoint now?'

'Yeah. Let's just say my gloriously gay grandson showed me the error of my ways. It was stone-age thinking. But at the time, with Mel, there was a lot of finger-pointing. A number of people let the police know that they didn't trust her and sowed seeds of doubt, so like Aaron, she got a lot of unwarranted attention.'

'Have you seen her in recent times?'

'Oh yes. She comes here occasionally. Usually to demand things. As much as I was sorry for being against her for all the wrong reasons back then, nowadays, she's a right cow. Can't stand the woman.'

CHAPTER 23

On the face of it New Zealand appears to be a great and enlightened place to live. We lead the world in so many things, but scratch a little bit below the surface and there are some horror statistics. We aren't the completely clean, green, land of milk and honey that we make ourselves out to be. King amongst the long list of our failings, abuse in care is one of New Zealand's great shames. In a time when the public spotlight was on churches and institutions and the appalling legacy of abuse of children and vulnerable people under their care, it was essential that everyone took it seriously. The recent Royal Commission of Inquiry into Abuse in Care had revealed the devastating effects on survivors and the scale of the coverups over generations. Finally, people were believing the victims of these crimes, and the perpetrators were being held to account – well, those that were still alive. Nowadays, with all this attention, making excuses and burying their heads in the sand was no longer an option, and many churches had addressed the issue head-on. Not all, but many, the Anglican Church amongst them. Part of my research into the case involved finding out as much as I could about the Church and its history. First port of call had been their website, which as well as having one of the coolest 3D virtual tours known to mankind also went into great detail about safeguarding and protecting the vulnerable – the protocols in place, how to make a complaint, who to contact.

That made my life easy. Cath Chisholm was the cathedral safeguarding officer at St Paul's, and although she hadn't been around at the time of the murder, she was a good starting point for one of the difficult conversations that needed to be had. In my mind I had pictured someone with the grand title and responsibility of safeguarding officer as being all cosy, mumsy-looking with soft edges and a demeanour that suggested she'd just finished baking a fruit cake and was about to put the kettle on. The woman that stood before me had a spiky, cropped, gloriously grey asymmetric haircut that defied gravity, wore a similarly edgy khaki tunic dress, which I could see had pockets, over a black turtleneck, and completed the look with cherry-coloured Doc Marten boots. I wished to God I had that kind of fashion sense and could pull off that kind of a look. Somehow I didn't think it would have the same impact if it was on me though. And it did make me realise I really needed to do some more work on my preconceptions about people.

'Thank you for taking the time to see me, it's much appreciated.'

'You're welcome,' she said as she led me through the rabbit warren of lower rooms to her office. 'Happy to help in any way I can, although, as I said, I wasn't here in 1999, when Reverend Freeman died.'

'How long have you been a part of this parish?'

Her office had a relaxed feel with big armchairs as well as the standard desk and chair, a tall tree-like pot plant doing pretty well in a space with little natural light, and a number of children's paintings stuck to the walls. It was a room where you would feel comfortable talking, and I had the sense Cath would be happy to chat herself. She indicated to one of the comfy chairs and I sank down into it.

'I've been in this role for five years, but we moved to Dunedin in 2005, so I've been a part of the congregation since then.'

'So you'd know everyone here quite well?'

'Yes, as well as you can. My whole *whānau* is actively involved here, have been right from the beginning. It feels very much like our church family, which is the way it's supposed to be, isn't it?'

That was the ideal. Although I wondered whether, like all families, the dynamics were not always perfect – people got pissed off with each other and there was that dodgy uncle no one wanted around at Christmas. Which led me to the whole point of the meeting.

'You know that I am reinvestigating the murder of Reverend Freeman? As part of that investigation I do need to ask some hard questions – so if I may be quite direct...?'

'Fire away,' she said.

'To your knowledge, was there any indication or evidence that Reverend Freeman had been suspected or been guilty of abusing anyone in the diocese?'

Her eyebrows raised a little. 'That is direct.'

'There's no easy way to ask it.'

'I like direct, and it was a question I was expecting. The straightforward answer is no, not to my knowledge. After you rang I went for a good look through the archives to see if there was any correspondence or complaints about the Reverend, but I came up empty-handed. There was nothing on record.'

'How comprehensive are your archives?' There was certainly enough space down here to store everything under the sun, but that didn't necessarily mean people would keep things.

'Not that great. A lot of the documents stored are the usual accounts and finances stuff. Also programmes and flyers for special events and services, that kind of thing. The correspondence is pretty good. We have been blessed with some very efficient and possibly over-zealous office managers over the years.'

Was that a wee dig at Delia?

Cath must have caught the look on my face, and laughed. 'The current manager and I are good friends, and yes, she is very, very efficient. The previous manager was what you would call a bit of an old biddy who knew everything that was going on around the parish and everyone's business. In fact, she would have been a very good person to talk with about the case. Unfortunately she's in a care home now. Alzheimer's has stolen a lot of her memory. Her daughter still comes here and keeps us updated on how she's going, but it is horribly sad. Reverend James goes and visits her, so you could ask him where she's at.' I made a mental note to ask him when I had plenty of time on hand for the sure-to-be wordy response.

'And there are no whispers off record about Reverend Freeman?'

'I can't tell you anything from back then, but in the short time you've been looking into the case and all of the chit-chat and discussion that's generated, not once has anyone brought up even the possibility of Reverend Freeman having done anything untoward, or something that may have provoked anyone to do him harm.'

'He sounds almost saintly.'

'Ah, no one's a saint. But everyone seemed to hold him in high esteem.'

I wasn't getting anywhere when it came to information about Mark Freeman. The thought about mistaken identity that had been niggling at the back of my mind elbowed its way to the front.

'What about the other priests in the parish at the time? Reverend James and Reverend Franklin?'

Had the target actually been one of them, and in the dark on a very wet night in Dunedin, the perpetrator had simply got the wrong man?

'Well, Reverend Franklin passed away a number of years ago, and you've talked with Reverend James, so you know what he's like. I don't think he'd be capable of hiding anything.' It seemed like everyone found him a little enthusiastic. 'But again, on record there were no written complaints or indications of any issues with them. And, likewise, in the recent conversations no one has raised any issues at all.'

'You're probably not the right person to ask this, and you mentioned you didn't think Reverend James could hide anything, but do you think there was any possibility of inappropriate things happening in the church at the time and for whatever reason, people covered it up, and are still covering it up?'

She took a very deep breath, and blew it out between pursed lips.

'I should let you know that there had been some difficult and unfortunate occurrences in the diocese a few years before Reverend Freeman was killed, but that was before his time, and before Reverend James's time too, for that matter, so they were not in any way involved. There were a lot of changes around here after that.'

I didn't recall seeing any reference to abuse or scandal in the original reports, and it did seem like something that should have been recorded as context and history to the case. I'd have to have a closer look at the files.

'Was that when your role, or roles like it, were put in place?'

'Yes. Abuse and preying on the vulnerable has to be taken very seriously. And let me be exceedingly blunt about this: I can assure you now that if some arsehole – priest or otherwise – was abusing any child in this parish, I'd be the first one down there with a very large knife to cut their balls off and force-feed them down their throat. And knowing the people around here, I'd be the first one in a very long queue. No one here would protect that kind of scum. We've all seen the kind of damage that's done to innocents when people look the other way and don't call that shit out. That is the case now, and I'm sure that would have been the case in the past.'

That was a fairly emphatic response. It made me wonder if she or a loved one had personal experience.

'Yet, given that the police back in the day had pretty much ruled out a random attack from some stranger, I have to consider that someone in the parish knows something and is protecting someone, whether it be themself, or someone they know and love.'

'That may be the case, and you may have to talk to a lot of people. But from my perspective and based on the information I have, at the time of Reverend Freeman's murder, none of the priests were suspected of abusing anyone, or doing anything that caused people upset. There had been no complaints. In fact, the only person who had complaints laid against them was Mel Smythe.'

'Oh, really?'

'Yes.'

'What sort of complaints?'

Cath gave a tight and amused smile.

'That she was going to lead our youth into a life of sin and depravity.'

CHAPTER 24

The wind had picked up, so I pulled my coat in tighter and zipped it up as I left the cathedral from the office side door. I'd given up on any attempt to keep it clean from my leaky boobs; dry-cleaning was inevitable. I spotted George further down the building, towards the carpark, fighting what looked to be an entirely futile battle against a wind-whipped eddy of fallen leaves. I headed down in his direction. My talk with Cath hadn't revealed any official concerns that Reverend Freeman, or any of the others, had been involved in abusing children, or any other vulnerable members of the congregation. And so far in my interviews, everyone had painted him in nothing but a glowing light. But I was very aware that people often didn't want to speak ill of the dead, and that sometimes it took a number of conversations before something about a person's dodgier behaviours slipped out.

'George,' I shouted out, and waved.

He smiled when he saw me, took a look at the non-compliant pile of leaves he was wrangling, abandoned the rake and headed in my direction.

'Did you have a good chat with Cath?' he asked.

'I did. It didn't give me any answers, but I got a bit more background information.'

'She's a nice lady to talk with. People like her.'

I could well believe it.

'Do you mind if I ask you a couple more questions, if it's not taking you away from your leaves?'

'They'll keep. And if I get lucky this flaming wind will blow them over to the neighbours and they'll become someone else's problem.'

'But the cathedral doesn't really have any neighbours,' I said. It sat like a little island in a sea of streets. A bit like Mont Saint-Michel, the urban Kiwi edition.

'Well, there's the flaw in my plans,' he said, and gave me a wink.

'So a question for you – and I'm going to be quite direct.'

'Considering who you've been talking to, I think I know what's coming.'

'What do you think I'm going to ask?'

'Well, I think you're going to ask me if Mark Freeman was a kiddy-fiddler of some kind?'

'Well, that's not quite how I would have worded it, but yes, you were here back in 1999, and had been for a while. Did you have any suspicion or had you heard anyone imply that he might have been acting inappropriately, abusing children – or anyone for that matter?'

'What are you thinking? That he was murdered by a vengeful parent or someone he'd been mistreating?'

'It's something we have to consider.'

He pondered for a moment, appearing to be contemplating what he was going to say.

'I've heard a lot of gossip over the years, and a lot of theories about why he was killed, but hand on heart, I can say child abuse wasn't one of them. I can't even recall anyone bringing it up. I think you're barking up the wrong tree there.'

'So you had no cause to believe or even suspect that Reverend Freeman had been abusing or acting inappropriately with children?'

'No, absolutely not.'

'And what about other priests in the diocese? Any concerns there?'

'When you have a role like mine, you spend a lot of time listening to people, and observing them. I never saw anything to cause me concern – from Mark, or from the other priests. If I had I would have spoken up.'

Coming from him that felt like the door was closing on that line of enquiry. There was only one other person I needed to raise the subject with and that was not a conversation I was looking forward to having. How did you broach the subject of potential child abuse with the wife of the victim and not come across as a cold-hearted bitch?

'But...' he added.

That word pulled me back from imagining that discussion. 'But?'

'I know people think the world of him, and he *was* a good man, don't get me wrong. But he wasn't perfect, and he could have a bit of a temper on him.'

'What do you mean?'

'Not with the parishioners, he was endlessly patient with them. But I did overhear the odd argument he had with his family.'

'With his wife and children?'

'Yep,' he said. 'He could be a bit tough on them.'

That piqued my curiosity. 'What do you mean by tough?'

'He had some pretty exacting standards with the children, and there were a few times I overheard him say some nasty, hurtful things to them when Yvonne wasn't around. Times when I thought, mate, that's a bit unnecessary. I felt sorry for them, but I didn't feel it was my place to say anything to him, especially as it wasn't meant for my ears anyway. I didn't want to be accused of sticking my nose in where it didn't belong.'

How many times had the police heard that sentiment from neighbours or workplace colleagues when they'd turned a blind eye to abuse or bullying because they were too afraid to get involved?

'What sort of things did he say to them? Anything that stuck in your mind?' I asked.

'It was a long time ago. My memory isn't as good as it used to be, so I couldn't quote anything specific, sorry, just uncomfortable recollections of a few rants. I don't know if that's a help or not.'

It was. This shone a new light on Reverend Freeman. Perhaps he wasn't quite as saintly as people had been making out. And if he could be that harsh on those he loved, perhaps he wasn't always so caring for those he didn't.

CHAPTER 25

I hadn't heard back from Mel Smythe and after trying her phone again, to no avail, decided to go ahead and visit her again at the boarding house regardless. Best-case scenario, she was home and I got to find out what she wanted to speak to me about. Worst-case scenario she wasn't home, I got a drive in the company car and some fresh air, and we'd get to play phone tag for a little longer.

She wasn't waiting on the front steps to meet me, as she was for my last visit, so I guessed she hadn't got the message after all. Despite not letting me see it last time, she'd told me she was in room six, which looked like it was up the stairs. Boarding houses certainly didn't get a good rap in Dunedin. A number of them were owned by what could only be called predatory landlords who took advantage of those in desperate need by providing facilities barely fit for human habitation and charging the most they could get away with. In the big scheme of things this one had a reasonable reputation. It was very tired and in dire need of some paint and TLC, but at least it didn't smell damp and it met fire-safety regulations. Well, I assumed those sprinkler heads in the ceiling weren't for decoration. And surely if you'd gone to the expense of retrofitting a grand old villa, then you'd keep those maintained. Judging by appearances, though, they were the only thing money had been spent on. It looked like the boarding house hadn't been redecorated since Laura Ashley wallpaper was all the rage. The main thing that stood out was how dark and depressing it was. Any hope of sunlight reaching into the interior stairwell was dashed by every single door being closed. The banisters were a mahogany-coloured wood, the wallpaper was a vintage dark green, and what remained of the threadbare carpet could only be described as work-boot-trod brown. There was a potted palm sitting in the entranceway that looked like it had lost the will to live. A single ineffective light bulb hung from a very ornate ceiling rose and did barely anything to penetrate the gloom. How on earth could anyone tolerate living here? I guessed it was cheap and was better than being on the streets, just.

I climbed the stairs up to the top landing and worked my way along past the bathroom and to the door marked number six. Well, the numeral 6 had been drawn on the door with a permanent marker, where once there might have been a brass one.

I gave a sharp knock and waited. There was no response, so I knocked again. Finally, there was the sound of a door opening, except it was from behind me.

'Can I help you?' The wizened face of a fairly elderly woman poked around the side, eyeballing me from behind a security chain.

'I was just wondering if Mel was at home. I was supposed to meet her here. Have you seen her today?' I asked.

The resident must have decided I wasn't much of a threat, because she closed the door, I heard a rattling of chain, and when it re-opened, she stepped out into the hallway. She was wrapped in a tatty pale-blue dressing gown that looked like it could have gone around her twice. Her slippers looked pretty new, though. The wild hair, beady eyes and well-loved face reminded me of that archaic woman-creature thing from *The Dark Crystal*.

'Who's asking?' The voice was just as antiquated. She had the inherent suspicion of someone who was used to people either wanting something from her, or being up to no good.

'I'm Detective Sam Shephard. I was here yesterday, talking with Mel, and she wanted me to call around again today.'

'She doesn't usually talk to the cops.' The tone told me she didn't believe a word of what I'd just said. Crystal Lady might have been old and pretty fragile-looking, but she wasn't shy in being forthright. I got the impression you wouldn't want to get offside with her.

'She was helping me with an old case, for a friend.' I added a smile for good measure.

She wasn't convinced. 'You're not here to take her away because she's in trouble?' She stepped towards me in what I guessed was supposed to be a threatening manner. She didn't quite manage it, but it was good to know that Mel had someone on her side, keeping an eye out, no matter how decrepit.

'No, nothing like that. She was helping me.'

'Oh, that's okay then.' She gestured towards Mel's door. 'I saw her this morning in the kitchen when I was getting some breakfast, but I haven't seen her since then. She must have gone out. Didn't say anything about it though.'

A wasted trip then. Never mind, it was good to have a change of scenery from the office or St Paul's, even if it was in a scuddy, depressing-as-hell boarding house. And I'd got to meet *Dark Crystal* Lady, which actually felt like a bit of a treat. Before I headed back downstairs and to the car I decided to give Mel another phone call to save me a trip if she happened to be nearby.

'I'm just going to try calling her again,' I said, and the old dear nodded her head.

'Good idea.'

There was the usual lag before my phone started making a ringing sound, but this time it was in stereo, the phone held against my ear and the fainter sound of ringing beyond Mel's door.

Crystal Lady and I looked at each other.

'That's odd,' she said. 'Mel wouldn't go out without her phone.'

'No.'

'I hope she's alright.'

'So do I.'

I moved back over to Mel's door and gave it another hard knock.

'Mel, can you hear me? It's Detective Shephard. Are you okay? Can I come in?'

Crystal Lady had moved right up beside me and had her ear to the door.

'Nothing,' she said. She reached for the door handle.

'No, let me do that. You wait there.'

I pulled out a pair of gloves I kept in my jacket pocket, put them on, and then tested the door handle. It turned. Not locked. I eased it open a little. The room had a smell of mustiness, and something else.

'Hello? Mel?'

Still no response, so I cautiously pushed the door open wider.

My heart rate immediately leapt several notches. That was not what I was expecting.

'What's your name?' I said to *Crystal* Lady, who was trying to crane her neck around me to see.

'Lorraine.'

'Lorraine, I need you to go and call an ambulance, and I need you to get them to call the police.'

I heard a gasp from behind me. 'Oh, dear mother of God,' she said, her voice cracking.

'Go!' I yelled.

She scampered off.

My eyes took in the form of Mel Smythe slumped back in an armchair directly across from the door. That should have been enough cause for alarm, but the blood ramped it up to a whole new level. What would have once been a white shirt was soaked vivid red, in two rose-like blooms from her left shoulder and right breast. The flow had worked its way down, creating a dark stain down the front of her jeans and onto the cushion of the seat. I quickly scanned the room. No signs of anyone else. I shoved the door fully open and heard the resounding thud of wood on a stopper, no one hiding behind it. No human-sized forms behind the drawn-back floor-length curtains in the bay window next to her chair. Her unmade queen-sized bed took up most of the room, the head against the wall opposite. It was a box base, so nowhere for someone to hide under. My eyes then found the old-style freestanding wardrobe in the far corner. The door was open and the few garments hanging in there were short jackets. There was a scattering of shoes in the bottom, but no legs.

Now I felt confident there was no one there, waiting to pounce, I strode across the room to Mel, reached out and placed my hand on her cheek. It felt warm.

First-aid training kicked in.

'Mel, can you hear me?' I tapped hard on her collar bone.

No response.

'Mel, can you hear me?' I tapped again.

Nothing.

I leaned over and checked for breath.

No chest movement, no sound, nothing.

Fuck.

She was a skinny woman but still taller and bigger than me, and the only way I was going to be able to wrestle her out of that chair was to drag her by the legs. As I picked up her feet and started to pull I took in the full extent of the blood. Jesus. It was probably too late and a hiding to nothing, but I had to try. I gave one last big heave, her body lurched and her head made a dull thud as it hit the carpeted floor.

'Sorry, Mel.'

Checked for breath again.

Nothing.

I knelt over her chest, laced my fingers and placed my palm on her sternum, in line with her nipples. Up this close I could see the bloody fingermarks on her shirt where she had tried to stem the flow, tried to stop her life from seeping away, could see the blood on her own hands.

I felt my eyes sting from the sudden welling of tears and a lump come into my throat.

One, two, three, four – I leaned forward and pushed down hard, shoulders above my hands. Five, six, seven, eight – felt the spring back of her ribs between each compression. Nine, ten, eleven, twelve – hard and fast, hard and fast. Thirteen, fourteen, fifteen, sixteen.

No one deserved to die like this.

CHAPTER 26

'You okay?'

Paul's head poked around the bathroom door.

'Not really.'

'Didn't think so.'

He pushed the door open with his foot and came in holding two mugs.

'Thought you might need some of the hard stuff.'

'Gin?'

'Better than that.'

He popped one down on the corner by my head and perched himself on the edge of the bathtub, down by my feet. I caught the chocolaty waft of Milo over the top of the scent of my vanilla bubble bath.

'Biscuits?' I asked.

With a 'ta-da' he pulled a packet of Toffee Pops out of his hoodie pocket. He extracted one from the pack and tossed it frisbee style to me. I caught it with a very sudsy hand.

Thank God Paul didn't feel the need to fill silences with conversation, and knew me well enough to give my brain time to find the right words, even if it took a while. Eventually some came.

'I don't know why I'm so rocked by today,' I said having nibbled the edges off the biscuit. 'It's really thwumped me. I've seen so many god-awful crime scenes over the years and witnessed plenty of the violence people can throw at each other – hell I've been on the receiving end. But this one, it's, I don't know, different.'

He nodded and gave me a tight smile. 'This would be the first time you've done CPR on someone and they haven't survived, wouldn't it?' he said.

I hadn't really thought about it like that. Was that what had brought on this massive funk?

'From what you described she was well and truly dead when you got to her and there was nothing you could have done. You tried, but she was already too far gone.'

I finished off the biscuit, pushed myself up into more of a sitting position and reached beside me for the Milo, cupping my hands around the mug.

'Yeah, I know, but it's not just that.' I blew at the surface of the drink and then took a tentative sip. It was the perfect temperature, so I drank more.

Paul sat quietly, sipping his drink too.

'I feel like a real shit.'

'What do you mean?'

'A shit person.'

He looked at me, puzzled. 'Why?'

I took a big breath and pushed it out with a *whumff*. 'I kept on misjudging Mel, and I think I was too influenced by what other people had said about her. People at the church had said she was difficult and that she had really let herself go, was down and out, basically a bum. Then yesterday, when she made me interview her outside, didn't want me to go into her room, I'd assumed it was because she was a hoarder, or it was filthy and she was ashamed of the state of it. I couldn't have been more wrong. It was really spare, hardly anything in there, she barely owned a thing, but I'd jumped to a conclusion based on how she looked, what I'd heard. She got on my nerves from the outset, and I couldn't see past that. I feel bad that I was so judgemental, and I feel bad that I feel bad, because I'm worried that I'm making this about me, and me feeling guilty, rather than it being about her, a woman who has been murdered.'

'Oh, you funny little thing,' he said, love and concern evident in his voice. 'You really do like to overthink things and beat yourself up.'

'It's my superpower,' I said. 'And to be honest, I also feel bad because it can't be coincidence that I start investigating the Mark Freeman case and suddenly one of the main players is murdered. I can't help but feel that I've opened this can of worms, and now suddenly someone is dead, because of what I've done. If I wasn't doing this, Mel Smythe would still be alive.' My voice was starting to waver. 'She'd said I should let things lie, leave the past alone.' It started to crack. 'And now look at what happened.'

'You can stop thinking like that right now.' Paul leaned forward, his voice firm. 'You were instructed to open the case – you were doing your job. If someone, somewhere, felt threatened by the police reinvestigating the case and took steps to protect themselves and silence someone who could potentially point the finger at them, then that's on them, not on you.'

My chin had started to tremble and I could feel the tears start to roll down my face.

'Oh, Sammy.' He dropped down onto his knees and shuffled along the floor until he was alongside me, prised the mug out of my hand, set it down, then wrapped his arms around me in a big, bubbly hug.

CHAPTER 27

The meeting room was abuzz with people and energy. No one liked the thought that someone had been killed in our city; it somehow suggested a failure on our part as protectors of our community. But the reality was a murder case provided a perverse level of excitement, a puzzle to solve, an opportunity to use our collective skills to bring justice to the fallen. It was an opportunity to remind everyone of our raison d'être.

DI Johns moved to centre-stage, and the buzz and banter dropped like an inverse Mexican wave, from the front to the back of the room, as everyone realised the show was about to get under way and sat down. He stood looking across us and nodding, smug that he could silence a crowd of his colleagues by merely walking five steps across the floor. Some people held authority with understated calm, some felt the urge to buy into theatrics. It didn't surprise me in the least that he felt the need to raise his hand like some gospel preacher to mute the last few whisperers.

'Thank you, that's enough. Quiet, please.'

Paul was seated beside me and gave me a little tap on the side of my leg. I kept my eyes straight ahead and tried not to giggle.

'As you will be aware, a homicide took place in the city yesterday. The victim was a fifty-three-year-old woman, Melanie Jane Smythe, a resident at the Blackwell boarding house on Stafford Street, and the death took place on the premises in her private accommodation.'

He could have just said 'in her room', but that wouldn't have sounded as grand and intelligent. Why use one word when you could use seven.

'Detective Sergeant Smith will be leading the case. I'll hand it over to him to bring you up to speed.'

Smithy shuffled his way to the middle of the room. He looked far less comfortable being in front of a crowd. He cleared his throat in a slightly eye-twitching way and began.

'Preliminary talks yesterday with residents who were in the building at the time indicate no witnesses to the crime, and no one had noticed any unusual activity, visitors or loud noises.' It was always kind of odd hearing him fall into formal speak when we were used to his more irreverent style of talking. 'Now the initial shock will have passed, the team will be going back to interview them at their temporary accommodation today and to take formal statements, including from those who were not home at the time.'

I did feel bad for the residents. Not only did they have to deal with the horror of having someone murdered in their building, someone who may have even been a friend to some, the entire house had become a crime scene, so they had been shipped out of their own home for a few days. Those who weren't home at the time wouldn't have even been allowed in to collect a toothbrush and a change of undies. Mind you, the motel accommodation they were placed in would be a step up from where they were. Still, being displaced and without your home comforts at such an awful time had to suck. And when they were allowed back, Blackwell House would never feel safe again – would forever bear the taint of death.

'ESR will continue with their forensic scene examination today. We can tell you that the weapon, a kitchen knife, was found at the scene, and this is being treated as a murder investigation. A post-mortem of the victim will take place today, but the initial impression from the pathologist at the scene regarding the nature of the injuries was that they were not self-inflicted.'

I could have told them that. Alistair had been the pathologist on call yesterday, so I had qualified inside information on that front. But also, from my amateur but up-close-and-personal experience, I could have told you no one could have done that to themselves, especially someone as scrawny and bird-like as Mel Smythe. It was a relief that the ESR people were here. Although police scene-of-crime officers in Dunedin could undertake basic forensic scene examination, for a major crime the experts from Christchurch were called down. Given the distance involved, it always made scene examinations take longer than if we had locals, but the time was worth it for the level of expertise. They felt like a big, sciencey security blanket. They also held more clout in a court of law.

Smithy went through the process of outlining the day's assignments. I noted none of them came in my direction, but wasn't surprised. It was probably a directive from The Boss. Also, no mention had been made of the possible connection between this case and my investigation into the murder of Reverend Freeman. That was a rather large omission as far as I was concerned.

DI Johns moved back to centre stage.

'Thank you, Detective Sergeant.' He scanned the room and set his eyes upon me. A knot formed in the pit of my stomach. 'Detective Shephard was the person who discovered the body of the victim when visiting her in relation to another case. I would like to take this time to remind everyone that we have strict protocols to follow at a crime scene to protect the scene and prevent contamination or destruction of evidence.'

I felt a rush of blood into my face and it seemed like every set of eyes in the room turned to look at me.

'Fucker,' I heard Paul whisper out the side of his mouth.

I should have known I'd got off lightly so far in this briefing, but that the spotlight would eventually come around to me and my apparent shortcomings. I couldn't believe the dickhead would criticise me for attempting to resuscitate the victim. I didn't know if she'd been there for five hours or five minutes. Of course I had to try and save her life. What would he have done in that situation? From what he was implying he'd have left her to die in order to preserve evidence. Heartless bastard. My eyes dropped to the floor and I had to take some deep slow breaths and count to ten. This week couldn't get any worse, and it was only Tuesday.

'Detective Shephard has also been working on a cold case. That of the murder of the Reverend Mark Freeman at St Paul's Cathedral in 1999. Of note is the fact Mel Smythe was one of the key witnesses in the Freeman case. We cannot discount the possibility the two cases are linked and that Ms Freeman was murdered on account of this connection. To that end I'd like to invite the detective to come up and give a summary of her progress on the case so far.'

What the fuck? A heads-up would have been nice. At no point this morning had he mentioned he was going to get me up there to give a briefing on the case. I'd have appreciated the chance for some preparation. Instead, now that he'd just castigated me in front of all my colleagues, he was going to throw me off the deep end and watch me flounder. The knot in my stomach untangled and reformed into a little pot of simmering rage. I abruptly stood to my feet, startling the people sitting beside me, including Paul, and strode with purpose to the front of the room.

I wasn't going to give him the pleasure of thinking he'd scored some sick point.

Fuck him.

I turned around to face the room, and took a steadying breath, ready to score a point or two of my own. I could feel the sharp bite of my fingernails digging into my palms, so had to consciously relax my fists. I had this.

'Thank you, DI Johns. As many of you are aware I have been tasked with reopening the Reverend Mark Freeman case. He was murdered on the steps of St Paul's Cathedral on the night of Sunday, the third of July 1999, sometime after the evening service. The investigation at the time was open for a number of years but failed to result in an arrest...' I let that hang for a second. 'It is important for everyone to note that DI Johns has a direct conflict of interest in the investigation as Reverend Freeman was the father of his wife, so the case needs to be dealt with sensitively, and any information or insight you may have is to come directly to me, please.'

I swear I could feel the heat on the back of my neck where his eyes were boring into me.

'He was also a part of the unsuccessful investigating team at the time, so, likewise, in the interests of making an unbiased and fresh review of the information and evidence, I'd appreciate it if any comments or leads that could be relevant come to me.'

I heard a sharp intake of breath from behind me and that hot sensation on my neck upgraded to daggers. It wouldn't have surprised me if he interjected at this stage, so I pressed on before he had the chance, and before the whispers and chatter now coming from the crowd became too raucous.

'A review of the postmortem notes has confirmed that the cause of death was a broken neck due to Freeman's fall down the steps. He had also suffered a stab wound to the abdomen, calculated to have been from a small knife. While this would not have been sufficient to cause immediate death, its presence indicates this was a homicide rather than an accident. No witnesses to the attack came forward in 1999.'

The murmurs had quietened down now. I had their attention, although I did note a number of them were looking at The Boss rather than at me. I caught Paul's eye and he gave an encouraging nod.

'I've undertaken interviews with the immediate family members: the Reverend's wife, Yvonne Freeman, his son, Callum Freeman, and daughter, Felicity Johns. Those confirmed their statements from the time and they weren't able to add any new information. One area of investigation that didn't appear to have been fully considered at the time, though, was the possibility of mistaken identity – that another of the priests had been the intended target.'

And thus I scored my third point. DI Johns must have known there was a risk I'd find shortcomings in the original investigation, and if he hadn't been such an almighty great ass I might have been a bit more discreet about highlighting them. But hey, he started it.

'To that end I have interviewed other members of the worship team from the time – staff, and also the current safeguarding officer. They're all adamant there had been no evidence or rumour of abuse or inappropriate behaviour from either Reverend Freeman or the other priests, which indicates Reverend Freeman was the intended target of the attack.'

I wanted to keep this as brief as possible – the more succinct I was, the less chance there was of my stuffing anything up and giving The Boss an opportunity to pounce. So I moved on quickly.

'We still need to interview Aaron Cox, a person from the congregation who received a lot of interest from the original investigating team. We are currently trying to locate him. Any assistance in finding him would be greatly appreciated.'

I paused to gather myself before addressing the final part of my report. I tried to keep my voice steady; this still felt very raw.

'As mentioned by DI Johns earlier, the victim of yesterday's homicide, Mel Smythe, was also a witness in the Freeman case. She had been the youth leader at St Paul's at the time of Reverend Freeman's murder and was present at the service on the night in question. I was able to conduct an interview with her the day before she died. That didn't reveal any new information, but she did contact me the morning of her death, wanting to talk urgently. Unfortunately, she was murdered before we had opportunity to speak. I...' I gulped. 'I discovered her body in her room when I went to meet up with her.'

It was the first time I had faltered. I paused for a moment, aware of the weight of silence in the room.

'We can't ignore the timing of her death, occurring just when the investigation into Reverend Freeman's murder has been reopened. It seems a little more than coincidence.'

My mouth suddenly felt dry, and I didn't have anything else to say. If anyone had questions they could come and find me. I'd had enough of being centre stage.

'Back to you, DI Johns,' I said and walked straight back to my chair without so much as a backwards glance.

Take that, arsehole.

CHAPTER 28

'Well done out there. You did a great job summarising the case, considering.'

Smithy and I were manoeuvring around each other in the kitchenette, making comfort drinks after the fiasco that had been the morning briefing. Well, I was making tea like a normal person while he made his special blend of tragic coffee.

'Thanks,' I said.

'Look, I'm sorry, I didn't know he was going to pull a stunt like that, otherwise I would have warned you so you had time to prepare.' I watched, slightly appalled, as he stirred three teaspoonfuls of sugar into the overly milky brew. It was moments like this that reinforced why I was a coffee snob. It was café flat whites only for me. There was no level of desperation that would make me go for instant crap, especially diabetes-inducing instant crap.

'Yeah, well, we all know his favourite game is Slam-a-Sam. You'd think, considering he was the one who asked me to reopen this bloody case in the first place, he'd be a little more supportive rather than trashing me in public.'

'Sorry, how long have you worked here?'

'Yeah, fair point. You'd think I'd have learned by now.'

Smithy gave small chuckle. 'It backfired though. You nailed it on the fly.'

We retreated along the corridor to the CIB room. For once I managed to get my drink back to the office without slopping some on the carpet, although, given how ugly it was, I'd never felt the slightest bit of remorse at adding to the ghosts of spills past.

When we got back to Smithy's desk, I popped the question that had been weighing on my mind. 'So where do I stand with the Mel Smythe case? What's my role there?' I asked.

He put his coffee down and set his hands on his hips. 'I've been thinking about that. You'll have noticed I didn't allocate you any tasks on the new case while we were in the briefing. Or The Boss, for that matter.'

One good thing about Smithy was he didn't beat around the bush. You knew where you stood with him, well, most of the time.

'He recognised there was still a conflict of interest?'

'I *told* him there was a conflict of interest.'

It was my turn to chuckle. I would have loved to have been a fly on the wall for that conversation. Although I was certain The Boss had taken Smithy's reminder far better than he'd taken the same warning from me, given Smithy was bigger than he was and they had things in common, like balls and dicks.

'So, what do want from me then?'

'You keep on doing what you're doing. Most of the team are investigating the new murder, and I've instructed them to keep their minds open: the murder could have been a result of some recent incident, or something as simple as a burglary gone wrong. But of course we can't discount the coincidence in terms of the timing – you're investigating the priest's murder, and, hey ho, suddenly someone who was there at the time dies. But, in saying that, we can't afford to take shortcuts and leap straight to that line of investigation at the exclusion of others.' With each 'but' he had both hands up, pointing out a path, first to the right, then to the left, like some slow-motion eighties boogie. It was the most animated I'd seen him in ages. 'So, given you're fully involved in that side of things, and have already formed a relationship with the people you've spoken with from his family and the church in general, you're the logical choice to continue being the point of contact there. Of course that puts a lot of the responsibility on you, but you can handle it.' I felt quite touched by the vote of confidence. 'Also, bear in mind there may be people from that first investigation who are going to be feeling pretty vulnerable right now and worried they might be in danger. You'll need to manage that. And more importantly, someone you're

following up on from that initial investigation might be the killer.'
He gave me that squinty look that meant I was about to hear something I might not like. 'You can be a bit too trusting at times, Sam.
No one is above suspicion. That's especially important, given the
closeness of the case to a certain colleague of ours. Use your radar,
and if it's telling you something's not quite right, listen to it.'

Fair comment.

The notion someone from the church could be responsible for
Mel's death wasn't the most comforting thought in the world. And
then there was the whole damn complication of The Boss.

I hoped like hell my radar was up to it.

CHAPTER 29

'Do you really think we should be having these kinds of discussions in front of Amelia?' I asked.

Paul shrugged and *booped* Amelia on the nose. An eruption of giggles came from the boopee, resulting in a delighted grin from the booper. It was contagious. They were on the floor together, enjoying tummy time, while I tried to fold Mount Laundry with the assistance of the cat.

'I'm sure lots of parents talk shop in front of their kids.'

'True, but I'm figuring most of them aren't discussing murder weapons.'

'Well, you never know. It's all about context. If they were game developers they might be, or crime writers, or journalists, or even murderers.'

'Yeah, yeah I get your point.' I threw a pair of underpants at him. 'Your daddy has got an answer for everything.' From the expulsion of more giggles, she thought it was funny, especially when he put the pants on his head. How the hell did I end up with a clown?

'But seriously, I think we're okay for now, but we might have to review that when she's a bit older and can dob us in to daycare, or starts drawing wildly inappropriate pictures and they call in the shrink.'

'As long as it doesn't turn her into a raging psychopath.'

'Well, it's a risk. She does have your mother's genes, after all.'

'Ouch.' I didn't refute it though. 'So what's the guts on the murder weapon?'

'That was, perhaps, a poor choice of words.'

It was a bit too close to the bone. Hadn't intended it that way. 'I spotted the knife beside the armchair when I was trying to help Mel Smythe. To me the position suggested she had pulled it out and dropped it, rather than the killer dropping it as they headed for the door. ESR might be able to shed more light on that when they've done the blood-spatter analysis.' If she'd pulled it out herself it would have been one of the worst things she could have done from a survival point of view. But then, I'm sure I wouldn't have been thinking clearly either if I had a bloody great carving knife sticking out of my chest. The mental image caused a rack of shudders. They didn't go unnoticed.

'You okay?' Paul asked.

'Yeah. It's still pretty vivid.'

He took my undies off his head and threw them back at me. They landed on Queen Victoria, who shrugged them off and flicked her tail, not amused.

'Hopefully ESR will come to light with fingerprints or some trace of the stabber,' I said. They always did a professional job, but like all things in these financially constrained times, under-resourcing and inadequate staffing meant results took longer than we would have liked.

'So tell me more about the knife?' Paul said.

'Unfortunately it was one of those SMEG brand ones that New World Supermarket had a big collect-the-sticker promotion for a few years back.' This was the 'spend more than you intended on your groceries so you could collect a million stickers to get a knife you didn't really need but went for anyway because it was "free"' promotion. Those sorts of promos sucked in the gullible, so yes, I think we had two.

'In other words, half the households in Dunedin will have one?'

'Yup,' I said. 'Well, at least the half that can afford to shop at New World.'

It looked like Amelia had had enough of scrubbing around on her tummy, so she flipped over onto her back. Her dad followed suit.

'I spent the day talking with the residents of the boarding house. None of them owned one of those knives, not that they admitted to, and they were all in agreement that there were none floating around in the shared kitchen.'

'Which implies, if none of them are lying or just plain unobservant, that the killer brought the knife with them.'

'Yes indeed. Premeditation.'

We both pondered upon that one for a while.

'Did the boarding house have security cameras?' I asked. I hadn't seen any on my visits, but my mind had been on other things at the time.

'Unfortunately not. We've canvassed other houses in the vicinity in case they have external cameras, but have come up zip. There were some further up the road, so we've grabbed their footage just in case we recognise anyone going past, but it's a long shot.'

A long shot was better than no shot at all.

'So if someone came along armed with a knife to pay a social visit to Mel Smythe, it begs the question why? I honestly can't help thinking it has to be tied into the Mark Freeman case. The timing is too convenient.'

'No argument from me there. As much as I understand the need to investigate the current case with a totally open mind, I think we should be putting more resources into your case. The two have to be connected.'

'Yeah. Someone got spooked by the Freeman case being reopened and panicked. Which begs the question: who wanted Mel Smythe silenced, and what did she have on them?'

CHAPTER 30

My first task for the day was to arrange an interview with Aaron Cox, AKA Andrew Cotton. The murder of Mel Smythe, and dealing with its immediate aftermath, had meant no opportunity to interview him for a day or two, but we were at the stage where it really needed to be done. He had the potential to provide the missing pieces of the puzzle of not just one, but two cases now, and given what felt like the zero progress I was making, I needed a break. The contact cell phone number Sonia had come up with was from the time he'd been living in Auckland. What were the chances of it still working when its owner seemed to be wanting to disappear into the back blocks of New Zealand? I wasn't about to hold my breath.

I tapped in the numbers and waited for it to connect.

Surprise, surprise, an automated voice informed me the number I had dialled was no longer in service. Bugger. That meant the only way to contact him was going to be an unannounced visit in person. That being the case, and given Waitati was around thirty minutes' drive away and that he lived up some remote, dodgy-looking, gravel country road, I'd definitely be taking company with me. Even I wasn't dumb enough to tackle that one alone. I'd have to try and see if Sonia was free this afternoon, as this morning she was out following up on some public tip-offs that had come through to the anonymous crime-stoppers phone line. The public response to our appeals for any information on Mel Smythe's murder had been fairly lukewarm. I couldn't help but wonder whether, had a well-connected young socialite from Roslyn or a university academic been killed, there would have been more public outrage than there was for a down-and-out on benefits and living in a dodgy boarding house.

It was time to consider plan B for the morning. Over the next few days I was going to have to go back and visit Reverend Freeman's family, and everyone I had spoken to from the St Paul's congregation. As well as asking them more about their relationship with and recollections of Mel Smythe, I would also have to ask the more uncomfortable question: where were you on Monday morning? Had a sneaking suspicion one or two of them might take offence at that one. And was pretty certain The Boss would take offence when he found out I had asked it of his wife. It may have been a little juvenile of me, but given my current mood, I quite liked the idea of offending The Boss.

I wondered what Smithy was up to. There were a couple of things I wanted to run past him. I wandered out of the CIB room and went in search of him, hoping he was still in the building somewhere. It was a good excuse to stretch my legs and combat the attack of the restlessnesses, which often happened after a sleepless night. Couldn't help but wonder why my body thought it was a good idea to combine being dog-tired and restless all at the same time. Bodies were weird. But little madam had had me up twice in the night. She was teething, poor sod. I knew I was a sook and complained enough when I got a mouth ulcer, so didn't begrudge her letting us know that having little fangs bust out of your gums was not fun.

My search for Smithy took me down towards the interview rooms, and as I rounded the corner of the corridor I was greeted by the sight of The Boss escorting what could only be described as an extremely unhappy man towards the elevators. He was around six foot tall, was built like a brick shithouse, and between the gang tattoos that extended up his neck and the string of expletives coming out of his mouth, the vibe he was emanating made me pause and back up against the wall to give them the maximum space to get past. The Boss looked as excited at the situation as his guest. I tried not to stare as they went past me. Moody Guy looked a little familiar but I couldn't quite place his face. He was so intent on delivering a verbal barrage at the back of DI John's head that I don't think he even registered my existence, which suited just fine. Constable Walters was bringing up the rear of the little procession. He was the tallest and buffest constable we had and was often asked to be on hand for the more intimidating customers. He caught my eye and gave me his best grimace and shoulder-shrug. That would be a fun elevator ride down.

Smithy was sitting at the table in an interview room, tidying away some notes, when I found him.

I indicated towards the retreating figures. 'That sounded fun,' I said.

'Understatement of the year.'

'Who was the guy? He looked kind of familiar, but I couldn't place him.'

It was hard to tell from Smithy's grizzled face, but I was pretty sure he became a little flushed. 'Take a seat,' he said, and indicated opposite. Given the rush of colour to his face and the tone in his voice, my suspicion-o-meter cranked up a couple of notches.

'Why?'

'Just take a seat. Trust me, you're going to need it.'

Comments like that usually presaged the delivery of some bad, if not tragic, news personal to the receiver of said news, but nothing about the current situation suggested that was the case. Which left only one alternative – some development I was not going to be pleased to hear about. I maintained eye contact with him all the while pulling out the chair and parking my butt on it.

'So are you going to tell me what's going on?' I asked.

I'd seen introverts at a rave look more comfortable. 'That,' he said pointing in the general direction of the departed, 'was Aaron Cox.'

'I beg your pardon?'

'We were interviewing Aaron Cox.'

'I'm sorry, but what the actual fuck?'

Now I understood why he had asked me to sit down. It reduced the risk of me picking up the chair and hurling it at him. 'Why was he in here and being interviewed by The Boss? And why the fuck wasn't I informed about it?' It may have been my generalised level of tiredness but my own mood had jumped immediately to extreme fire risk.

'Hey, you don't need to be like that,' he said, hands up in supplication. 'It was not my idea, I can assure you. When The Boss found out Cox had been located, he insisted on him being picked up and brought in for questioning.' That explained why Moody Guy looked a little familiar. It was the same man from the photos I had been studying, but with twenty-five years of wear and tear, twenty extra kilograms and a shaved head.

'On what grounds and for what case? Because I thought it had been made perfectly clear that any involvement Johns had in my case was a clear conflict of interest, so unless he had some stunning reason to suspect that Aaron Cox was involved in the Mel Smythe murder in a way completely independently of the Freeman case, then he had No. Damned. Right. To. Step. In.' Those last six words were also emphasised by the percussion of my fists on the table.

'Look. I advised him against it, but he pulled rank and was insistent. For some reason he has the hots for Aaron Cox. I don't know what happened twenty-five years ago between them, but he was like a dog having rediscovered his favourite bone. Certainly gave me the feeling he believed Cox was responsible for the murder of Mark Freeman, but they just hadn't found the incontrovertible proof.' Johns' name hadn't been down as the author of any of the reports I'd read that related to Cox, but as an officer at the time he would have been fully briefed on the case and must have interacted with Cox in some way. And I knew from bitter experience that if Johns got an idea into his skull he couldn't let it go. If that idea was that Cox was the murderer, then there would be no persuading him otherwise.

'And how did that go down? Because judging by the swearing and fucking furious demeanour of the man, he was not happy about being dragged in here and questioned by some arsehole with a grievance.'

'Well I can tell you that it was a very short interview, because The

Boss went in with his usual subtlety, and as soon as Cox twigged that he was one of the original investigating crew, then he went apeshit and insisted on having a lawyer present. I believe the word "stitch-up" might have been mentioned, and as you can imagine someone didn't take kindly to being accused of corruption, and it all went extremely pear-shaped from there.'

'Jesus fucking Christ.' I stood up so abruptly the chair fell over backward. I didn't bother setting it back on its feet, and instead shoved it further away with my foot. 'Johns has completely fucked up any chance of my having a constructive conversation with Cox about the case, and I'm fairly certain he now won't help us shed any light on who may have killed Mel Smythe, not when he's treated like a criminal by that dickhead.'

'Hey, tone it down, you're preaching to the converted here, Sam.' Smithy had put a warning growl into his voice. 'It's happened. There's nothing you can do to change that, and neither of us are happy about it.'

I swung around to face him, hands on hips. 'So what am I sup-posed to do now? What exactly am I supposed to do now that idiot has blown it with my best potential source of information into the case?'

'Well, for a start you can take a breath and calm the hell down. And then you will do what you always do when faced with a steam-ing pile of his shit that no one else wants to deal with.'

'Oh yeah, and what is that?'

'Piss him off by sorting it.'

CHAPTER 31

This case was getting under my skin in more ways than one. After being so monumentally pissed off, I felt the need for some fresh air to cool my head and rethink of my plan of attack. I didn't set off with any destination in mind, just put one foot in front of the other, my head a swirl of people and reading and evidence and conversations, but my subconscious took matters into its own hands. Before I knew it, I found myself walking up the front steps of St Paul's Cathedral. How the hell did I get here? It was like no matter what I did, I ended up back at the cathedral. It was my magnetic north, but I can't say I was happy with the attraction. When I reached the top of the stairs, my eyes were drawn through the open double-doors to the grand cross suspended at the far end of the building. It was a bit late to stop now, so I took a deep breath and crossed the threshold.

It felt like stepping through into another world. The traffic noise and street bustle of The Octagon melted away and was replaced by what I could only describe as negative noise, an absence of sound – but an absence with an echo. In a weird kind of a way it felt comforting, as much as vast, empty spaces could. I was very aware of the sound of my footsteps as I walked up the central nave and sidled into one of the pews several rows up to the right. My eyes were drawn upward to the beautiful, vaulted stone ceiling then ran along the length of the church to the massive perspex cross suspended in the modern chancel addition at the end. The sun was angling in from the side and striking it in a way that threw little lines of red, purple and green onto the opposite wall. My mind found the transition from the old to the new jarring, so my eyes fell back to some of the traditional stained-glass windows that seemed to befit the *mana* of the building better than the brash modern postscript.

Again, the play of colour and light from the sun shining through them was mesmerising. Although it was officially public visiting hours, there didn't appear to be anyone else here. It wasn't the tourist season, so the regular throng of cruise-ship visitors and coach tours was thankfully absent, as were any staff. That was a relief, as a part of me felt slightly embarrassed that I'd come here at all.

I had to remind myself that a congregation was about people, not a building, and despite me finding this place vast and unsettling, not everyone did. And while it didn't feel that lively today, there was a vibrant community here that did bring it to life. Sitting in this space my mind set to imagining what that community was like back in 1999. Clearly there were points of tension. So far no one had anything glowing to say about Mel Smythe, and there was uncertainty and suspicion about Aaron Cox. They were your classic outsiders, viewed with distrust, the first ones to have the finger pointed at them when something bad went down. I couldn't help but feel a pang of sadness and guilt when I thought of Mel. It would be interesting to see if people looked upon her a little kindlier now that she'd died, especially in such shocking circumstances. I was reminded about what I'd discovered about her – that her life and politics were unappreciated by the older members of the congregation. I made a mental note to talk with members of the youth group from that time, see if they had a different impression of their feminist lesbian youth leader. Maybe to them she was edgy and cool, someone unafraid to think beyond the strictures of the church, and they could relate to her better than to their own parents. They would also probably have an opinion about the man who'd been paraded to them as the gold standard – evidence that anyone could be saved by God, no matter how lost.

The creak of the external door opening startled me out of my reverie, signalling my time of solitude was over. I listened as a single set of footsteps walked up the side aisle to the right, and when they came alongside, I discreetly turned my head to find out who else had sought out this place of refuge in the middle of a week day.

Tourist or worshipper? My eyes widened and snapped back to the front as I recognised the visitor.

Fuck, fuck and fuckity-fuck.

The man had briefly caught my eye but kept on walking, coming to a stop several rows ahead and then shuffling between the pews into a small chapel area off to the side, settling in behind a pillar, so out of my line of sight.

I let out the breath I hadn't realised I'd been holding. He didn't seem to have recognised me. But then why would he? We'd only crossed paths for a few seconds back in the station, and at the time Aaron Cox was fully intent on bawling out DI Johns, not paying attention to a random detective who had the misfortune to be in the hallway at the same time.

But what the hell was he doing here? I'd have thought, given the circumstances, setting foot in this place would be the last thing on earth he'd want to do. He hadn't exactly been made welcome here after Reverend Freeman's murder, in fact by the sounds of it the congregation went into pitchfork-and-torches mode and basically drove him out of town. Yet, like me, here he was.

What the hell was I going to do? A large part of me wanted to quietly skulk out of the building and scamper down the stairs unnoticed. But another part of me was thinking an opportunity had been handed to me on a plate to have a conversation with the man on neutral territory. What was the worst that could happen? Actually, I could imagine a lot of bad things that could happen, but I was unlikely to get a chance like this again, so I took an almighty calming breath, mentally put my big-girl panties on and stood up. The sound of my heart thudding was even louder than my footsteps echoing through the building as I approached him. Courtesy of the pew configuration it was pretty obvious I was making my way directly towards him. He turned to watch me, a puzzled and then a suspicious look crossing his face as I got closer. I stood at the end of the pew he was sitting in, then took the plunge and sat down, landing on the little pile of red hymnbooks tucked into the corner and having to move a little closer to the now alarmed-looking man.

'Can I help you?' he said. His voice was raspy, like his vocal cords had been fried by a lifetime of smoking.

'You're Aaron Cox, aren't you?' My hand went to my heart like I was indicating, yes, it's me, to a kid. 'I'm Detective Sam Shephard.'

As soon as I said the word 'detective', I could see his hackles rise.

'What the hell are you doing here, Detective? And why are you following me?'

Me following him? Well it proved that he wasn't very observant.

'Actually, I could ask you the same question? In case you hadn't noticed, I was already here in the church when you came in, you walked straight past me. So why did you follow me here from the station?' It wasn't quite the line I'd rehearsed in my head, but turning it around on him felt like it could be a way to connect, or at least allay some of his suspicions.

'Why the fuck would I follow you from the station?' he said, with up-flick of his head. 'I don't even know who you are.'

'Well, you did see me there just before. I was in the hallway when you came out of the interview room with Detective Inspector Johns.'

'That fucking tosser. What an arsehole. I had other things on my mind. The fucking pope could have been standing in the hallway and I wouldn't have noticed him, so why the fuck would you think that I'd notice you?'

I didn't think I was that invisible, and he really could have done with a broader range of adjectives. The guttural click of the Ks echoed around the cathedral and seemed to magnify with the acoustics. It wouldn't have surprised me if someone from the church made an appearance any moment now to see if everything was okay. I couldn't help but look over my shoulder before focussing back on him.

'Well, you did seem rather intent on reminding the DI about his lack of legitimate parentage at the time, so I guess you could have missed me.'

I saw the corner of his mouth curl a little. 'So what do you want, then?' he asked.

'To ask you some questions about the Mark Freeman case.'

'You're kidding me, right. After being grilled down at the station by those arseholes you really think I'm going to sit here in a fucking church – *his* fucking church, I might add – and answer more questions. Firstly, I don't have a lawyer present, and the way you guys are, you'll be trying to pin that woman's murder on me too. You're all the fucking same. And secondly, I wouldn't trust any of you to listen to anything I had to say anyway.'

'What do you mean?'

'You all have this idea in your head about who I am, and no amount of talking or explaining will ever change your mind about me. Despite what you think, I am not some criminal scumbag who has never let go of his past. Yes, that was my life once, but that was a long time ago. My life is simple now, under the radar, and I want it to stay that way. After Mark was killed, the police came after me with everything. I didn't kill him – there was no evidence to say I killed him – but they wouldn't let it go. Those arseholes had it fixed in their brain that the Māori ex-gang guy with the tats must have done it, so they hounded me and hounded me, racist fuckers. But you know what? They had nothing – nothing – and they never will have anything on me, because I didn't fucking do it.'

For someone who didn't want to talk with the likes of me, he was saying a hell of a lot. I kept my mouth shut and fought the urge to ask questions. He was on a roll, it was better to let him put it all out there. Somehow this had turned into a confessional, although he didn't have anything to confess, other than an over-usage of expletives. Although, given what he'd been through, they were fully justified expletives.

'And now it's the same again, with that woman killed. You guys will hound me and hound me because according to you I'm the scum of the earth. And I admit that I'm no angel, and that after Mark's death and all of that fucking stress I fell back into old habits for a bit, what with the police, and then the people from the church, the so-called righteous Christians driving me away too, hypocritical bastards, but I got myself on the straight and narrow again, ditched the booze and the drugs, been sober eighteen years now. So no, I had nothing to do with Mark's death, and I had nothing to do with that woman's death. And no, I don't want to talk with you, because you cops are all the fucking same.'

I had so much going on in my head, taking in the details from his rant, that it took me a moment to realise he'd stopped talking.

'Why did you come here?' I asked, my voice quiet in this hallowed space. 'I mean, you just said the people from the church, from this place, drove you away. Yet you're here. Why would you do that if it's got so many bad memories for you?'

He looked at me then in a way that made me feel like I was being assessed. It was as uncomfortable as hell, but I held his stare until he seemed to have come to some kind of decision. He expelled a large breath and leaned back against the pew, brought his interlocked hands to his mouth and sat for a moment, eyes down, almost in prayer.

When he spoke, his voice had lost the fire and indignation, and was instead quiet, pensive: 'The simple answer is I miss him. I miss Mark. Even after all these years.' He looked at me again. 'You may find it hard to believe that someone like me and someone like him could have been friends. But we connected in a way that I'd never had with anyone before. Could talk about anything, and I didn't feel like I was being judged. And before you say it, I know people in the church thought that I was his pet project – you know, convert the bad guy and parade him like some trophy – but it wasn't like that. It was the most genuine friendship I think I've ever had with anyone. In my previous life, if you had friends it was because they wanted something from you, or you had to behave in a way that made you worthy of their friendship. With Mark I always felt there were no strings attached, there was no agenda. And I miss that.'

Friendship was the most valuable thing on earth. If it weren't for

Maggie, my life would be so much less rich and fulfilling, and I'd probably still be that slightly immature and irritating-as-hell woman-child that she put up with and brought down to earth – in a good way, in a needed way. Yes, I had Paul, but that friendship and partnership was completely different to what I had with Maggs. So I completely understood where Aaron was coming from and why the lingering memories of that friendship and his longing for it would have endured over the decades.

'Good friends are a gift,' I said.

He simply nodded his head in agreement.

'Do you have any thoughts on who did do it? Who killed your friend, I mean, although if you have any thoughts on Mel Smythe, that would be useful too.'

'Well, I can't make any comments on Mel's murder. Poor woman. We didn't see eye to eye, which was more my fault than hers. Back then I still thought of women as ... Well, let's just say I'm more enlightened nowadays. She did piss a lot of people off, though. And it has to be someone tied to Mark's death. Any idiot can see that.'

'And Reverend Freeman?'

'Well, of course, I don't buy into the it-was-me brigade,' he said with a low laugh. 'As well as me the police also spent a lot of time looking at other people outside the Church. I reckon they should have been looking more inside.'

'Why?'

'How he died. From my *previous* experience' – he looked at me askance, having emphasised the 'previous' – 'if someone had wanted him dead, they wouldn't have pissed about with some small knife. They would have done him good and proper.'

'So you think they didn't want him dead?'

'I don't know what to think, but it feels odd.'

It was something that had crossed my mind too.

'Anyway, I've probably said too much.' He rose to his feet. 'Do me a favour and get those bastards off my back. I had nothing to do with any of this. Never did.'

'Yeah. I'll do my best.'

'Appreciate it.'

I watched as he edged his way to the end of the pew. He reached the aisle, paused then turned and looked at me that way again. Assessing.

'You know, Mark and me had a lot more things in common than you might think.' He tapped his fingers on the wood. 'We both had daughters who got in trouble.'

'What do you mean in trouble?'

'In the biblical sense,' he said, and walked away.

CHAPTER 32

'I need to ask you a question, but it is rather personal and rather delicate.'

The afternoon light was lovely, shining into the sitting area in Felicity Johns' home. I could really see why they had made this addition to the house – to capture exactly this. It was a haven in what could sometimes be a gloomy Dunedin. Gemma, the wee Westie, must have agreed, as she was stretched out asleep in the sun. Felicity placed a cup of tea in front of me and carefully sat back into the armchair with her own.

'That sounds ominous,' she said. 'What were you wanting to know?'

'There is no easy way to ask this, so I will be direct.' Sometimes I hated the level of prying into personal lives that this job required. Asking questions like this felt in some ways on a par with the awful job of informing next of kin about the death of a loved one. Both were difficult and emotionally charged, although this was more awkward. 'In the course of my investigation into your father's death it was brought to my attention that at that time, as a teenager, you had fallen pregnant. Was that the case?'

Her drink stopped halfway up to her mouth then continued. She blew into the tea several times, eyes downcast, before she set it back on the table without taking a sip.

'Before I respond to that, can I ask if this conversation is on the record?'

Her question and the fact she didn't outright deny it was rather telling.

'If the information that comes from this conversation ties into your father's case in a relevant way, then yes, it is on the record and it would be shared with my colleagues. If it turns out that information is not relevant to the case, then it is a confidential conversation between you and me. It won't go beyond this room.'

She sat there, rocking gently on the edge of the chair, before leaning back. 'Thank you,' she said.

'I know it's a difficult question, but in order to get to the bottom of your father's death, I have to consider and understand everything that was going on in his life at the time, including within his family. I'm sorry if this makes you uncomfortable or causes you pain – that's not my intention.'

'I know, that's okay. You're just doing your job. I appreciate that. But I'd also appreciate that this didn't go out of this room.'

'As I said, if it doesn't seem pertinent to the case then it stays between us.'

She licked her lips and blew out a long breath. 'Yes. When I was fifteen years old, much to my horror, I found myself pregnant.' The fact that she was choosing to speak about it indicated that, in her mind, it didn't have anything to do with her father's murder. Or perhaps she had decided that not saying anything would make a worse impression, make me think she was hiding something, and ultimately have a worse outcome for her. Either way, I appreciated the trust she was placing in me and my judgement.

'I take it that Greg doesn't know about it.'

She slowly shook her head. 'No. It's something I've kept to myself. There are some things you just don't want to share with those you love. Or need to share.' It was one hell of a secret to keep to yourself, but I could understand why. But how would The Boss react if he found out his wife had withheld something so deeply personal? How would that make him feel about the trust in their relationship? I fervently hoped, for Felicity's sake, he wouldn't find out.

'Can I ask what the circumstances were?'

'Love.' She gave a wry smile. 'Well, I thought it was love at the time. And so did he. We were both so young, same class at school, playing about with all of those overwhelming urges and feelings. I'm sure you can remember what it was like at that age, all lust and raging hormones with a healthy dose of fear of God. The fear made it even more exciting, in a way.'

Excitement and love weren't something I associated with encounters at that age.

'Not enough fear of God though, and not enough sense, because we didn't use any protection and – I'm still surprised that I was surprised, which shows how naive I was – I fell pregnant. Sex before marriage was a big no-no in the Church, and it was that classic thing where we were constantly being told that if we had sex we were sinning, so in our minds using contraception would be admitting to sin, so we didn't. God, who understands teenage logic?'

Raging hormones and critical thought didn't always go hand in hand. It wasn't usually the brain doing the thinking.

'So what did you do?' I asked, although I could guess what the outcome was – I hadn't seen any notes on record of her being pregnant or having a child, and from what I had seen and heard at the station there didn't seem to be a twenty-five-year-old in her or DI Johns' lives.

'I was only fifteen – so young. There was no way I wanted to have a baby, no way I could have cared for it. I was just a baby myself. I ... I didn't have a choice. For me there was no other option. I had to have an abortion.' Even twenty-five years later I could see the emotion twist her face, watched her bite her lip, her eyes well up.

'Did your parents help you sort that?' I asked, my voice soft.

'Good Lord, no. They ... No, I couldn't.' Her hands waved as much as her sputters. 'They didn't know. There was no way I could tell them. I was the daughter of a priest, for God's sake. It would have brought so much shame and embarrassment to them if they found out – if anyone found out. And...' she paused for a large breath '...I was too scared to tell them. I was too scared of how angry they would be, how disappointed they would be. And I couldn't face that. And I was scared if they found out I was pregnant they would make me have the baby and then adopt it out. They would never let me have an abortion. You can't imagine how terrifying it was.'

It was shocking and scary enough when I found out I was unexpectedly pregnant as an adult, so what must it have been like for a teenage kid? All of the thought processes and decision-making I had to go through, and wondering how it was going to affect the rest of my life and Paul's, were huge.

'So, who did you turn to? Who helped you out?' I hoped to God she hadn't attempted to abort it herself. My mind leapt to a terrified teenager taking, at risk of her life, terrible measures. Then my mind tried to grapple with how awful it must have been for her not to be able to confide in her loved ones, and to have to go through all that, scared and alone. Had she ever been able to confide in others, talk it through, process such an immense and life-changing thing? Or was that still something she was burying deep? I found my eyes swimming and had to blink the tears back. For me, despite not having planned it, having Amelia had turned out to be one of the most amazing things in my life. But would I have made the same choice if I had been a terrified teenager rather than a bewildered adult? Even as a grown-up it wasn't a straightforward decision, but I couldn't imagine my life without my daughter now. Stuff having to make tough decisions about a pregnancy when I was that age, though.

'I really needed someone to talk to, to tell me what to do. There was only one person back then I could think of who would be able to help, who'd know what to do.' She hesitated a moment before continuing. 'And that was Mel Smythe.'

Well, that took me aback. And judging by the hesitation and the look on Felicity's face, she realised the complexity of the situation now that Mel was dead. That was assuming she knew.

'Are you aware that Mel Smythe was the victim of a homicide earlier this week?'

She nodded slowly. 'I'm still trying to get my head around it.'

Gemma had decided she needed a pat. Felicity obliged.

'Did you have a close relationship with her?'

'I wouldn't say it was close, and I haven't seen her for years and years. But it's an awful thing to happen and I'm still quite shocked.'

It would be a lot to process, given the circumstances.

'She was your youth leader back then, wasn't she? So when you went to her, she was able to help you with the pregnancy?'

'Yeah, she did. She was the one who talked me through all the options. She took me to the doctor, and went with me and supported me at the hospital when it was time to get it done. She was amazing really, a life-saver. I don't know what I would have done otherwise.'

Yet again I felt that pang of guilt. I had misjudged the woman. Mel Smythe clearly showed a level of care and compassion that was lacking in the other adults in Felicity's life, and that was lacking in the Church people who'd ultimately rejected Mel herself. I felt grateful that Mel had been able to intervene safely on behalf of a very vulnerable teenager in an untenable position. Alas, my personal experience with youth leaders hadn't been as positive.

'And the boy? Did he know you were pregnant?'

'Yes. I didn't want to tell him, but Mel insisted. She said he had to be a part of it all the way so he would learn from it too. He was a member of the youth group, as well as being in my class at school, so she knew him well. She said something along the lines of "if you were old enough to have sex, you were old enough to deal with the very real consequences". Don't get me wrong, she wasn't cruel about it or anything. She was really pragmatic and kind. But she didn't want us to make the same mistake again.'

They were fortunate kids.

'How did he react to that?'

'Not well. He didn't believe me at first, because we'd only done it a few times. But when it sank in, he was pretty scared. We both were. And then, well, with that and everything that happened with Dad, there was too much going on in my world. We broke up. It was all a bit much for us to take in. God, we were so young.'

'Is he still in Dunedin? I'm going to need to know his name.'

'Do you really?' she asked.

'Yes. Again, unless it is relevant to the investigation, I won't share it, and I won't be making contact with him unless it is needed in the course of the investigation.'

'I don't know if he's still here. I know he went away to Wellington for uni, but he may have come back. I didn't keep track of him. Didn't want to. I needed to put all of that behind me.'

'That's quite understandable.'

'But if you need to know, his name was Timothy Williamson – Tim.'

'Thank you. Did you ever tell your parents?'

'No, I didn't tell them anything. And I've never said anything to my mother. It was one of those things where initially I wasn't going to tell her – as I said, too scared. Then part of me wanted to because, you know, sometimes you really need your mum. But then with Dad being killed, and the aftermath of that, I couldn't bring myself to add to her worries. And then it just felt too late to tell her, that too much time had gone by. There was no point in saying something, it wouldn't achieve anything other than to drive a wedge between us, because she'd have been all, "why didn't you tell me?", and it would have spiralled downhill from there.'

That was a hard relate from me. There was a raft of very personal things I'd never confided in my mother. In retrospect, some of them I should have, but, like Felicity, it had reached a point where it felt the moment had passed and it was too late. It would serve no purpose than to cause pain, or worse, a rift.

'What about Callum? Did you tell him?'

'No, I didn't tell him either. It isn't really the sort of thing you talked about with your brother, is it? I mean, we didn't talk about periods or anything in our household, let alone something like this. I suppose if I'd had a sister, then perhaps I might have told her, but although we were really close, it didn't feel right to share my worries with Callum. And then everything happened with Dad, and life got even harder, so, you know.' She shrugged.

When I thought about it, we didn't share intimate details in our family either. Last thing my brothers would have wanted to know about were my gynaecological issues.

'How soon after all this happened was your dad killed?' I noticed she'd mentioned his death several times now, so it must have been soon after.

'It was all in the same week. The worst week of my life.'

Jesus. That didn't bear thinking about. What utterly shit timing. But then the timing itself was interesting. You had to ask if it had a bearing somehow on what happened.

'So you hadn't told your parents. And other than Mel and the boy, Tim, you haven't ever told anyone? Not even as an adult?'

'No,' she said, her voice cracking.

'You've carried that all this time?'

'Yes,' she said, tears flowing down her cheeks now.

'Oh, Felicity, that must have been so hard,' I said. I hated seeing people in distress. I knew she was The Boss's wife and part of an investigation, but I couldn't help myself, I had to get up and go over to give her a hug. After holding on to so much for so long, she deserved it. She was weeping freely now and gripped me hard. Gemma was concerned, and jumped up against us, trying to wiggle her way in. Felicity gave a small laugh at the dog's attention and let go. I took the opportunity to grab a box of tissues from the nearby sideboard, and Gemma took the opportunity to jump up onto her mum's lap. I handed the tissues over and waited for Felicity to regain her composure.

'I'm sorry,' she said, 'I shouldn't be such a mess and crying all over you.' She blew her nose with a stomach-turning intensity.

'That's okay. It's a huge thing you went through, having to make that kind of a decision about a baby when you were so young, and then everything that happened with your dad on top of it all. Have you considered getting some counselling? It could help, especially now, with so many memories being dug up by the investigation. It would give you a chance to talk freely with someone.'

'Maybe I should, because I feel like I could explode right now. What with Dad's case, and now Mel's murder. There's so much going on. Too much going on.'

One thing that had been nagging away in the back of my mind

was how on earth did Aaron Cox know that Felicity had been pregnant? Who had told him? And had he then told Mark Freeman? Had they talked about it? But if that had been the case, surely Reverend Freeman would have challenged his daughter about it. He would have said something to her, and surely he'd have told his wife. I needed to have a serious conversation with Mr Cox.

'Can I ask you, how much did you trust Mel? Do you think she would have told anyone else about what happened?'

There was emphatic head shaking going on. 'No, absolutely not. She wouldn't have told anyone on principle. She swore that she wouldn't tell Mum and Dad, and explained that even though I was underage, the law protected my privacy and they didn't have to know. And besides that, she was cool, you know. She was very women's rights, a feminist. She looked out for her sisters. I think she would have helped any woman who got into trouble; that's how she was back then.'

'Back then?'

'Yeah. I heard that she's fallen on hard times in recent years and managed to alienate herself from pretty much everyone.'

'My understanding was that after your father was murdered, the people of the congregation pushed her away.'

'Yeah, they did. I felt really bad about that, because I knew she had a good heart. Look at what she'd done for me. But some adults in the congregation didn't like the influence she had on us, and without Dad there to defend her, they forced her out. It felt like a witch hunt.'

'Was your mother part of that? Did she have misgivings about her too?'

'She didn't approve of Mel, but she wasn't part of the backlash. After Dad was killed Mum was in survival mode, and she was too busy dealing with her own grief and ours, and trying to protect us from everything going on with the police to be concerned with all the politics and finger-pointing going on at the church. We pretty much just hid away.'

So who told Aaron Cox about Felicity's pregnancy? The health professionals involved didn't come into consideration, particularly those involved in something as sensitive as a termination. They fully understood the importance of patient confidentiality, and the ramifications for both the patient and themselves professionally if they breached it.

So if Mel Smythe hadn't said anything, and Felicity's family didn't know, that left Timothy Williamson. Unless, of course, Mel had lied.

CHAPTER 33

'Hello? Is that Sam?'

The incoming call had flashed up the name of Amelia's childcare centre. Wonder what they wanted? We'd been sorting out the admin and paperwork side of things, i.e., paying the bill. Hopefully there wasn't a problem there.

'Yes, that's right.'

'Hey, it's Angela from the childcare centre ... Um ... I was just wondering who was coming to pick up Amelia today? Usually one of you has been by now, but no one has arrived. We're closing in fifteen minutes.'

'Oh.' Paul was supposed to be picking her up today. That was odd, I hoped everything was okay. 'Sorry about that. I'll give Paul the hurry-up. Someone will be there shortly. Thanks for ringing.'

Shit. Well, I hoped it was Paul collecting her today.

I pulled up his number in my phone and hit call.

Fortunately he answered straight away. 'Underground Airlines. How can I help you?'

Could he feel the eye roll? 'Hardy, hardy ha.' Frigging goof ball. 'Look, daycare just rang to see when you're picking up Amelia? They're closing in fifteen.'

'Ummm, weren't you picking her up today? he said.

'I thought you were picking her up.'

'No, you were.'

Silence.

'Oh fuck,' he said.

'Oh fuckity-fuck,' I repeated.

'It's been what, just over a week and we've already screwed up?'

'Knew it would happen one day, but not quite this soon.'

He laughed. 'I guess you've got to see the funny side. Where are you now?'

'I'm in the office? You?'

'I'm out at Brighton.'

'Shit, okay.' My eyes glanced up to the clock. 'I can rattle my dags and scramble there.'

'Thank you. Sorry.'

'Me too – we're both idiots.'

'Yup.' He made an air-kiss noise. 'Love you, Dipshit.'

I smooched back. 'Talk soon, ya dork.'

Fuck.

❧

Thank God Angela had laughed at my profuse apologies at pick-up, and Amelia was none the wiser for her negligent parents' lack of organisational skills. I was assured that everyone had been a numpty at least once, but was kindly reminded not to make a habit of it. Although she did a good job of hiding it, I suspected Angela was a bit pissed off. Even though I'd been able to scamper back to the car and get up the hill pretty quickly, I was still ten minutes late. Appropriately chastened I had skulked out very tail-between-my-legs.

'Here's to parenting fail 101,' I said as Paul and I chinked glasses. We didn't usually go in for booze on a week night, but hey, needs must.

'Cheers, Big Ears.'

'Let's not do that again.'

'Amen to that.'

Amelia was tucked up in bed, the aftermath of dinner was strewn all over the bench and Mount Laundry was languishing on the armchair it had come to land on. It could stay that way for now. We were slouched together on the sofa and the wine was taking the edge off.

'Can I ask you a question?' Paul asked. 'It's work related.'

'Of course it is. I'll let you know after you've asked the question.' Some people could leave their work behind at the end of the day, but we weren't those people. We'd figured out pretty early on in our relationship that one of the things we had in common was an unhealthy inability to switch off. In some ways I was relieved to find out it wasn't just me, that it was in fact an inherent part of the job. Which might explain why the divorce rate amongst the police was so high. Too many long-suffering partners turned into surrogate therapists and endurers of unpleasant, less-than-desirable, end-of-day pillow talk. There could only be so much of that you could handle before it tipped the balance between love and self-preservation. So far for us, the 'two brains work better than one' element made post-work chit-chat empowering and synergistic, but I had vowed to myself that if I ever began to feel that home life was being weighed down by work life, then for the sake of the relationship we'd have to put a stop to it.

'It's to do with Mel Smythe.'

Paul was all too aware of the additional personal burden I carried when it came to that unfortunate woman. I felt grateful he thought to ask permission before launching in. To me it said a lot about his respect for me and that he didn't take his privileged position for granted.

'I'm listening.'

'Something really interesting came up in the investigation today. Otto was looking into her bank-account records, seeing if there was anything out of the ordinary – usual stuff.'

'I'm guessing she'd not been hiding millions in the bank and was just living in that hovel by choice?'

'Correct ... Well, it wasn't millions, but – and it's a pretty big but – the day before she was murdered, she had not one, but two large deposits appear in her bank account.'

That was an elephantine but.

'Well, the timing couldn't be more interesting if it tried.'

'I know, right?'

'So how large was large?'

'Five thousand large.'

'Total?'

'Each.'

Wow. Ten thousand might not have seemed an outrageous amount – in the movies it was always in the millions – but for many people, particularly someone like Mel, living on the bones of her arse, that was huge.

'Who gave her that, then?'

'Therein lies the problem. They were cash deposits, so we can't trace them back to the source and find out what they were for.'

'But you've got a theory?'

'I have, but I wanted to quiz you first.'

'Okay then, yes, fire away. I'm intrigued now.'

'You had a chance to talk with her before she died. Did she say anything to you about her financial circumstances?'

I drained the last from my wine glass and looked at its emptiness with sadness. It had only been a small one, and timed for just after her royal ladyship had been fed so she wouldn't get the benefits of my indulgence in six hours or so's time. As much as I would have loved a refill, the single would have to do.

'I don't recall her saying anything specific about that. But given she lived in that awful boarding house and ... well, you saw her room and how few possessions she had, I'd guess she was struggling for money.' I thought back to that day, sitting outside in the sun with no idea about the hideous events that were going to unfold, and my body gave a little shudder. 'I know she'd asked the church for help on a fairly regular basis, and considering how they had treated her in the past she must have been pretty desperate to front up on their doorstep and do that.'

'So she said nothing about money? Hadn't been expecting a windfall, won Lotto, had a hot tip for a bet on the races?'

'No. I do recall her saying she hoped to get out of the place soon, but I took that to mean in general, because I'm pretty sure all of them would have loved to be living somewhere a little more salubrious, rather than she had already booked the movers.'

'That huge amount of money out of the blue gets us asking all sorts of questions. Where it's from, of course, and why she got it. But also why on earth she banked it. She was a beneficiary. If I came into a heap of cash in her circumstances, I'd be hiding it in the mattress rather than putting it in the bank where Work & Income could discover it and then penalise the hell out of me.'

'Christ, yes. If you want to get people asking all sorts of awkward questions when you're on assisted living, have a chunk of money turn up.'

Why would you bank cash? She can't have thought that through. The government was very quick to cut your benefits and grab back any money if you were reliant on them for a living. It was their special way of making sure the downtrodden stayed downtrodden. And she wasn't a stupid woman. Back in the day she had worked in education. Maybe someone else had deposited the money into her account. 'You're sure it was her that banked the cash? You've checked video footage from the bank?'

'Otto's onto that next. We've got the branch and the timestamps so we'll be able to see if it was her or someone else who did the deed.' Paul had seen my longing look into my empty glass, so proceeded to take care of supplying the next best thing to a top-up – a cup of tea.

'Can't wait to see the results of that search.'

'Pretty confident it wasn't her. Whoever it was, we'll be needing to have a wee chat.'

Indeed.

Timing was everything.

Mel Smythe had been rich one day, dead the next.

CHAPTER 34

There was a scrap of daylight left, and despite wine and food on board, I had a massive case of restless legs and needed to go for a run. Paul was one of those weird people who liked to do the dishes and was happy to clean up the bench. He also knew me well enough to recognise when it was in his best interests to shoo me out the door to blow away some cobwebs, rather than have me fidget my way around the house annoying the crap out of him. The timing had worked okay on the boobs front, as I'd recently fed Amelia, and by wearing two sports bras, the bounce didn't hurt. It was only going to be a short run to scratch the itch, and what with the late hour and lack of lighting, I decided to pound the streets and head up Kenmure Avenue and along the ridge on Highgate, rather than take on my favourite routes through the lush bush and low-lit paths of the Green Belt. It was also a welcome opportunity to ogle at some of the nicer houses in Dunedin and fantasise about the kind of home we'd have if we ever managed to save up enough of a deposit for a mortgage. Couldn't see that happening anytime soon, though.

A tranquil evening stillness had settled over the city and the last vestiges of pink smudged the horizon. This was just the tonic I needed after what had turned out to be one hell of an intense day. This and the wine. Between being undermined by The Boss and being left out of interviewing Aaron Cox, and then the shock of inadvertently being trapped in the same cathedral with the man, not to mention the little info-bomb he dropped on leaving, followed by the discomfort of confronting Felicity Johns about what had been up until then her secret past, I was spent. I fell into an easy rhythm, let the metronomic effect of one foot after the next, one breath after another, soothe my mind, centre my thoughts. I tuned out, and before I knew it my feet had taken me past Roslyn Kindergarten and on past the Falcon Street playground. Amelia might have only been six months old, but she'd already enjoyed many a ride down that epic slide, strapped onto the front of her dad. It always resulted in squeals and giggling, and sometimes the squeals and giggles were from Amelia. The closer I got to Roslyn Village, the more thoughts of work started to intrude, so by the time I had crossed the Highgate Bridge, after a brief pause to take in the stunning vista across the city and down Stuart Street, a word worm was intruding, playing in sync with my steps: *Mel, money. Mel, money. Mel, money.* Then, by the time I'd reached the Dairy in the Dip, another word dropped in and totally screwed up my timing by elevating it from a two-step to a waltz: *Mel, money, dead. Mel, money, dead.* I found myself jogging awkward triplets down the road.

To my mind there were only a few reasons why you might instantly acquire money that could get you into serious trouble – the kind of trouble that could result in a knife between your ribs. The first reason was drugs. The dollar figures involved put it in the realm of possibility, but from what I'd seen of Mel's living arrangements, she certainly didn't have the space or facilities to produce pot or meth. Well, not in her room anyway. She could have been a dealer, but again, I found that very unlikely. Besides, the people involved in that industry were as cunning as shithouse rats, and there would be no way that they would put any transactions through the bank account of a down-at-heel beneficiary. Too easy to get red-flagged by the banks and then nek-minnit the police would be invited to take a closer look.

The next reason was a money-laundering scam. The vulnerable were caught out way too often with this by some predatory bastards. When you didn't have enough money to pay the bills, or even eat, if a gift horse suddenly came along, it wouldn't occur to you to give it a dental inspection. Money laundering needed to be done through bank accounts, but the turnaround time was so quick that the scammers had often disappeared into the mist before anyone was able to find a trail. Social media and the environment it created had made it so much easier for those scum to operate. But scams like that didn't usually result in murder. These people were keyboard warriors – they didn't want blood on their hands. The only thing I could think of that would have put Mel in physical danger in that scenario would be if she'd been taken in, but then turned around and tried to scam the scammers. Keep a hold of the money, threaten to go to the police.

Which led me to my third train of thought.

Blackmail.

Mel Smythe, destitute for an eternity, suddenly comes into some money just at the time a historical crime is being reinvestigated. Precisely when someone carrying guilt from the past might be getting a little nervous. The timing was too significant to ignore. So the question had to be asked, what did she have on someone, or some-ones? Who were they? And if she knew something significant, why hadn't she come forward with that information during the first investigation? What was her motive for waiting until now to make use of that knowledge for her own gain? Opportunism? In my mind blackmail seemed to be the most logical reason for this tragic course of events. Was Mel Smythe capable of it? Absolutely. Despite what Felicity had told me about Mel being supportive and a life-saver back in the day, from what Delia, Reverend James and the other members of the congregation had said about her, she had turned into a bitter and challenging person.

By this time I'd almost reached the Māori Hill roundabout, which I'd planned as my turn-back point. My ruminations having brought me to some kind of conclusion, I did just that and headed for home.

CHAPTER 35

First task in the Shephard-Frost household this morning had been a definitive conversation about who was picking the kid up from daycare. Neither of us wanted to experience that level of mortification again. Paul stuck his hand up first with the trade-off that if he picked her up and cooked dinner he would get out to the gym tonight. Sounded fair. One of the juggles we hadn't considered in this new family thing was how the hell we could both fit the exercise we loved and needed to keep healthy, sane and pleasant to be with, around work and parenthood. It was a work in progress.

The morning briefing hadn't presented anything new in terms of developments in the Mel Smythe investigation, or any special surprises sprung by The Boss. I had settled in at my desk with an industrial-sized cup of tea to revisit some of the masses of material from the Reverend Freeman's case. With the murder of Mel Smythe I had a new mental filter to examine the transcripts through. What may have been an innocuous comment that went unnoticed on my first read might now have more relevance and need follow-up and clarification. Given Aaron Cox's bombshell news in the cathedral, I also wanted to reread his transcripts in case there were hints there about Felicity Johns' pregnancy that hadn't been picked up on at the time. I was completely engrossed in the task at hand when a loud and abrupt voice yanked me out of the zone.

'My God, Sam, you need to see this.' Otto wasn't usually given to displays of schoolboy-like excitement, so the almost squealy tone in his voice had me heading straight over to his desk.

'I'm guessing this isn't your usual cutesy social-media reel with an abundance of guilty-looking dogs doing dumb-nut things.'

'It's waaay better.' He paused. 'Or not, depending on how you look at it.'

I stopped by his shoulder and focussed in on his computer monitor.

'Westpac Bank sent through the video feeds from the ATM machines where Mel Smythe's deposits were made.'

'And again, I'm guessing from your excitement that it wasn't Mel doing the depositing.'

'You are correct. It was not Mel, and I think you are going to be a little surprised at who fed the machines five grand.'

'You could just tell me,' I said.

'Where would be the fun in that? And besides, you wouldn't believe me.'

That got my curiosity piqued. 'Well, get on with it. Don't keep me in suspense.'

'Us in suspense,' Paul said, picking the exact right moment to enter the room. He came and stood beside me by Otto's screen.

'Okay,' said Otto, 'this first one is from the Westpac South Dunedin branch ATM machine at 2.34pm on Sunday, the day before Mel Smythe's death.' He hit the play arrow and a face came into focus.

'Holy fuck.' The words escaped my mouth before I could stop them. 'That's Callum Freeman. What the hell is he doing paying Mel Smythe that money?'

'It gets better,' Otto said. 'Same day, 1.45pm Westpac Moray Place.' He opened the next attachment and hit play.

The next face caused me to gasp out loud. 'Holy double fuck a duck.'

Paul and I looked at each other.

'Oh crap,' he said. 'That complicates matters. What a fucking mess.'

'What was that, Detective?' It was almost like DI Johns had a gift for entering a room at precisely the wrong moment. Three panic-stricken faces swapped looks, and Otto quickly hit the *oh shit* button to close the media player and flicked his browser tab back to Facebook.

'Sorry, Otto was just showing us a clip of some cute dogs wreaking havoc in the kitchen,' I said. There was an awkward silence, so, like all panic merchants, I filled it with more detail than necessary. 'The owners were going to need the professional cleaners in to deal with that mess.'

The Boss literally growled. 'I'd like to think you weren't wasting police time on social media, Detectives. Or do you not have enough work to do? Because if I recall, we have a number of cases that needed to be sorted with some urgency, so I don't need to remind you where your priorities should lie.' He approached Otto's desk and made to look at what was on the monitor. He was greeted with a 'play again' message on Facebook with the little circle arrow thing. 'Hmph,' he snorted. 'Have you received the ATM surveillance clips from the bank yet?'

Oh Jesus.

'No, not yet,' Otto said. 'I'll give them a follow-up and see where they're at.'

Hopefully my mouth wasn't gaping, because I'd never witnessed Otto tell a bare-faced lie before, but given the circumstances the man deserved a medal and an Oscar. Paul was standing next to me as rigid as a pole, and I could feel the heat rising in my face. Please let The Boss assume my blushing was a result of being sprung watching cutesy stuff, not because we were desperately hiding something.

'You do that,' he said. 'And in the meantime, you can all get on to doing some actual work. I don't want to see you wasting time on bloody pet videos again. Understood?'

'Yes, sir,' I said. The phrase was also muttered by my two colluders.

It felt like an eternity before he finally left the room, and the moment he was out of earshot there was a collective exhalation of breath.

'Holy shit,' Paul said.

'What the hell are we going to do now?' That was Otto.

'I have no fucking idea.' That was me.

No matter what we did, we were on a hiding to nothing.

The face in the second ATM video was Felicity Johns.

CHAPTER 36

We couldn't divulge anything to DI Johns about his wife's predicament at this point in time. And even if we could, who wanted to draw the short straw and have to tell him? None of us were that brave, or that stupid. After consultation with Smithy, we'd decided the intricate politics of the situation was way above our paygrade and the consensus was he would talk with the district commander about the appropriate course of action. This was the sort of situation that needed to be carefully managed, because once the close relationship between a potential suspect in a murder enquiry and a senior officer of the police was known, all eyes would be on us to ensure the investigation was above board and no one was being shown favour. If there was even the slightest whiff of impropriety, the media would have a field day and any defence legal team would be rubbing their hands together with glee. No one wanted that to happen. Justice had to be served. And despite none of us being particularly fond of The Boss, we still hoped for his sake that we wouldn't end up putting one of his nearest and dearest behind bars. And of course we all fervently hoped he didn't have a hand in it himself – wasn't personally involved in some way. He was an arsehole, but none of us thought he was a homicidal arsehole. But it was something we couldn't assume or take for granted. It was an uncomfortable sensation.

Until the directive came through though, the investigation had to go on. And the clock was ticking. Now we suspected that two of the Freeman family had been blackmailed, we had to find out if this was really the case and why – and if it had stopped there. My gut feeling was it was to do with the pregnancy, but then why did they pay up so long after the fact? And it still didn't answer the question about the timing. Why now?

Also, if Mel was desperate and bold enough to blackmail them, had she also thrown caution to the wind and blackmailed anyone else? Someone from the original case with something to hide. Someone with a lot to lose.

We needed to interview Felicity Johns today. A: before she had to deal with the nightmare that would be her husband finding out about the teen pregnancy and the money. Jesus, I wouldn't want to be having that conversation. Poor woman. Imagine his reaction. The Boss wasn't known for his interpersonal or his anger-management skills. And B: before she got talking with her brother. We had the problem of chat to deal with. The stakes were high for Callum and Felicity. We didn't want them collaborating to try and protect each other, but we couldn't stop them if they did. To that end, within an hour of receiving the video footage, Smithy and I were knocking on Felicity Johns' door. Under normal circumstances this conversation would be taking place at the station, but we couldn't risk her being spotted by her husband and him asking awkward questions before the hierarchy had the opportunity to bring him up to speed, in a confined space, and with people who were higher up the food chain than he was that he'd be less likely to yell at.

Felicity Johns looked surprised at first, and then wary when she saw who was standing unannounced on her doorstep.

'Detectives. Is there a problem? What can I do for you?'

'Apologies for the lack of warning,' I said, 'but we've had some information come to hand that we need to discuss with you, and it couldn't wait.'

Her mouth opened then shut, like she was about to say something but changed her mind.

'It's to do with a large deposit of money you made into Mel Smythe's bank account the day before she died.'

Her face reddened and her mouth dropped open again, gaping like a fish. I half expected her to slam the door in our faces, but instead, she took a deep breath and pushed it open wider.

'You'd better come in,' she said.

She didn't even wait for us to enter before turning and heading into the reception lounge off to the side. I guessed the formality of the situation warranted the formal room. I shut the front door behind us and followed them in.

'Take a seat, Detectives.'

In the time we'd taken to get to the lounge she had regained some of her composure, and it didn't surprise me in the faintest when she got straight to the point.

'I know it looks really bad that I paid money to Mel Smythe, especially now she's been murdered. But I had no choice – she put me in an impossible situation.'

Felicity had known Smithy for a long time as a work colleague of her husband, and I thought she and I had built up a rapport in the times I'd come to talk with her about her father's case, so I felt that I could be fairly direct with her too.

'No, it doesn't look good,' I said. 'When did she get in touch with you to make her demands, and how did she make contact?'

Gemma the dog had strategically settled herself down on the floor between us and her mistress, head on paws, keeping watch.

'She rang on Saturday morning, caught me when I was out at the Farmers' Market. Thank heavens Greg wasn't with me. I don't know how she knew my number. I hadn't given it to her, and hadn't had anything to do with her for years, decades.'

So the day after I'd been to visit her and had informed her the case was being reopened, Mel Smythe was busy trying to extort money out of people. Had she spent the night hatching grand plans to get herself out of the boarding house and to line her pockets? That was some warped kind of opportunism.

'Can I ask: now, with you finding out about the money, Mel being killed and how that looks, does that mean everyone is going to know about my history?'

'No. At this stage only a select few officers who need to know have been informed of your background.' Smithy spoke quite formally, but then he dropped to a softer voice, addressed her as a friend. 'And we haven't told Greg.'

She nodded, apparently reassured. 'Thank you.'

'Can I ask you a question?' I said. 'How did you know that Mel Smythe was the victim of the murder? That information has only just been released to the public. It took a while to locate her next of kin.'

'Greg,' she said.

I suspected as much. That further justified our need to keep The Boss separate from the case. Little slips of information could inadvertently derail the case, any subsequent prosecution, or even give the bad guys a heads-up.

'Has he talked with you much about your father's case?' Smithy asked. 'And now Mel Smythe's case too?' He would be thinking the same thing I was.

'No. He's pretty good at being discreet about any cases he's working on, wouldn't disclose anything confidential. And he knows I don't really like hearing about them. I had enough to do with a murder investigation in my past, and that still upsets me, and he is sensitive enough to respect that. All I really know about Dad's case was that he'd asked you to investigate, Detective Shephard, and that he'd been told to keep out of it. So I have no idea on how far that's progressed, really. He let Mel's name slip, but I think that was because he knew her connection to Dad, and well, it could hardly be coincidence that something bad happened to her just after Dad's case was reopened, so he thought I should know.'

She bent forward and scratched the dog's head, which was received with much tail-wagging, then leaned back in the chair.

'Look, I know Greg isn't the most liked person in the force, and yes, he can be difficult, but he is a good man, and he wouldn't do anything wrong or unethical on purpose. I mean, the whole reason he asked you to look into Dad's case was because Mum's ill, she's dying, and he didn't want her going to her grave not knowing who murdered our father.'

'That is understandable,' I said. Although it was safe to say his attempt at being a thoughtful son-in-law and providing closure had backfired spectacularly. 'So, tell us about the phone call. What did Mel Smythe say exactly?'

As if to invoke the memory she picked up her cell phone and cradled it in her hands.

'When she first rang she asked if I remembered who she was? Which was stupid. Of course I remembered who she was. How could I ever forget her when she'd helped me out so much. And then she said, "Well, it's your turn to help me out now." That's when she told me she needed money, she needed five grand, and that if I didn't give it to her, she would tell my mother all about our secret.'

She paused and brushed away some imaginary dirt from the arm of the chair.

'As you can imagine I was pretty shocked to hear from her at all, let alone when she made her demands. It brought a whole lot of memories back and I was quite frankly a bit of a panicky mess. I didn't think to question it at the time, because how would Mel have known I hadn't told Mum? That it would be something I could be blackmailed over? I could have called her bluff and said Mum already knows, it's not a secret, so no, you're not going to extort money out of me. Bugger off. God, I wish I had thought of it, but at the time her call kind of tipped me over the edge and I realised with everything going on right now I didn't want Mum to know about all that. I couldn't let her find out. So I panicked and the only way I could see to get out of the situation was to just give Mel the money.'

Smithy was being very quiet. I wasn't surprised. This conversation had to be triggering a few personal experiences for him that had had a profound effect on his family. The questioning was going to be up to me. I was going to have to be good cop and bad cop.

'So you paid the money.'

'Yes.'

'And she wanted it in the bank, not cash in hand, delivered in person?'

'Yes. Then I wouldn't know where she lived, and she wouldn't have to look me in the eye, I guess. Coward's way out.' The hurt was beginning to tell.

'But how did you know she wouldn't take the money then keep coming back for more?'

She had been picking at a spot on the chair arm, but looked up to reply. 'I didn't, but at that time, what choice did I have? The fact she blackmailed me in the first place had proved I couldn't trust her anymore.'

'And after you paid the money, *did* she come back for more?' I asked.

'No, I never heard from her. She didn't acknowledge receiving the money or anything, which was weird. I thought she'd at least do that. But then I found out why, of course: someone had killed her.'

The outright and obvious question needed to be asked.

'Did you kill Mel Smythe?'

Her face crinkled into an embodiment of shock, mouth agape. 'No, and what a dreadful thing to ask. Of course I didn't kill her. Why on earth would I?'

'To stop it happening again, to shut her up.'

'But that wouldn't make any sense. Why on earth would I have paid her the money and then turned around and killed her? That would be stupid.' She was gesticulating wildly now. Phone forgotten and dropped in her lap. 'Look, I'm a cop's wife. I know full well the depths you will go to to find a murderer, that you'd look at phone records and bank accounts, you'd be digging everywhere, nothing would be sacred. I'm not dumb enough to risk that. It was bad enough trying to sneak around behind Greg's back to find five grand in a way that he wouldn't notice. Not that it matters now. I'm sure he's going to find out everything.'

Didn't envy her that conversation.

'So, how did you find the money?'

'Someone very wise once said to me every woman should have a separate, secret stash of money. Just in case you ever found yourself in the awful position some women do of being in a violent or toxic relationship and you had to escape. You should always have a plan B. Mine was cash, hidden at home. I've been quietly slipping away twenty dollars here, twenty dollars there since we first got together. Nothing big, nothing that would get noticed. But over the years it adds up.'

I had come across other women who had done similar things and found themselves in a position of needing it. It wasn't the silliest idea.

'Was that advice from your mother?'

'Hell, no. She was the grand romantic, didn't think anything could ever go wrong in her and Dad's relationship. God had meant them to be together. Obviously God's plan didn't work out.' She'd calmed down now and gave a wee shrug. 'You know, she's never re-married, never found anyone else since Dad. I don't think she's even tried to. Probably thinks it would be betraying him somehow. No, it was Mel who suggested it. She told us girls at the youth group, all those years ago, that a woman would be smart to make sure she had escape options. That you should trust people, but not blindly. So ironically it was Mel's own preaching that meant I had the money to pay her.'

CHAPTER 37

Callum Freeman seemed a much-diminished version of the man I had talked with in his home last week. The interview room had that effect on people. It wasn't that it was so big that they looked small, or so empty that you had nothing to compare their size too, and it wasn't a trick of the light. It was just that the demeanour of most people who ended up in these rooms changed – because they knew they had some explaining to do.

Today he had the privilege of explaining several issues to both me and Smithy. As the two case leaders, our Venn diagrams had a clear overlap now.

We were still trying to keep The Boss out of the equation. Smithy had now briefed the district commander, and he was going to have a word with DI Johns, but as far as we were aware that hadn't happened yet. In the meantime, we had to tread very carefully.

'Would you care to explain to us why, the day before she was murdered, you deposited five thousand dollars, cash, into Mel Smythe's bank account?' I asked. I had my elbows on the table between us, giving Callum the full benefit of my attention, while Smithy leaned back in his chair, arms crossed loosely across his chest, looking casual but in one of the most ominous ways imaginable.

Callum's eyes kept darting to my colleague. 'I didn't have anything to do with her murder.' His voice sounded diminished too.

'That wasn't the question. The question was why did you deposit the cash into her bank account?'

'It's difficult to explain.'

'Try me.'

If he was looking to Smithy for sympathy, he wasn't going to find any there. Smithy adjusted his position on his seat. The small movement seemed to make a large impression on Callum. He was still floundering around for words.

'How about I make this simpler for you,' I went on. 'When did Mel Smythe get in contact with you?'

'She rang me out of the blue on Saturday.'

That confirmed one of my other questions – about the mode of contact. Although talking on the phone left a digital footprint, unless it was recorded, it didn't give away specifics about a conversation like a text message or DM could. It was a smarter, more secure move, even if it still left a trail.

'Prior to that call, when was the last time you would have talked with her?'

'Well, that would have to be twenty-five years ago, around the time of Dad's death. I hadn't heard from her since. Well, not until, you know, that call.'

'And what exactly did she say?'

He sat there for a moment, eyes downcast, concentrating on his slowly twiddling thumbs.

'What did she say, Callum?' I put on a stroppy voice, and he jerked to attention.

'She told me she wanted five thousand dollars.'

'Yes, and what for? You can't tell me that you'd pop five grand into the account of anyone who came up to you and said, "I need money". Did she threaten you?'

'Yes.' I had to strain to hear the response.

'You can be a little more forthcoming, or are you going to make me ask every little separate question and reply with one-word answers. Because if you're going to do that, then we will be in here for a very long time.'

He started drumming his fingertips on the table. 'She said that if I didn't pay her the money then she was going to talk to my mother.'

It sounded kind of pathetic, hearing a middle-aged man saying he was afraid someone was going to tell his mummy something he didn't want her to hear. Most blackmail of men involved threats of going to spouses with proof they were shagging the staff, or to the police about actions that were a little, or a lot, against the law. We knew Felicity had a valid reason for not wanting their mother to know the juicy piece of information Mel Smythe had on her. But Callum? The fact that he straight-up paid the money indicated whatever she had on him, it must have been good.

'Your mother?'

'Yes.'

'And what information was she threatening to share with your mother that was so potentially damaging you, without question, parted with five thousand dollars?'

I would notice if a cool five grand disappeared out of my and Paul's savings account, so either Callum had his own money hidden away, or he preferred an inquisition by his missus over Mummy knowing something she shouldn't.

He gave a very large sigh and started picking at the quick around his fingernails.

'Hey. Are you going to share with us, or would you like to invite back the lawyer that you waived earlier, and we start preparing your bed downstairs in the cells?' The sound of Smithy's voice startled Callum to attention, his eyes flew back up, his mouth fell open.

'Mel wasn't threatening me.'

'Then who was she threatening?' I asked.

'She threatened to tell Mum about something that would have been bad for my sister.'

'You mean Felicity?'

'Yes, Flossie.'

It was the first time I'd ever heard her referred to by that name. Maybe the siblings were closer than I thought.

'Would you care to elaborate?'

'Mel Smythe knew something, a secret about Flossie from long ago, from when she was younger. Something Mum didn't know about, but which would really upset her.'

'And this secret was so bad that you were prepared to pay her the money to protect your sister?'

'Yes.'

'And what was so secret?'

He blew out a big breath. 'When Flossie was fifteen, just before Dad died, she got into trouble. She got pregnant.'

Smithy and I looked at each other. From what Felicity had told me, no one else in her family knew about the pregnancy. And she specifically said she hadn't spoken with her brother about it.

'Go on,' I said.

'At the time, she turned to Mel Smythe, and Mel helped her out, helped her get, you know, an abortion.' He looked extremely un-comfortable saying that word.

'And how did you know about this?' I asked. 'Did Felicity confide in you? Your mother didn't know. But did your father? How did you find out?'

That was too many questions at once, but I was curious now. The stories weren't marrying up.

'She didn't tell me anything. I overheard it when we were at youth group one day. They were downstairs in one of the rooms under the cathedral and they didn't know I was there. She was talking with Mel about going to get it done, begging her not to tell Mum and Dad, and I heard Mel promise her she wouldn't say anything, that it would be their secret.'

'And how did that make you feel, finding out your sister was in trouble?'

'I was shocked, of course. We were a Church family, a priest's kids. Her having a baby would have been the end of the world as far as our parents were concerned. So in a way I could understand why she felt she couldn't go to Mum and Dad about it. And I'll be honest and say they were pretty protective of her. They wouldn't let her go out with boys – she wasn't going to be allowed to start dating until she was sixteen, and then she would only be allowed to see Christians. They were a bit control-freakish with her. They certainly didn't know she had a boyfriend.'

'But you did.'

'Yeah, I knew. I wasn't stupid. But I didn't say anything to them because he was a really nice kid, and I knew she'd get in so much trouble. I thought they were mean to her, too strict, I wasn't going to spoil her fun.'

'Were they that strict with you too?'

'Pretty strict, it wasn't much fun being the Reverend's kid. But they weren't as bad with me. I was a boy.' He gave a little shrug. 'Double standards.'

So if he were to be believed, that protective streak he showed towards his sister had started when they were young. It didn't answer one very obvious question though. Why was *he* black-mailed?

'So if you overheard this conversation in secret, then how did Mel Smythe know you knew about the pregnancy? How did she know she could blackmail you?'

'Because I challenged her about it – not then, not in front of Flossie. I went and talked to her later, another day. I needed to know what was going on, I was worried. We had all heard the terrible stories about people getting abortions down back alleyways and bleeding to death or getting infections. The kind of stuff our parents liked to scare us with to keep us on the straight and narrow. I had to know what the plan was, that she'd be safe.'

They must have had a close relationship, because I couldn't imagine my brothers showing that level of concern. And if they did, they would have probably been more intent on dealing with the boy involved than my personal welfare. Callum's worry would have been touching if the person who had extorted money from him wasn't now dead.

'But Felicity didn't know you'd talked to Mel?'

'No, and I don't think Mel told her either, because Flossie never ever talked to me about it. Not then – not ever.'

It seemed like this family were pretty good at keeping secrets from each other. And Mel had been good to her word for years, until opportunity arose and her need for money overcame any last vestige of her scruples.

'Were you aware of Mel making similar threats to other people?'

'What do you mean?'

'Did she say she was going to threaten anyone else?'

'No, she said nothing like that. Did she though?' He sounded anxious. 'Did she blackmail other people too?' Who was he worried about? 'It wouldn't have surprised me if she did. She'd turned into a nasty old woman.'

'So what made you think you could trust her? That she wouldn't take your money and tell your mother anyway?'

'I couldn't trust her. She held all the cards. But what choice did I have?'

'Would protecting your sister extend as far as ensuring that the threat was never made again?'

'Are you asking if I killed Mel to shut her up, to keep Flossie's secret?' He looked offended by the question, but there was an underlying hint of fear. 'No, of course I didn't kill her. Keeping a teenage pregnancy secret would never be worth killing someone over. It wasn't that important, especially as it was all so long ago, way in the past. That would be crazy. Why would I risk everything for that?' It was a good point, but people had done worse.

'Where were you on Monday morning?'

'I was at work all day, and everyone will attest to that. I didn't leave the office. So no, I didn't kill Mel. Besides, if I was going to kill her, I would never have bothered paying her the money in the first place.'

'So why did you pay the money?'

'For Mum's sake. She's sick, and she's dying, and finding out about all that is the very last thing she needs right now. It would be awful if she found out and it tainted her and Flossie's relationship, awful for both of them. I paid the money because there are some things she doesn't need to take to her grave.'

CHAPTER 38

I was not entirely sure how to play this conversation. I needed to ask Yvonne Freeman some fairly pointed questions relating to Mel Smythe, but do it in such a way that she didn't suspect there may have been more going on with regards to her children. The need for tact was both professional and personal. Professionally, I had to ensure I didn't inadvertently give her information that would sway her responses. The last thing we wanted was for her to tell us what she thought we wanted to hear, or withhold information altogether because she thought it would protect her children. And on the personal front I still had the vivid memory of both Felicity and Callum making it crystal clear why they didn't want their mother to know about Felicity's pregnancy. That in her advanced state of disease, it was better that she never knew.

Yvonne Freeman was carrying the tea tray over to the table where I was seated. She had chosen a Royal Doulton tea set with a beautiful rose design this time. I recalled that my nan had a similar set when I visited her as a child. The tea pot was wearing a strawberry-design cosy, and the sugar bowl had one of those little lace doily things, weighted around the edges with coloured beads. A small plate held some short-bread biscuits. There was something about a good old-fashioned tea tray that epitomised hospitality, and I wished more people made the effort. I had to smile to myself at the hypocrisy of that observation, as tea bags and mugs were the order of the day in my household. One day I might have the time and inclination to get more lah-di-dah with guests to our home, but that was likely to be with the 'tea party with the toys' phase that I hoped Amelia would go through.

Even in the short time since my visit last week, Yvonne Freeman seemed to have become a little more frail, diminished, and she was moving with exaggerated care.

'Can I help you with that?' I asked, getting to my feet.

'Oh no, I'm okay, almost there.'

She slid the tray onto the table with minimal cup rattling and we both took a seat.

'How have you been keeping?' I asked. From what her children had said, her cancer was quite advanced now, and they didn't think she had too long. All things considered it was impressive that she was still living independently in her own home. How long that would last was hard to say, but I was pretty sure that her children would be keeping a very close watch on her.

'I have been better,' she said with a tight smile. 'But it could be worse.' What was it about her generation that they downplayed everything? Or did the 'I don't want to be a bother' thing. My father had been exactly the same when he was close to the end. It was like they were all competing for a prize on who could be the most stoic. He who died with the least grumbles won. Maybe the reason she was still living alone was because she was too stubborn to admit she needed the extra support.

'You do look like you're feeling a bit sore today. So I'll try to keep this as quick as I can.'

'Thank you, but I'm okay. The doctor has just increased my pain medication, and added something to help with the anxiety, and it's all making me a bit tired and wobbly, so I have to be very careful. The last thing I want to do is have a fall and break a hip. Wouldn't that be a great way to end things?' She gave a weary laugh. 'So I do apologise in advance if I seem a little off.'

That explained her slightly laboured expressions. Pain and anxiety meds would wipe you out.

'I'm sorry if opening your husband's case has caused you stress and you needed something to help with that. It wasn't our intention.'

'I know, but it wasn't just for that. The anxiety drug was more for the worry about the fact I won't be on this earth much longer. The fear of the great unknown, and how you're going to die. Will it be awful, will it hurt? All those things. You'd think being a Christian I wouldn't be so scared about how it will end, but no, that hasn't helped at all. I can understand why some people would choose to die on their own terms, before it got to that stage.'

Ooof, that was painfully direct. I wasn't sure how you responded to a statement like that.

'Well, just let me know if you need a little break.' And then I resorted to the manners that my mother had instilled in me. 'And thank you for the tea.' It felt a little lame.

'That's okay,' she said, and played Mum.

'I needed to talk with you today about Mel Smythe.'

Yvonne finished pouring and passed my cup over. 'I heard this morning the woman killed in that boarding house was her. They had it on the radio.' It hadn't taken long for the news agencies to report the victim when her name was formally released.

'Yes. So as well as the investigation into your husband's death, we are having to look into Mel Smythe's murder and see if there are any connections there.'

'I guess it does seem odd that something happened to her just when you reopened Mark's case.'

'Yes, the timing is interesting.' I took a sip from the tea and pressed on. 'When was the last time you heard from her?'

'Gosh, it would have been a long time ago. Probably not since that year after Mark's death. She moved away from the church, so we lost touch a long time ago.'

From everyone else's accounts she didn't so much as move away as was driven off, but I wasn't going to dwell on that point.

'So she hadn't been in contact with you at all in the last week or two?'

'No. Why? Had she been in touch with other people? I can check with Callum and Felicity.'

This is what I had feared. Yvonne Freeman may have been doped up to her eyeballs, but she was still sharp and quick on the uptake. How could I word this without outright lying?

'As part of the investigation into her murder, and because of the timing, we are asking everyone involved in your husband's case if she had made contact with them. So we will be contacting your children too and other people from the church.' It was only a partial lie. And now I needed to ask her something much more confronting. 'Along with everyone else involved I also need to ask you about your whereabouts on Monday morning and early afternoon?'

'You think I murdered Mel?' She sounded quite affronted. 'You think I'm capable of murdering someone? I can barely walk.'

Theoretically anyone was capable. But she'd made her point.

'As I said, we are asking everyone involved with Mark's case as a matter of procedure, to rule people out.'

'Well, I don't think what I tell you will help much, because I would have been here, resting. I don't get out much anymore. But there won't be anyone who can vouch for me on that, unless one of the neighbours can. And I can't remember which day the hospice nurse visited. Was that Monday or Tuesday? I could check?'

'That's okay. I can follow it up.'

'Sorry, I'm not much help.'

I took a moment to tackle a piece of shortbread – a weakness of mine – and washed it down with a mouthful of tea.

'The last thing I wanted to ask was, if you could think of any reason why anyone would want to harm Mel Smythe? Anything related to your husband's death? Any reason why someone might feel threatened by her?'

Even as the words came out of my mouth I realised, yet again, I was asking too many questions at once. I really needed to work on my interviewing skills. But it was hard, because in my mind these questions were all interconnected, although I was yet to figure out exactly how.

Yvonne finished sipping her tea. 'From what I've heard from other people, she wasn't a very nice woman to deal with anymore.' This seemed to be a recurring theme. 'And back then, I found her attitudes towards some things challenging. She was quite the modern miss and pushed the boundaries on what was proper, but Mark seemed to think she was okay. But, now that this has happened, looking back I can't help but wonder if maybe she had something to do with Mark's murder after all. The police talked to everyone and ruled her out. But with you reopening his case, it has got me to wondering if someone knew that she did it, and that this is somehow God's justice.'

If it was, it was pretty harsh justice.

CHAPTER 39

Our little home had become quite the haven after the intensity of the day job, but the work didn't let up once we got here. There was the keeping up with the cute demands of the kid. Although Amelia outwardly appeared to be coping well with daycare, we had noticed some subtle tells that she was still getting used to the routine, and that the stimulation of a busy daycare with lots of other kids, and their energy and bustle, was a totally different proposition to what she had been used to at home. Where it was showing was during hell hour. Before heading off on maternity leave, a number of work colleagues, regaling me with stories of the trials and tribulations of parenthood, had mentioned hell hour. I thought they had meant figuratively. But no, as we had discovered, hell hour was a thing. I guess her grizzling and screaming wasn't exactly a subtle tell that she was struggling to adjust, and for the last few days her level of clinginess meant that after she got home one of us had to be holding her at all times. It made cooking dinner fun, and the moment we sat down to actually eat, she was guaranteed to cut up rough again. One good thing, I supposed, was she didn't exercise favouritism. She was an equal-opportunities misery-guts. So if Paul was holding her and I was eating, she'd want me. Then if we swapped and I was holding her, trying to shovel food into my face one-handed while Paul was trying to scoff his dinner, she'd reach out for him. Rinse and repeat. Hopefully this was just a phase that wouldn't last until high school. Fun times.

As much as I loved the wee poppet, the best part of the day was when we were pretty sure she'd finally settled down to sleep and we got to collapse onto the sofa with a cup of tea and a bikkie.

Now we had attained parental bliss, Tori the cat decided to be needy. After a long and frankly emotional day at work, the sleepless nights catching up with me and just generalised feeling of blahiness about the progress of the cases, plural, it felt like things were getting on top of me. One thing in particular had tipped me over the edge, and despite my best intentions, I'd kind of had enough.

'We need to have a serious talk about the expressing at work thing,' I blurted out around a mouthful of biscuit.

Paul paused mid-tea-sip. 'Okay, what's on your mind?'

I finished swallowing. 'How would you feel if I gave up trying to express and we just shifted Amelia to bottle feeds?'

He looked at me like I was slightly nutty. 'Why are you asking me how I feel? That's totally your call.'

Bless him, that was the right answer, but I needed to hear more than that.

'I know. My body, my choice, and all that. But still, I wanted to ask your thoughts because you have a stake in what's best for our girl.' I let out a big sigh, and blew onto my tea. 'But, to be honest I really don't think I can juggle the whole breast-feeding and working thing, but I still want to try because I feel like it's giving in, but—'

He lifted his index finger and placed it gently on my lips.

I shushed.

'Jesus, Sam, I'm frankly surprised you've managed it this long and that you even considered the whole milking-yourself-at-work thing.' He dropped his hand and gave mine a squeeze.

I snorted. 'Milking myself?'

'Well, you know what I mean.'

'So you won't think I'm a failure if I stop?'

'Hell, no. You've given it a decent shot, but if it's not working and it's getting too much, then it's time to move on. I think it's the sensible thing to do.'

'So you don't have a problem with it.'

'If I did have a problem with it, I wouldn't be stupid enough to tell you.'

I looked up to see if he was taking the piss and caught the wink. He got a thump on the arm for his troubles.

'Seriously though, that makes me feel quite relieved.' It wasn't just getting Paul's agreement that enough was enough, and that as parents and as a couple, we were singing from the same song sheet. It was knowing I could, with clear conscience, flick off one thing that added a massive level of complexity to my day. Well not an entirely clear conscience – I was sure my overdeveloped sense of guilt would give me a fair amount of stick about it and would regularly quote the *breast is best* mantra at me. I'd just learn to mute it with time.

'I'm pleased to hear it,' Paul said. 'Of course, the only flaw in your plan is Amelia. We'd better hope that her ladyship isn't a prized milk snob and decides that only your homegrown vintage will do.'

'If she's anything like her mother, when it comes her booze, quantity is more important than quality and she won't be fussy.' I raised what was left of my tea in a toast.

'True,' Paul said and clinked my mug.

'You didn't need to agree quite so quickly.'

'Oops, my bad.' He leaned over and kissed my cheek. 'I know it's your boobs, but can I make a suggestion that we wait until the weekend before trying her out on formula?'

'Good plan. Let's make it Sunday.'

'Why Sunday?'

'Because of our regular Saturday visitor. We're going to have to wean my mother off the idea of me exclusively breast-feeding, and I ain't ready to tackle that one this week.'

CHAPTER 40

Lunch-time expressing was done. It was kind of ironic that after our discussion last night I found the task much easier today. I was ditching it just when I'd learned to tune out from the physical task at hand and occupy the time thinking about the case and planning the rest of my day. It no longer irked me or icked me out. True to form, I was peaking just when I'd decided to stop.

I headed from the family room, along the corridor in the general direction of the kitchenette to pop the results of my efforts in the refrigerator and rinse out the pump pieces. The novelty of it all had worn off for the rest of the staff too, who were now used to seeing my expressions – the amusing term Paul used for breast milk – in the fridge and no longer made comments, rude or otherwise.

I was humming my radio-induced earworm du jour when I rounded the corner and ran headlong into The Boss.

Literally.

Shit.

Luckily I had capped the bottle of expressed milk, so when the hand I was carrying it in collided with his torso it sloshed but didn't spill. Unluckily, the other hand was carrying the pump body, and despite me carrying it carefully to avoid any possible drips, somehow the collision deposited a few splatters onto his navy-coloured suit jacket.

'Fuck.' He looked down at me, the objects in my hands, his jacket, and then wiped at it with a face screwed up like he was cleaning off dog shit, not a few harmless spots of milk.

'Shephard. We need to talk. My office, now.' He turned on his heel and marched off, clearly expecting me to follow.

I didn't. 'I just need to put these away first,' I said.

'No. Now.'

Great. That didn't bode well. I followed DI Johns into his lair and made to sit down.

'Shut the door behind you.'

A 'please' wouldn't have killed him. It was slightly difficult with my hands full, and to be honest I would rather have left it open, but given the change in his situation in the last day I could understand why he might want to have a private conversation. I nudged the door closed with my foot but slightly misjudged the force required so it closed with a slam.

We both flinched.

He watched me as I settled myself into the chair and then continued to stare at me without speaking. It was just getting to the point of being awkward, and I was beginning to feel creeped out, when it dawned on me: for once in his life The Boss was speechless. Here was a man who didn't know how and where to start.

He got there eventually. 'You should know the district commander has informed me of developments in the Freeman Smythe cases, including about my wife.'

Well fuck, this was awkward. By the time he got to the part about his wife, his voice had got loud and very strident. Now he sat there, lips pursed, eyeballing me like he was waiting for a response. I didn't know what to say.

The last time we'd been together in this room, having a conversation, he had been giving me his extra-special brand of 'welcome back from maternity leave' and had been directing me to investigate a cold case. Little did he know the can of worms he was opening. I could see he had regrets aplenty, and the investigations were still ongoing – there was ample opportunity for more to go wrong yet. Part of me had the urge to be petty and let him sweat it out, but my Boss-o-radar was telling me this wasn't the time or place.

I kept my voice very even as I said, 'I'm truly sorry that your family has been so deeply drawn into the murder investigations.'

He was sitting, elbows on desk, hands together, tapping his fingers together in sequence. The tapping stopped.

'You're sorry? You're fucking sorry? The district commander has basically stood me down from duty while the investigation takes place. The very least you could have done was given me a heads-up on the depth of my wife's involvement in all of this. It would have been a fucking courtesy. I cannot tell you how humiliating it was to be hauled up before him and have no idea what was coming. This whole bloody thing has turned into a fiasco.' I sat there gripping the items in my hands even tighter. 'God, I wish I'd never asked you to reopen the Freeman case. Look where it's got me.' The way he said it made it sound like everything was my fault. But blaming me was his forte, it wasn't about to stop now. 'It's an utter shit show.'

It took me a few moments to realise he'd paused his rant, and was again waiting for a response.

'It's certainly become rather complicated,' I said, giving the understatement of the month.

'Complicated? It's a hell of a lot more than complicated. Little did I know there's been a lot of lying and covering up going on. Behind my back – behind everyone's back. You can't imagine what it's been like for me.'

Actually I could, but now wasn't the time to point that out.

'First, I find out you've been keeping the extent of things from me, and then I find out, from the district fucking commander, that my wife was once pregnant and had an abortion –not because she told me, but because it comes out in a murder investigation. How do you think that made me feel? My own wife kept that kind of a secret from me. She didn't feel she could tell me about it. Would she ever have told me if it hadn't come out in this God-awful mess?'

I started to say something, but he spoke right over the top of me. For someone who initially couldn't find the words to say, he was on a roll now. Unfortunately, it had turned into a self-pity roll.

'And now she wants me to forgive her – *expects* me to forgive her. But how can I do that? How can I forgive her when she's betrayed me like that?'

He was making this into a him thing, like some put-out, pouty teenager. I'd had a gutsful and couldn't hold my tongue any longer.

'Don't be so bloody self-absorbed. There is absolutely nothing to forgive. She didn't do anything to hurt you. She does not owe you an explanation – she doesn't owe you anything. If Felicity chose not to share something awful and traumatic that happened to her in her childhood, then that was entirely up to her. So don't you condescend to "forgive her" something from her past that didn't affect you and where she did nothing wrong.'

'But she broke my trust.'

'Bullshit.'

'I beg your pardon? You mind your language, Detective.' The usual defensive growl had returned to the conversation, but I ignored it. I was frankly surprised at the deeply personal turn this conversation had taken. The Boss had lowered his guard and I didn't think I was likely to get another opportunity to make my point and plead his wife's case.

'She did not break your trust in any way.'

'Yes, she did. There's the matter of the money.'

'That's a separate issue. Her not telling you about her abortion, something that happened well before you were on the scene, was her own business. And I can't believe you're making this all about you. Don't be so fucking selfish. Imagine what it was like for her. Being a fifteen-year-old girl and pregnant, and not being able to talk to your parents about it because they were so wrapped up in the church and being all Goddy Goddy. Not being able to talk with them because you thought they would condemn you, and would never *forgive* you.' I emphasised the 'forgive'. 'Can you imagine that? Can you conceive of how it would feel not being able to talk to your own family about something so life-changing and immense? Thank Christ she had Mel Smythe to take care of her, someone to make sure she got the treatment she needed, and safely. But she essentially went through that terrifying ordeal alone. And now you're making it about you.'

The face staring at me from across the desk looked anything but chastened, but I hadn't finished yet.

'You should be supporting her and telling her how sorry you are that she had to go through all that. Don't you dare leave her in the situation again where she is so judged by her loved ones that she feels alone in the world. Don't you do that to her. Pull your head out of your arse.'

'I will not be spoken to like that.'

'Well, I don't care, you are going to be. Someone needs to say it. There are some things you need to face.'

'That's very easy for you to say from the cheap seats, but now she is embroiled in the murder of Mel Smythe, and that very much has an effect on me. It could have a devastating effect on my career and everything I hold dear. So don't you go lecturing me about being selfish, thank you very much.' The voice had transitioned from dangerous and indignant to justifying. He was still missing the whole damned point.

'Yes, the fact that she paid money to Mel Smythe – hush money – and now that woman is dead makes everything very much more complicated and leaves you both up in the air until we complete the investigation and find out who is responsible, and, worst-case scenario, find out *she* is responsible. Yes, it's all a fucking mess. But she is your wife and she has been through hell – then and now. First an unwanted pregnancy and abortion at a hideously young age, closely followed by the murder of her father. And now, being extorted by the very same woman who had come to her rescue when she was a kid and being a suspect in her murder.' I was wildly gesticulating now and suddenly I realised I still had my hands full of expressing equipment.

The ridiculousness of it hit me and I dropped them to my lap.

'Do you love her?' I asked, quietly.

The Boss looked taken aback, but then seemed to deflate before my eyes.

'Of course I love her.'

'This investigation is going to have to take its course, and yes, at present your position is unfortunate. But at some point you are going to have to decide what is more important to you: your career or your wife.'

He just looked at me.

'So if you had to make a choice today between your career or your wife, what would it be?' It was a bold question and very personal, but it was the only way I was going to get it into his thick head what the stakes were here. If he was prepared to damage his relationship because he was feeling betrayed by something before his time and out of his control, and was worrying how everything looked to his colleagues, then he was a fucking idiot.

It felt like an eternity before he replied.

'You'd better leave, Detective.' He got to his feet, walked around the desk and pulled the open the door.

'I thought as much,' I said, as I got to my feet and made my escape for the exit. 'You know what? You deserve what you get.'

His hand clamped down on my shoulder as I walked past, stopping me dead in my tracks.

'Well you thought wrong, Detective. Of course I would choose my wife.'

CHAPTER 41

My mother and I may have had our differences, but when she visited our wee ritual was one of my favourite things. I'd never tell her that of course. It was a Saturday morning, and as usual she had perfectly judged her drive from Gore to arrive around the time I was feeding Amelia before putting her down for her morning sleep. As was customary, Mum made us a cup of tea, criticised my housekeeping skills while pointedly folding the laundry, and bided her time until the kid had decided she'd had enough tucker.

As soon as Amelia had come up for air, and before I could even pack my tit away, Mum had claimed the child, then gently winded her and settled onto the sofa with her granddaughter draped across her ample chest. In no time at all Amelia was clapped out, head on Mum's shoulder, her sweet little mouth slightly agape, breathing little dreamy breaths onto Mum's neck. The sight of the old gal snuggled in and looking so content more than made up for the little digs at our parenting style, the 'in my day we let them cry it out' asides, the 'she needs to have more routine with her feeds not just when she demands it' conversations and the 'you'll spoil her if you pick her up again' comments. We were getting close to introducing solids, and, of course, with the decision to introduce formula for the middle-of-the-day feeds, I was quite certain the 'advice' was only going to increase. It was clear she adored her granddaughter, and the way she fawned over Paul, you'd have to be blind not to realise she doted on her son-not-in-law. She wasn't as demonstrative with her love for me, but underneath it all I knew it was there. It would just be nice to see it sometimes. I wondered if she'd spent such blissful moments with me when I was a babe, or if life with two very busy little boys and running a farm household meant such moments were a rarity. If they did happen I had no memory of them.

'How's work going?' she said.

I was quite taken aback that she'd asked. She didn't often inquire into my working life. She'd never really come to accept my choice of being in the police; her thoughts were that a good profession for a girl was to be a nurse or a teacher. The situation wasn't helped by the fact my job had put not only myself, but her, in the path of danger. And any thought of it affecting her granddaughter was intolerable. My taken-abackness was promptly replaced with suspicion.

'It's going well.' It wasn't entirely a lie.

'And how is poor Amelia settling in at the nursery?'

And there it was, the little ping.

'She's doing just fine. It's probably her parents taking longer to adjust to it all than she has.' One-hundred-percent truth.

'And you couldn't have waited longer before going back? You know you could have taken more time off.'

'I know I could have, but we couldn't afford that, Mum. You only get paid parental leave for six months. I would have loved to have spent longer home with her, but there was no way we could wangle it.'

'Modern parenting, I suppose. No more stay-at-home mums like in my day.'

Hers were slightly different circumstances and she may technically have been 'stay at home' but she had still been working. I wonder if she gave my sister-in-law, Saint Sheryl, the same kind of grief when she went back to work, or if that was different because she wasn't her flesh-and-blood daughter, and because Sheryl was a nurse.

'There still are plenty of them,' I said, 'and all power to them if they can manage it. It's not for us though.' As much as part of me would have loved to have been able to stay at home, to be honest, I don't know if I was cut out for it. Yes, there were elements of my work that sucked, and a few people who made life difficult, but I loved what I did. Solving crime, bringing people to justice, finding comfort for victims and the families of those who'd lost their lives, feeling like what I did made a difference. And to be frank, I needed the stimulation. I suspected I'd get bored and frustrated with a life of domestic bliss. I certainly wasn't cut out to be a domestic goddess. Six months of maternity leave had driven that home. Fortunately for me, I wasn't aware of anyone dying from a lack of vacuuming, bed-making and not managing to get out of their PJs all day. It helped that Paul didn't care less if strange new life-forms were growing in the shower.

'How are you getting on with that murder you are looking into with the church minister? The old case? I saw your appeal for information in the newspaper.'

I had to have a quick think about how much information had been put out in the public arena and whether there had been any mention of the link between that case and Mel Smythe's murder. From what I was aware we were keeping that under our hat for the moment.

'It's coming along slowly. It was a long time ago; people's memories fade.'

'And do people actually come forward with new information after all that time?'

'They do, but we have to take it with a grain of salt. But you never know if someone might not have felt comfortable or safe talking back then, but does now, with the passage of time.'

'Well, I hope you sort it out and find who did it to that fine man.' The way she described him made me sit up and take notice.

I leaned forward. 'Did you know him?' I asked.

'No, not personally, but Cathy and Jim, Alistair's parents, did. They went to church at St Paul's for a while.'

'Yes, I know, Alistair told me, and I'm going to talk with them. From the way you said he was a good man, I thought you meant you knew him yourself.'

'Oh no, but, you know, he was a priest.'

Which made him automatically a fine man in her eyes. In this case it may well have been true. I'd only had glowing endorsements for the Reverend Mark Freeman so far, but history showed it wasn't an assumption you could make about all men of the cloth.

'Just because he was a priest doesn't mean he was a saint,' I said.

'I'm surprised to hear you say that, Samantha. You were very much in team God when you were young. You used to always be at church or hanging out with the youth group.'

I did not need to be reminded of that.

'Are you okay there with Amelia?' I asked. Anything to change the direction of conversation. 'Do you want me to take her for you – you're not getting uncomfortable?'

'No, I'm good.' She turned her head to peer at her granddaughter and gave her a little kiss on the forehead. 'She's happy snoozing here.' Amelia gave a little wriggle and a sigh. 'All the ministers I met have been good people, so I can't understand why someone would have wanted to kill one. And I don't understand why you of all people would imply that they might not be.'

'Might not be what?'

'Good people.'

'I wasn't implying that.'

'It sure sounded like it to me. I thought you really liked the minister where you went to church.'

My palms were starting to feel slippery. 'I did.' The minister wasn't the problem.

'Anyway, I guess church was another one of your fads, because you dropped it fast enough. One minute you were all "let's go, let's go", the next minute you didn't want a bar of it. It was just like when you dropped the Girl Guides, and that sport you did, the judo.'

'It was taekwondo and I didn't drop it, the club stopped operating because the coach moved away to Christchurch. I didn't have any choice.' The self-defence skills learned there had proved very handy, given my profession, but at the time I didn't love it enough to trail all the way to Invercargill to carry on. I'd give her the Girl Guides though, that was something I outgrew. There was only so much concentrated activity with a group of tweeny girls this tom-boy could take. But it pissed me off that she lumped all of the activities I stopped participating in under the 'Sam's a quitter' um-brella. It never occurred to her there may have been good reason. Even thinking about it was making my mouth grow dry, but I looked at the little girl asleep on her chest, and a little part of me wondered if maybe it was time to have that conversation. No more secrets. This case had certainly stirred up enough memories, and setting foot across the threshold of the cathedral had been challeng-ing to say the least.

I swallowed back the big lump in my throat.

'Did you ever wonder why I stopped going to church?' I asked. My voice sounded small to my own ears.

'What do you mean?'

'Did you or Dad wonder why I stopped going all of a sudden?'

'Oh, we just thought it was because you got bored with it, or you'd only been going because of a boy, or friends or something, and they left so you did too.'

Wow. They really thought I was that shallow, even taking into account I was a teenager? Part of me could imagine Mum might think that – nothing I could do was good enough in her eyes – but Dad? I hoped that Dad didn't think like that. That he might have been puzzled and had asked himself why, at least.

'You know what, Mum? It was nothing like that. Not like that at all.'

'Well, why did you stop going?'

Shit. Moment of truth. I took a deep breath, felt my heart beating hard in my chest.

'I left because of Mr Bennett.'

'Mr Bennett? Wasn't he the youth leader? I remember him, he was a very nice man.'

My heart beat even harder.

'He wasn't that nice.'

Deep breath.

'He ... he groped me, he kissed me and tried to...' I wrung my hands together, hard. 'He sexually assaulted me.'

There. The words were out there. They couldn't be hidden any more. My ears were ringing and the edges around my vision were greying. I consciously slowed my breathing, tried to calm the flood of memories and emotions that were threatening to overwhelm me.

'Don't be silly. He wouldn't have done anything like that.'

Clarity slapped me in the face. I couldn't help the gasp of breath and the tears that sprang into my eyes. Not to mention the instant knot of rage. The feelings of anxiety and fear had rapidly been replaced by anger and betrayal.

'I tell you something as huge as this and that's the first thing that you can say? That I'm silly and he wouldn't have done a thing like that?' Jesus fucking Christ. 'Do you even hear yourself?'

'Well, I mean to say, teenage girls can have big imaginations. He was your church youth leader. Maybe you just misunderstood the situation. It's happened before.'

'Mum. I didn't misunderstand him sticking his tongue down my throat, I didn't misunderstand him grabbing my breast and trying to stick his hand down my pants. I did not misunderstand that at all.'

'You don't need to speak to me like that, and keep your voice down. You'll wake Amelia.'

My voice didn't stay down.

'Well, what do you expect? I share something I've carried for years and years, my deepest, darkest secret, and your automatic response is to not believe me. How do you think that makes me feel?'

'I didn't say I didn't believe you.'

'But you immediately jumped to his defence.'

'Well, I'm struggling to understand why didn't you say anything at the time?'

Why didn't I say anything? I'd been asking myself that very question for years. So many of those thoughts had circled back to 'who would believe me?' A hallowed church leader versus a teenage girl.

And then there were the old cherries: 'you had a schoolgirl crush' or 'you led him on'. And this very conversation vindicated every reason I had for not speaking out.

'Why do you think? Who would have believed me? And you've exactly proven my point. Even my own mother doesn't believe me.'

'Well Sam, if you'd said something at the time.'

'Jesus, I was fifteen years old, Mum. Being accosted and groped was huge, and gross and I was scared. It made me scared of him. I didn't want to be around him and certainly not alone with him, and I didn't know what to do. So I left.'

'Well, why didn't you say something when you were older? You're a detective, for heaven's sake. You could have reported him later on, when you joined the police.'

And yet again, that just made it even harder, because all of those questions would have come up again: 'Why didn't you say anything at the time?' 'If it was that bad, why didn't you report it to the police?' The implication being that you were making it all up to spoil the reputation of a good man.

'Well, he's dead now.'

'Oh, that poor man. What happened?'

'And yet again, straight away, your immediate concern is for him.' I got to my feet, paced to the door and back, unsure of what to do with my limbs, what to do with myself. I finally turned back around to face her. 'He crashed his motorbike, if you must know. Crashed it into the side of the bridge at Balclutha. And I was sorry for him, but I wasn't sorry. After that it made it impossible to say something because it would have been my word against all those people, yourself included, who thought he was a good man, and everyone would be saying I was making it up and slandering him when he couldn't defend himself. And I would be the one to be made to feel in the wrong for something that sleazy bastard did all that time ago.'

By this stage I was right royally wound up, and damn it, I was in my own house with my baby, so I didn't even have the luxury of storming out to blow off some steam. I should have known it would go down like this. Should have known I would get zero support from my mother. Why had I even said anything?

'Sam,' Mum said. She'd put on that voice I remembered from childhood when one of us had got too wound up. The voice that radiated quiet calm, but also had a steel edge that made you realise any instruction was non-negotiable. 'Sit down. Sit yourself back down.'

I retreated back to the chair, but I took my time about it.

We stared at each other for a bit. All the while she quietly rubbed Amelia's back.

'Let's take this back to the beginning,' she said. 'I'm sorry if you thought I didn't believe you.' That was probably as close as I was going to get to an apology. 'And I'm glad your father wasn't alive to hear about this. It would have broken his heart.'

Her referring to Dad was completely unexpected, as were the tears that sprang to my eyes at the mention of him. What was even more unexpected was my realisation that she was crying too.

'No one ever wants to imagine their child could go through something like that. It was hard to hear it, and please believe me when I say some of how I reacted and what I said was only because I was shocked and spoke without thinking.'

'So you do believe me?'

There was so much riding on this question.

'Sam, you may have done many things over the years I don't entirely agree with, but as far as I'm aware, you've never lied to me. Except for that one time when you covered for your brother and told me he'd been home when he'd snuck out to the Clintons' party.'

'You found out about that?'

'Of course we did. Gore's too small a town.'

'But I didn't get into trouble.'

'He did.'

We both had a little chuckle, a release valve on the tension.

'I do believe you, Sam, but I have to say it upsets me to think you didn't feel you could talk to us about anything, especially something as important as this.' It wouldn't be Mum if she didn't find a way to make me feel guilty when she'd been the one who behaved badly. If she'd had herself as a mother, she would have understood exactly why it was impossible for me to speak up at the time. But then maybe she did. Maybe Nana McKay had been a bit of a battle-axe too, and Mum had her fine example of caring and compassion as a model. I promised myself that Amelia would never, ever doubt that she was loved and had her mother fighting in her corner, no matter what.

'Anyway. We can't change that now, can we?' she said.

'No,' I said. 'We can't.'

Amelia gave a cute grunting noise and adjusted her position on Mum's chest. Mum gave her a wee snuggle and kissed her forehead.

'You know, perhaps it's just as well you didn't tell us at the time.'

'Why?' I asked.

'Your father absolutely adored you and if he had found out that some lecherous bastard had laid a hand on you, he would have been down there like a shot to cut off his balls.'

CHAPTER 42

It was becoming more and more apparent that the people I was talking to about this case were being economic with the truth. Instead of being completely up front, they were choosing to drip-feed information in a way that was starting to feel manipulative, and I was getting heartily sick of it.

'How did you know about Felicity Freeman's pregnancy?' There was no point beating about the bush. 'According to Felicity only two people knew about it – her boyfriend and Mel Smythe – yet you dropped that bombshell as a parting shot when we talked here the other day.'

Aaron Cox looked at me in a way I couldn't quite interpret. Was it cagey? Annoyed? I couldn't quite pick it. Or was trying to label it as one emotion too simplistic and it was a blend, a complex range, and needed to be reviewed in the way connoisseurs judged whisky or wine. This human is displaying classic avoidance, but with underlying base notes of guilt, embarrassment – and is that a whiff of existential dread?

'I'm not entirely sure how to answer that question,' he said.

'Well, it's fairly straightforward. I don't know that I can phrase it any other way.'

He sighed and leaned back in the pew. 'The answer isn't, though.'

Nothing about this case was straightforward.

'Well, let's try a different approach then. Let's start with why did you tell me about her pregnancy the other day, yet you didn't mention it in any of your interviews back in 1999? I've been through and checked all of the transcripts. Not a word. And you endured a lot of interviews. The police seemed intent on finding anything that would connect you to Reverend Freeman's death, yet you didn't mention the one thing that could have taken the focus off you.'

We were meeting in St Paul's Cathedral again, this time by design and at Aaron's insistence. It was neutral territory, and, oddly now for me, safe territory.

'Time is an interesting thing,' he said. 'As you get older you get to see things that seemed important to you at the time with a different perspective. It gives you the space to rethink your choices – which is a double-edged sword, because in examining them, and realising that perhaps you didn't do the right thing, you then have to live with the guilt that that brings.'

He paused and looked up to the sun-struck cross suspended from the ceiling.

'And you find yourself needing some form of absolution, of forgiveness.'

I could feel the chill wave as the hairs on my arms stood up.

'What are you telling me, Aaron? Are you saying that you did, in fact, kill Mark Freeman after all?'

When he had assured me that he hadn't been the murderer, I had believed him. When I had read through the transcripts and looked at the complete lack of evidence, I had believed him. Could I have been so very wrong?

'No, I didn't kill Mark Freeman, not directly. But I have been left wondering all these years if it was my actions that triggered the events that led to his death. That somehow I was to blame. That's been a heavy burden to carry. And then when Mel was murdered as well, I've had to do some soul-searching.'

His denial that he'd a direct hand in events was a relief, but he'd now raised more questions.

'Was that why you came here the day we met, after they'd interviewed you at the station? To seek forgiveness?'

He inhaled deeply and closed his eyes. 'Yes. Sometimes God works in mysterious ways. I think God brought you here that day too. If you hadn't been here, if we hadn't connected the way we did, I don't know that I would have ever said anything, would have had the guts to. I think you were meant to be here.'

In a strange way, sitting here again today, after the catharsis of finally sharing my own church-induced trauma, was comforting. This place didn't feel as cold and intimidating as it had last week. It no longer triggered the borderline panic attacks I was having at the beginning of the investigation. Although I was well beyond being labelled 'Team God', as my mother put it, there remained some vestige of the peace and connection I used to find in churches.

'Is that why we are here again today?' I asked. 'For confession? Forgiveness? Absolution?'

'You forgot sanctuary,' he said, with a wry smile. 'Holy ground.'

I couldn't help but smile back. 'So what are you wanting to confess? Why did you think your actions may have led to Mark Freeman's death all those years ago?'

He leaned forward, elbows on knees, hands slowly rubbing together.

'Twenty-five years ago I overheard a conversation I shouldn't have. It was downstairs in one of the rooms. They didn't know I was there. I was never meant to hear – no one was.'

It wasn't hard to guess between who. 'Mel and Felicity?'

'Yeah. Mel was talking her through the abortion procedure. They were going the next day, Friday. She was trying to calm Felicity down, reassure her.'

'Did you get the feeling that Mel was pressuring her into it?' I asked. That would have put a whole new complexion on the termination.

'No, no, nothing like that. It was clear that Felicity wanted it to happen, needed it to happen, but she was terrified her parents would find out.'

'Why was she so afraid of what her parents would think?' It felt like the answer was kind of obvious, but I still wanted Aaron's take on it.

'Because they were a minister's family. They had to live up to higher ideals than other kids. She was worried about the shame and embarrassment it would bring them, and that her parents would be angry with her.'

I certainly wouldn't have wanted to have to live up to that level of expectation, having to live a perfect life, with everyone scrutinising any deviance from the straight and narrow.

'And from what you knew of the Freemans, was she right to be afraid of their response?'

There was a sizeable pause before he spoke.

'At the time I thought they would be shocked, as anyone would be with that kind of news. But I thought they would understand. As I told you, I've been in the same boat myself as a parent. My youngest got into trouble too. It was young love – and they made a stupid mistake. Passion got in the way of brains. Was I disappointed? Yes. Angry? A little. But mostly I was concerned for my little girl, her future. It was hard, but we worked through it as a family. I thought Mark would be the same.'

I had a feeling I knew where this was going.

'But?'

'I thought I was doing the right thing by telling him about Felicity's predicament. That it would give him the time to think it through and mentally prepare for when Felicity told him herself. And if she didn't tell him – and this was the father in me thinking – I thought he had a right to know.' He leaned back and looked straight up at the vaulted ceiling. 'It's one of my greatest regrets, I wish I'd never told him.'

'He didn't take it well?'

He gave a scoffing laugh. 'That is a bit of an understatement. He went off his nut. Called his daughter all sorts of names that were pretty rough. I'd never seen him like that before.'

'What did he do?'

'He was going to go and have her up about it. Challenge her, demand an explanation.'

I didn't think a pregnancy required much explanation.

There was a sinking feeling of premonition before I asked the next question. 'When was this? When did this conversation take place?'

He turned and looked at me then, and I could see the answer in his tormented face before he even uttered the words.

'It was the night he was killed,' he said in a whisper. 'I told him just before the service.'

He wiped his eyes with the back of his hand.

My recollection of the witness statements from the night he was killed was that the service proceeded as normal and no one commented on unusual behaviour from Reverend Freeman. No one had flagged a change in temperament, or that the Reverend had seemed angry or distracted. It wasn't fire and brimstone from the pulpit.

'And did he challenge her that evening?' My other recollection was that at no point had Felicity Johns mentioned that her father had confronted her about the pregnancy; nor had Callum for that matter. The impression she had given was that he didn't even know.

'Not before the service. Parishioners were in the church by that stage so there were people around. He wouldn't have had a chance to get her alone in private.'

'But afterwards?'

'Yeah. He did. It was bad.'

'You saw it?'

'I heard it. When he started in on her, I had to go. I wasn't going to stand around and watch the man bailing up his daughter. They were in the Neville Chapel, the one over there, off to the side.' He indicated the small chapel. Was that why Aaron had chosen that particular spot when we first talked? Atonement?

'But you listened?'

'Yeah. Voices carry here, especially loud voices. Part of me felt I had to stick around, in case he went too far you know, in case I needed to step in. I was out of sight, by the entrance.'

'You were worried that he'd hit her?'

'I didn't think he would, he wasn't that kind of a man. But men can do bad things when they're angry, they can lose their heads.' It sounded like the voice of experience. Given his gang background, it probably was. 'I had unleashed this. I'd told him his daughter's secret, so I had to stay, make sure she was safe.'

'Why didn't you say any of this to the police when they interviewed you back then? That was important information that could have changed the direction of the investigation.'

'Like I said, I felt responsible. I don't know if it had anything to do with his death. It may have been a coincidence, but you know, I thought about my own daughter and how she would have felt in those circumstances. If when she'd told me she was pregnant I had reacted like that and told her she was a whore, that she was going to burn in hell.' I must have gasped slightly because he paused and said, 'Yes, those were his words. He said ugly, ugly things. Things which I'm sure he would have felt bad about later on. But at the time, he was angry.'

'So you kept quiet because you thought maybe Felicity killed her father?'

'I don't think she had it in her, but ... well, you never know, and if she did, I felt it was my fault. I forced the issue. Stuck my nose in where it didn't belong. I suppose I didn't say anything because I felt I had to protect her from all that attention. I owed her that.'

There was a flawed logic to that, and in a small way I applauded his loyalty, but that loyalty had meant the Freeman family had not seen justice for their husband and father's murder for more than twenty-five years.

'So you were still in the church. You didn't see them leave, or see any of what happened outside?'

'No. Felicity didn't stay. When her father started ripping into her, after he called her those dreadful things, she just ran.' He pointed over towards the side door, out onto Stuart Street. 'She didn't stick around for more abuse, she took off. I didn't blame her.'

I put myself into the shoes of a fifteen-year-old girl. A fifteen-year-old who had just been through the trauma of an abortion, who was probably still sore and scared, and was then confronted with her worst nightmare: the pious rage of her own father. I would have run too.

She had kept this rather significant altercation a secret from the police back in 1999, and she had withheld it from me too, even when we were having a pretty frank conversation about the whole episode. Was that because she was holding an even bigger secret?

'What did the Reverend do after that?'

'I don't know. As soon as I saw Felicity leave, I snuck out the door. I didn't want to be caught eavesdropping, and I sure as hell didn't want to talk to Mark after that. No way. I was off.'

'So the last time you actually spoke with Reverend Freeman alone was before the service, when you told him about Felicity?'

'Yeah.'

None of the other parishioners had mentioned a massive argument between the Reverend and his daughter. I'm sure they would have noticed something as huge as a screaming match in the church. They must have all gone. But had everyone gone? I thought about the timing of when people had told me they'd left to go home. When the Freemans had gone. Yvonne. Felicity. Callum. Yvonne was definitely the first; that had been confirmed by a number of people. But there was a cloud of confusion as to whether Callum left next, or Felicity. Felicity had said Callum, and Callum had said Felicity. Had someone gone and come back?

'Who else was there, Aaron? Who else saw it?' And who else had kept it a secret?

'The congregation had all gone. And Yvonne had already left. She'd had a headache, so had gone home shortly after the service...'

'But?'

'Callum may still have been there, I'm not certain, I lost sight of him.'

Interesting.

'But I definitely did see someone else.'

'And who was that?'

He hesitated a little.

'It was Mel Smythe.'

CHAPTER 43

'Why didn't you tell me about the altercation between you and your father on the night he died?' I was feeling a little pissy by this stage, and judging by the look on Felicity's face, it showed in my voice. She didn't say anything and dropped her eyes to the floor. 'We've had a number of conversations now, and you have had plenty of opportunity to bring it up, but you haven't. In fact, you've not been very forthcoming about a number of important issues, and I want to know why.'

She took a very deep breath. 'I didn't say anything earlier because I knew how it would look.'

'Well, leaving it until I have to prise it out of you makes it look even worse,' I said. 'In fact, you had told me your parents didn't know about your pregnancy and abortion, yet clearly your father did. You lied to me. It makes it look like you're covering something up.'

Silence.

'Are you?'

This time the interview was taking place at the station, not in the comfort of home with a canine support buddy. We didn't need to worry about The Boss hovering around or interfering, as he had been placed on paid leave for the remainder of the investigation. Although I felt a bit bad for him, it made things a lot simpler for the rest of us. Simpler and a damn sight more comfortable. There would have been no comfort for Felicity though. With him at home and now aware of the many secrets being withheld from him, those hard conversations must have happened. It wasn't only the less-than-flattering lighting in the interview room that made her look pale and tired. I doubted there was much sleep going on in her household.

'No, there's nothing left to hide,' she said.

She still avoided looking directly at me, and at this point I'd given up on assuming anyone was telling the full truth. There had been a shit-tonne of lying, and lying by omission, going on.

'How about you tell us about the night your father was killed: what happened after the service finished?'

'God,' she said. Even her voice sounded tired. 'Everyone left pretty quickly that night. I guess that was because of the weather. Everyone just wanted to get home. A few of the regulars stayed behind to talk, as always, but even they left earlier than usual.'

Once again Smithy was sitting in on the interview, but we'd decided ahead of time I would be the one asking the questions.

'Why did you stay until after everyone else left? I understand that your mother had already walked home. Why didn't you go with her?'

'I wish I could have. I was feeling pretty tired and washed out after ... well, you know.'

'We need you to state why for the recording.' That was Smithy interjecting, but he spoke with care.

She nodded. 'Sorry, of course. I was still feeling uncomfortable after the abortion on Friday.' It was a dreadfully harsh word, and I could understand why she was reluctant to use it. 'But Dad had asked me to stay on. I had no idea what for at that stage. I assumed he wanted me to help with tidying up or something.'

'Was there anyone else there who may have overheard your father?'

Again, the hesitation.

'I'm not entirely sure,' she said.

'What do you mean?'

'There may have been one or two people at first, but once Dad got going, I don't know. It's a big building. We were off to the side, and I had my back to the nave so I couldn't see, but then, as you can imagine with Dad having a full-on rant, I wasn't paying attention to anything else.'

'So who did you think may have been there?'

She had been slowly wringing her hands, but stopped when I asked the question.

'I don't know if I should say because I might be wrong. I don't want to get other people in trouble.'

'Felicity, we're talking about a murder here. The murder of your own father. If other people were there, we need to know. It's not for you to judge what might be important and what might not. That is our job. Who do you think was there?'

She blew out a long breath, and then looked at me, a frown creasing her forehead.

'I think maybe Callum was still there. Callum and Mel.'

My eyebrows shot up. Callum. But she didn't mention Aaron's name. Mel we knew was there, if Aaron was telling the truth, but this confirmed that Callum had been there. Aaron had mentioned Callum may have been there, but that he had lost sight of him. But then again, he'd been trying to remain hidden himself. Maybe there had been three others present, all trying not to be seen. It was frigging hide-and-seek, the cathedral edition. And now we could add Callum's name to the list of those being selective with the truth. He'd only told me he'd overheard the conversation between Felicity and Mel, when he'd learned about his sister's pregnancy. Had he also overheard the Sunday-night confrontation?

'Okay. Thank you. We needed to know that.' Hopefully my expression had remained impassive. Long shot though, I wasn't known for my poker face.

Aaron had hinted that the confrontation had been pretty brutal, so I softened my voice when I asked the next question. I knew this was going to be tough.

'So when your dad took you aside that night, what did he say?'

I was glad I'd had the foresight to place a tissue box on the table.

She took a long, shuddering breath. 'Oh, God. He just launched straight in, no warning, no nothing. I didn't see it coming. He said he knew all about my pregnancy, and knew that I'd had the termination, and he just went out of his mind. My God, he was so angry. And he called me things. Awful, awful names that no daughter should have to hear coming from her father's mouth. And I couldn't even defend myself from it because he just wouldn't stop.'

She paused to blow her nose and take a few moments to compose herself.

'Do you need a glass of water?' I asked.

'No, I'll be fine,' she said.

I somehow doubted that. 'I know this is really difficult, but, for the record, I need to know what sort of things he called you.'

'Why do you need to know that?' she whispered.

'Because if there was anyone else there who overheard the confrontation, we need to know what they may have heard, in case it may have caused them to react in some way.'

She nodded slowly, understanding what I was trying to say.

'Did you see Mel or Callum afterwards, when you left?'

She shook her head. 'But there may have been other people there too, though. Not just Callum and Mel.'

'I know, and we are looking into that.' Even now, in her precarious position, this woman was still trying to protect people. 'Felicity, what did he say?'

She closed her eyes, pursed her lips. 'He called me a whore, a Jezebel, and a heathen and a murderer.' Such awful words to rain down on a teenager, hateful words from someone she loved. 'He said he was ashamed of me and that I was a disgrace to our family. And then he went on and on about how it would make him look bad, and that I was a selfish bitch for not thinking about what it would do to my family ... and him ... and his position ... in ... the Church.'

The tears were flowing freely now, the words were punctuated with sobs. She took several moments to get herself under control.

'My own father called me a slut. He said he disowned me, didn't want anything to do with me. That I was no longer welcome under his roof and that I deserved to burn in hell.'

A huge part of me wanted to reach over to her, to wrap her in a hug, comfort her. This was the ultimate rejection from her dad. Sometimes I hated the formality of the job. The need for professionalism, particularly under the watchful eye of the video camera, when what was really required was humanity and compassion.

'What did you do then?'

An image of a fragile young woman lashing out against the tirade jumped into my mind. Could she have been carrying a knife? Her own anger and shame boiling to the surface and striking at the cause of the pain? Could she have stabbed him? In a blind moment of sheer hurt and desolation, could she have plunged that knife into him to try and make it stop? And had her father then staggered out of the church, following his daughter, shocked, bleeding, and then come to his demise by falling down those steep and unforgiving stairs?

'I ran,' she said. 'I ran. I fled. I had to get away from him, get out of there, I ran for the door.'

Her testimony matched what Aaron had said. My imaginings were just that: imaginings. There had been no evidence of blood inside the cathedral, and her father had been wearing his raincoat when he died. He'd changed out of his robes and was a man wrapped up for the weather. A man on his way home.

Another thought struck me then, a thought that rocked me and brought instant tears to my eyes. For fifteen-year-old Felicity Freeman, the last words she ever heard from her father were of condemnation and shame. The last words she heard from her father were that she was a whore.

CHAPTER 44

The seat had barely cooled when Callum Freeman was invited into the interview room. In a sequenced manoeuvre worthy of a Hollywood blockbuster, we had carefully orchestrated it so the siblings didn't meet up in the building, nor have opportunity to contact each other by phone. We didn't want them conferring on anything. Although a part of me wondered if we even needed to bother with the theatrics, as I was getting the impression that this was a family that didn't actually talk with each other. Well, not about the big things.

The energy coming off Callum was quite different to his previous interview. Whereas last time he had been a bundle of nerves, this time he had an air of resignation. An attitude of 'here we are again'.

We sat silently in the room, waiting for Smithy to return from walking Felicity down to the foyer and farewelling her from the premises. Callum didn't attempt to make conversation and after the emotional rollercoaster that was Felicity's interview, I was very happy to sit quietly and gather my thoughts. I was jolted out of my reverie by Smithy pulling out the chair beside me. He gave me a nod and we got straight into it.

'On the night that your father was killed, after the evensong service had finished, did you witness an altercation between Felicity and your father?'

Callum Freeman had a naturally pale complexion. It bleached a shade paler.

'We have eyewitness accounts that after most people had left for the evening, your father had a loud argument with your sister. Were you there when that occurred?'

He closed his eyes momentarily and blew a long breath out through pursed lips. 'Yes, yes I saw it, I was there.' He looked at me then, face grim.

'Why didn't you mention this when we talked with you yesterday? This was a significant event and you have had plenty of opportunity. In fact, you told me Felicity had already left for home before you did. You lied to me, and I want to know why.'

'It was for Flossie's sake. It was bad enough everything coming out about her pregnancy and abortion, and that whole sorry saga. I wanted to spare her the anguish of having people know about how Dad treated her that night too. And when you didn't ask me about it yesterday, I thought no one else had said anything or knew about it either. So I kept quiet because some things are better left alone.'

'Well, people did know about it, so choosing not to say anything to us now, or to the police back in the original investigation, makes it look like you had something to hide.'

'I know it looks bad, and I should have said something, but honestly, I thought Flossie had been through enough. And besides, I didn't want our mother ever finding out about what happened that night, because she would be so upset if she knew, and she doesn't need that right now. You haven't told her about this or the abortion, have you?' His voice had a pleading tone to it. His protective urges towards the women in his life were touching, if misguided.

'At this point we haven't divulged anything to your mother,' Smithy said.

I let the silence sit for a moment before continuing.

'What exactly did you see happen that night?'

He sat forward, elbows on the table, fingers interlocked. 'It was after the service, and I thought everyone had gone home except Flossie and Dad. Mum had long gone. I was just going over to see if Flossie wanted to walk back together when I heard Dad start up.'

'Whereabouts were you in the church?' I knew where Aaron had been hidden – near the entrance, on the stairs down to the gallery, and had an idea of the view he would have had. He hadn't been able to see Callum.

'I was behind one of the pillars, down by the pipe organ. I could see Flossie, but Dad was out of sight in the small chapel.' That explained why Callum was out of Aaron's line of sight. The angles would have prevented him.

'And you couldn't see anyone else in the cathedral?'

'No, just Dad and Flossie. Well, Flossie – but I could hear everything Dad said.'

'And what did he say to her?'

He shifted in his chair. 'It was awful, I don't know that I want to repeat it.'

'We need to know exactly what he said.'

'He said he knew all about the pregnancy and the abortion. Someone had told him all about it.'

'Did he say who?'

'No, he didn't mention any names. But I can guess.'

'Who do you think would have told him?'

'There was only one person who could have: Mel Smythe. No one else knew, besides Tim, and he was hardly going to confess to the father of the girl he got pregnant,' he said.

After Felicity had revealed Tim's name I had checked the list of congregation who had been present that night. Tim Williamson was one of them. Had he heard the Reverend's rant too? I added it to my mental list to follow up.

'It had to have been Mel,' Callum continued. 'She'd promised she wouldn't tell, but she must have. The bitch.'

There was a lot of bitterness in his statement. Enough to do something drastic? His alibi for Monday was solid, though.

'How would you describe his manner?'

'Oh Jesus, he was angry. So angry. I had never seen him like that before.'

'So this reaction was not typical? He hadn't acted that way towards Felicity or yourself before?'

'Not this bad. He could be pretty harsh at home, especially if Mum wasn't around. But I had never seen this type of rage before.'

It did make me wonder if there was a deeper, more sinister, reason for that level of reaction to Felicity's pregnancy.

I had to ask. 'Callum, did you have any reason to believe that your father may have been abusing Felicity in some way? Sexually abusing her?'

His mouth formed a shocked O, and he started stuttering. 'No ... no way ... absolutely not. Dad would never have done that. I didn't see anything that had me worried about sex abuse. Ever. And Dad was too tied up with Mum. He adored her. They were a very gushy couple. It was embarrassing. The only way that anything could be interpreted as abuse was in the way he was so hard on her, and controlling in who she could and couldn't see, when she could go out, that kind of thing.'

'So why do you think he reacted so badly in the church that night?'

'I don't honestly know. All I know is that he was on a full-on rant, and he called her the most awful, awful things.'

'What did he say?'

Callum's voice became quiet, as though whispering the words would make them less hurtful. 'He called her a slut and a whore, accused her of sleeping around. He said she was a murderer and a heathen and that she would burn in hell. But that wasn't the worst of it.'

He paused, licking his lips.

'He told her he was ashamed of her and that he no longer called her his daughter. He disowned her and told her she was no longer welcome in our home. He threw her out.'

I could see his eyes brimming.

'How did hearing those things make you feel?'

'I was shocked. So shocked to hear that coming out of his mouth. And I could see Flossie, I could see her face.'

'Did hearing those words make you angry?'

He looked up at me. 'I'd be lying if I didn't say it made me angry. He was hurting her so much, you could see she was utterly stricken. He was still yelling after her as she ran away, still calling her awful things.'

'And what did you do after you saw Felicity run off? Did you confront your father? Did you make him pay for how he treated your sister?'

Had he been the one carrying a knife that night? Did Callum Freeman go too far to defend his sister's honour?

'No.' His eyes were downcast again. 'Dad was so angry I didn't want to go near him in case he ripped into me too. I stayed hidden, stayed where I was until he went downstairs to change and I could escape out the side door and go home.' He drummed his fingers on the table. 'And you know what? I really regret it. I regret that I didn't stand up to him right then and there in front of her, tell him he was being an arsehole and was out of order. And I feel ashamed – ashamed that I was too much of a coward to defend my sister in what must have been the toughest time of her life.'

I had to remind myself it had been a seventeen-year-old boy dealing with a situation most grown adults wouldn't know how to cope with. In fact, the other adults apparently in the room had kept in hiding too. Neither Aaron Cox nor Mel Smythe had come to Felicity's rescue in that moment. It would appear that they had all slunk off into the night. In fact, given that Reverend Freeman had changed and had turned out the lights before locking up and leaving implied some time had elapsed between the argument and when he had been fatally assaulted. So who waited? Who bided their time outside in that terrible weather for Mark Freeman to exit the cathedral? And why? Did they not want to spill blood in the house of God? It could have been any of them, or none of them.

'Did you talk to Felicity afterwards, let her know you had seen what happened?'

'No, I didn't get the chance. When I got home she was in her room, and then, well, Dad didn't come home and Mum sent me back down to the church, and that's when I found him. Then it all went crazy. After everything that happened, and then with us all trying to come to grips with Dad dying, I decided that it was best for everyone if the argument was never mentioned, that Felicity never knew someone else had heard.'

Oh, foolish child. His teenage self did not realise that what his sister really needed at that time was for someone to tell her that her father was wrong, very wrong, that she did the right thing, that she was loved and she would be okay.

CHAPTER 45

My mind was awhirl with the intense conversations of the last few days and it felt like the thoughts and themes were beginning to coalesce, but I couldn't quite define the shape. The two cases, past and present, were merging into one, and the talk amongst the team was that although we were narrowing the suspects, unfortunately there was no clear winner or winners. For want of solid evidence we were relying on 'he said, she said', and alas that would not stand up in a court of law.

Previous experience had told me the best course of action in that situation was to get on the move. I was an active thinker – when my brain was computing, I had to move. I knew that trait used to drive my teachers and my mother nuts, but now I had made the connection between my brain and my feet, I rolled with it. Consequently, I was walking past the playing fields at the Alhambra Union Rugby Club on my way to the Botanic Garden, my default think space. I noted that even in the middle of winter on what could only be described as a brisk day, there were still a handful of die-hard students out there wearing shorts and kicking around a ball on what looked like a fairly sodden pitch. The bare legs made their standard black puffer jackets and colourful beanies seem somewhat redundant.

In the case of Mel Smythe, there was the hope that ESR would be able to come to light with trace evidence from the scene. No matter how careful people were, they always left something behind. There was also the hope that now her name had been released in the media and people were able to make connections, eyewitnesses to her activities on the day and in the days prior, and anyone she might have met with, could come to light. Some poor staff were also undertaking the mind-numbing task of screening the various video feeds we'd acquired for familiar faces, or vehicle number plates. The small piece that completed the puzzle could come from anywhere.

In the case of Mark Freeman, we weren't holding out any hope for new forensic evidence, or that techniques developed in the last twenty-five years would shed new light on the existing materials. Instead, my feeling was that the people involved would give way soon. The pressure from the last few days had certainly illustrated that the players were wearing down, running out of omissions, untruths and outright lies to hide behind. Someone would make a mistake, let something slip.

I thought about all those still in the game. Unfortunately for The Boss, a few of them were his nearest and dearest – Felicity, Callum. And of course, as a left-field option in the Mel Smythe case, the big kahuna himself. On the St Paul's congregation side there was Aaron, Mel herself, and fellow left-fielder, Tim Williamson.

How many of them would have had access to knives? A small, possibly pocket knife twenty-five years ago, or a Monty-great carving knife recently? Of course the carving knife was left at the murder scene in Mel Smythe's room. But where was the other? Had the killer ditched the evidence? Logic would say that you would get rid of anything that could possibly link you to a crime. But what if they had kept it? People kept murder weapons for a variety of reasons, from having a trophy, to never having the opportunity to discard it discreetly, to feeling the need to keep it as a nihilistic memento, a strange form of self-flagellation to remind themselves of their sin and how depraved they were. Which was why Callum's name insisted on floating to the top of my mind. From all witness reports, after seeing his father's unfortunate verbal assault on his sister he ran home with his tail between his legs. But what if he hadn't? What if he'd garnered the courage to confront his dad and went back? Was that yet another piece of information he'd neglected to disclose? I wondered if a gut feeling working on no evidence would be enough to get a warrant to search a home for a knife that if the perpetrator had any sense they would have got rid of years ago? Seemed a little unlikely.

A buzz on my wrist notified me of an incoming message. I pulled my phone out of my pocket and smiled when I saw who it was from. Sometimes I swore that woman was psychic and knew exactly when I needed to hear her voice, or in this case her text.

How's it going? Haven't heard from you lately. Still alive?

She knew damned well I'd laugh at that passive-aggressive little dig.

Sorry, who's this? I messaged back.

Being someone who couldn't text and walk without risking getting run over or serious injury I stopped and moved to the side of the footpath.

A photo appeared on my screen of Maggie about to feed a doughnut the size of her head into her mouth.

I sent her a photo of my shoe attached to my leg on the way to the gardens:

Walking and thinking.

Uh oh. Thinking what?

Families are weird.

Yours or someone else's?

Not mine for a change.

Yours isn't exactly functional.

True. We're not as bad as this one.

Has it got a mother in it as formidable as yours?

I had to have a think about that. Yvonne Freeman was a tough woman who had endured a lot. And given that neither of her children felt they could tell her some pretty important things, back then and now, maybe she was.

Possibly?

Oh dear. Lucky them.

Lucky indeed. A few possibilities began to congregate at the back of my mind.

I needed to go talk to Smithy.

CHAPTER 46

Oh, how I wished we could be like Poirot, or Alleyn and the grand fictional detectives of the Golden Era. That we could gather all the suspects in a room together, lob in some truth bombs, stand back and watch the fireworks as everything unravelled. The killer or killers were always revealed, the innocent aghast, and some dramatic struggle ensued before the detective saved the day. Alas, those kind of techniques were frowned upon nowadays, and quite frankly I didn't think would work in these two cases. I was sure if locked in a room together and told all the details they were so desperately trying to hide from each other, despite the potential consequences, every one of those players would still try and protect each other. Protect each other from the truth, from hurt, and protect reputations. The family and church family bonds were strong. Almost as strong as the guilt.

Smithy, Paul, Sonia, Otto and I had sat together yesterday afternoon and thrashed through all of the permutations we could come up with. It had been an interesting discussion and I was relieved when my inklings were taken seriously. We decided our plan of attack and set to our tasks. Paul, Sonia and Otto were going to concentrate on following up on the physical evidence in the Mel Smythe case. We were still waiting on the full ESR report, including DNA testing. The early information they had sent on fingerprints had come up a blank. Our perpetrator had worn gloves, which given it was frigging cold and the middle of winter wasn't a huge surprise, not to mention anyone who had watched any TV crime series or read crime fiction knew to wear them to avoid identification. Toxicology from the postmortem was yet to come in – important in case Mel had been under the influence of drugs or medication which may have impaired her ability to react or fight back when she was stabbed. Then there was the foot traffic / road traffic CCTV. All vital in building up a case.

Smithy and I were going to deal with the people. They were the wildcards. At this stage in the investigation it was a matter of finding the lynchpin and giving it a wee tug to see what happened. To that end, we had decided to go with the person everyone seemed so desperate to protect and not upset. The person in the gravest position.

I tapped in the number and waited while it rang.

'Hello?' Even with that one word the voice carried a profound weariness.

'Hi, Mrs Freeman, It's Detective Sam Shephard here.'

'Oh, Detective. Hello.'

'I hope I didn't wake you up?'

'No, no, that's okay. I was already awake.'

'That's good. Look, something has come up and I was wondering if I could come around and talk with you today?'

'Oh. May I ask what it's about?'

'It's just some questions I wanted to clarify with you about Callum and Felicity. Are you free this afternoon?'

'Is there a problem with them? I hope nothing's wrong?'

'I can't really discuss it on the phone. It would be best in person. How is 3.00pm?'

'Oh, yes, that will be fine.'

'Thank you. We will see you then.'

The wheel was in motion. We would see what happened.

CHAPTER 47

Smithy and I walked down the ivy-hedge-lined driveway to the collection of flats that Yvonne Freeman lived in. It was drizzling today, the dreary-grey-day kind of rain that was enough to be a hassle, but not enough to bother putting a raincoat on. I noted there was only one car in the five-bay carport. Was it Yvonne's? Although each unit was of the same brick design, the occupants had all managed to put their stamp of individuality on them. In Yvonne's case it was with pots filled with perfectly trimmed topiary, varying from spheres to cone shapes to what looked like a pūkeko.

'So we're agreed, I'll do the talking?' I asked.

'That's the plan. You know her best.'

'I know she serves great tea.'

'You would say that.'

I don't know why I felt the need to make light of this serious visit. I guessed it was because we were about to test whether I had come to the right conclusions or was seriously off the track. In an ideal world I would have conducted this interview alone; being faced with two detectives could be quite intimidating for anyone, let alone a very ill and frail woman. We wanted her to feel comfortable enough to talk to me, and I was acutely aware of the power imbalance. I had pitched for DC Richardson to come with me, as another smallish female detective would be less threatening than an over-six-feet-tall lug like Detective Sergeant Smith, but given the gravity of the situation and the complication of DI Johns' intimate involvement with the case it was decided the presence of a senior officer as a witness was necessary.

'I'll stay in the background and try to be as inconspicuous as possible.' From that comment Smithy was all too aware of the impression he made on people, and he knew that for some weird reason people felt they could tell me anything. Although the way people had been withholding things recently, I was beginning to wonder if I'd lost that knack.

I walked up the three steps and across the concrete porch, and knocked on the front door. Half a minute passed and I couldn't hear any movement within so I knocked again.

Nothing.

I turned around and looked at Smithy, who was waiting at the bottom of the steps, leaning against the low wrought-iron fence. He looked at me and shrugged.

'I hope she's okay,' I said. She'd been looking pretty unwell last time I visited so I hoped she hadn't had a medical emergency of some kind.

'I'll check around the back,' he said, and headed off past the neighbouring flat to get access from the side. I gave the door handle a try, in case it was unlocked. It wasn't. I walked further along the patio to where there were sliding doors that opened onto the living space. They were obscured with net curtains, but if I put my face up to the window and cupped my hands around my eyes, there was enough backlighting from the kitchen windows at the rear to make out furniture and objects inside. I couldn't see any sign of her or detect any movement. I was just about to try the same thing at her bedroom window when an unexpected voice gave me a hell of a fright.

'Excuse me, what do you think you are doing?'

I turned around, trying to suppress the guilty look on my face, to see an elderly woman at the bottom of the steps, hands on hips, looking like she wouldn't hesitate to take me on. It was neighbourhood watch at its finest.

'Sorry, I'm Detective Sam Shephard. You may have seen me here the other day. I was supposed to have an appointment with Yvonne at three, but she doesn't seem to be home. Do you know where she might be?'

The neighbour dropped her hands from her hips, and the relaxation in posture made her look half the size. 'Oh. No, she's not here. She popped out about an hour ago, I'd say.' That relieved my mental images of her lying collapsed on the floor.

'Did you talk with her? How did she seem?'

'The poor thing looked really tired and a bit upset. I've been very worried about her. You know she isn't very well.'

'Yes, we were aware she is sick. Did she mention where she was going?' Here was hoping.

'No, she didn't say.'

At this stage Smithy arrived back from around the house. Neighbour lady looked quite alarmed to see him.

'He's a colleague,' I said quickly, to reassure her. 'Look, thanks for your help. We really do need to get in touch with her urgently, so if she does arrive home, could you please let us know?' I handed her a business card and she took it with interest.

'I hope it's not serious,' she said.

'We're just following up on a routine investigation.' Sometimes the white lies were simpler.

We had just started walking back up the driveway when there was a call from behind us. 'Detective? Wait.'

I turned back around.

'When she left she did say something a little odd.'

'Oh, what was that?' I said.

'She asked if I could look after her cat.'

CHAPTER 48

'Why does the comment about the cat make me nervous?'

'Do you think she's done a runner?' Smithy said.

We were back in the car in a fug of damp wool, courtesy of Smithy's jersey.

'No. Neighbour lady didn't mention her carrying bags. I hope she hasn't done anything stupid.' The humidity emanating from our clothes now we had begun to warm up had started to fog up the windows. 'We really do need to find out where she is. I'm going to make a few phone calls.'

The first was to Yvonne Freeman herself. I put the call onto speakerphone so Smithy could hear what was being said.

After ringing for what seemed like an eternity it clicked over to the sound of her voice: 'Yvonne here. Please leave a message.'

In order to leave a time-stamp trail I obliged. In reality I hadn't expected her to pick up.

'Yvonne, it's Detective Shephard here. I stopped by at your home at 3.00pm for our appointment, but you weren't home. I hope everything is okay. Can you please give me a call?'

I looked at Smithy and he raised his eyebrows.

Next up was Callum Freeman. He did answer. At this time of day he would most likely be at work.

'Callum. It's Detective Sam Shephard here. Listen, I had made a time to meet with your mother this afternoon, but she wasn't at home when I called. Is she okay? Do you know where she is?'

I could hear voices in the background and the sound of Callum's voice telling them, 'Sorry, I just have to take this call, I won't be a minute.'

Then he came loudly back across the speakers.

'No. As far as I'm aware she should be at home. And she was expecting you?'

'Yes.'

'That's not like her to not be there for an appointment.'

'Have you heard from her at all today?' I asked.

'I haven't talked with her, but she did send a text message earlier.'

'Can I ask what she said?'

'She just said she hoped I had a good day, and' – his voice dropped a little quieter so his colleagues couldn't hear – 'I love you.'

'Does she often do that?' I asked.

'Message?' he said.

'Say I love you.'

'No, I guess not. I must reply actually. I haven't done that yet.'

Little hackles of alarm were starting to rise.

'If she gets in touch, can you please let me know? I do need to talk with her.'

'Sure, Detective,' he said, and hung up.

At this point it was getting a bit too stuffy in the car. I turned the key in the ignition so I could crack the window. I almost immediately regretted the decision as the air that flowed in felt bitterly cold.

'One more,' I said to Smithy.

'The hospital?' he asked.

'Okay, maybe two more.'

I pulled up the number and tapped it. The phone picked up on the fourth ring.

'Detective Shephard? Can I help you?' She must have added me to her contacts. I caught another familiar voice in the background checking if he'd heard right.

Crap.

'Hi, Felicity. I was wondering if you'd heard from your mother at all today. I'd made an appointment to meet her at her place this afternoon, but when we arrived she wasn't there. Do you happen to know where she is?'

'Oh, she wasn't home? No, I don't know where she is then. Is everything alright?'

Well, that was the question.

'I was just about to ask you that. So she hasn't been in touch with you today?'

'Ah, not to talk to, but she did message me earlier.'

'And what did she say?' I was trying to keep my voice neutral, but it may not have been working.

'Ah ... she was just wishing me a good day, said love you, that kind of thing. Why? Do you think something's wrong?' From the change in the tone of her voice, my concern was contagious.

At this point I could hear the basso voice in the background getting more insistent and after a brief interchange it came over the speaker so loud and clear we both flinched.

'Shephard. What's going on?' The Boss didn't sound that happy.

'We're just trying to locate Yvonne Freeman. You don't know where she is, do you?'

'Why? What's happening?'

'We just need to find her to clarify a few things.'

There was a pause. Even the silence sounded angry.

'Stop being cagey and tell me what's going on.'

At this point Smithy interceded. 'Boss. Smithy here. Look, it's nothing for you to concern yourself about. We had arranged an appointment with Yvonne this afternoon and she wasn't there, so we were just wanting to check that she is alright. She hadn't been in touch to say she was sick and was getting medical help or anything?'

'No. And I hope you haven't been harassing her and making her ill.' Although the comment was very direct, it was delivered in a different tone from the one he used with me. The boys' club tone.

'No, we have been very mindful of her condition and we've been keeping any contact to an absolute minimum. We were just concerned when she wasn't there for our meeting just now. It would be helpful if you could let me know when she does get in touch, so I know she's alright.'

A harrumph came from the other side. 'Very well. But you make sure you let me know what's going on.'

We both heaved a sigh of relief when that phone call was over.

'Hospital?' Smithy asked.

'I don't know. From what the neighbour was saying, Yvonne wasn't in urgent need of medical care. I got the feeling she would have had an ambulance there in a shot if there was. To me it sounds like Yvonne was saying goodbye to everyone. And then that comment about the cat. Smithy, I'm worried she might be planning to do herself some harm.'

What I was most worried about was that by rattling the tree to flush out the others, I'd actually driven her to do something drastic. Something I'd be responsible for.

'Jesus, you know, you might be right. But if she was going to do that, surely she'd do it at home?' he said.

I could appreciate the logic of that, but so much of this case had been about protecting people, about secrets and hiding things from each other. But it had also been about absolution and making amends for events twenty-five years ago.

Where would I go if I needed to seek forgiveness, to make amends?

Of course. It hit me with dead certainty. She'd go to the place it had all begun. I turned the ignition.

'Smithy, I know where she is.'

CHAPTER 49

St Paul's Cathedral was shrouded in a mantle of mist, and loomed up against a backdrop of foreboding skies. Climbing back up those front steps, the prickle of goosebumps erupting on my skin echoed the apprehension I'd experienced on that first day of the case, that same sense of dread. Jesus, that felt so long ago now. The bleak weather had emptied out the centre of town. There were only a few people down in The Octagon, a few hardy individuals walking under the shelters either side of the central carriageway. Even the roads were quiet, with just the occasional passing *schusssh* of car tyres on wet asphalt. Smithy and I reached the top of the steps, a sense of urgency driving us up quickly. The outer doors were open, but the inner ones were closed to keep out the chill. I pulled at the nearest one and entered that hallowed space. The brightness of the lighting was a stark contrast to the lowering dusk outside, and the beauty and tranquillity of the quiet space belied the reason we were here. I quickly scanned the pews and could see no one, but that didn't mean anything. There were many nooks and crannies in this building someone could retreat into if they didn't want to be discovered, even by the few staff working downstairs.

'Where do you want to start?' Smithy asked in a whisper. What was it about churches that made people want to lower their voices, not make a noise, even when there was no one else within earshot?

Where should we start? I thought about Yvonne Freeman and her history with this place. She had been far more than just a parishioner here, a member of a congregation. She had been a priest's wife, which in its own way was a hallowed role. This building wasn't just a place of worship – for someone who'd had a lifelong love of God and a responsibility to support her husband, this place had been the centre of her world. Until her world had been violently shattered. I gazed up to the great vaulted ceilings, and my eyes ran down the length of the nave to the beautiful, suspended semi-transparent cross. I felt the peace that emanated from its walls and asked myself, if I were seeking a place to end my pain, would it be in here, in a sanctuary? Or if I were someone with a deep-rooted faith, would I see that as defiling the house of God?

The Reverend Mark Freeman had not met his fate inside the cathedral.

My eyes remained fixated upon that cross as I said, 'I think you should search inside, there are a lot of rooms downstairs as well. Check them out. I'll check outside.'

He turned to me, puzzled. 'You think she'd be outside in this weather?'

'Maybe. I've got a feeling.'

He snorted. 'Grown men quake and stock markets crash when you get a feeling.'

'Thanks.'

'I'll be quick as I can in here, then come out to find you. Good luck.'

He headed off to the left to do a lap around the interior, and I turned and headed back out the door.

In the short time we had been inside the drizzle had intensified into a steady rain. It made me grateful that I had thrown on a coat after all. Even though it was only around 4.00pm, what little daylight there was struggled to penetrate the cloud and a gloom had descended upon the city. If my hunch was right, I knew exactly where Yvonne Freeman would be, but there was a fear in my heart about what state I would find her in. I took a big breath, plunged out into the rain and headed directly towards the small side stairs to the left, the stairs Reverend Mark Freeman had tumbled down to his death. There was no one there at the bottom, but as I got halfway down I could see a lone figure off to my left, next to the rose garden. I slowed my descent, assessing the situation, trying to take in as much detail as I could as I approached her.

Yvonne Freeman was sitting on the grass with her back to me, leaning against the kerbing of the memorial rose garden, at the place where the plaque to her deceased husband lay. She was coatless and saturated, and must have been terribly cold. I reached the bottom of the stairs and moved slowly in her direction, skirting out wide to the side. She was sitting in a pocket perfectly obscured from the view of anyone walking in The Octagon, or even on the main stairs up to the cathedral, by a massive plinth, the solid banisters and the retaining walls. Only someone exiting the church offices by the side door would come across her. She was hiding in plain sight.

As I came further round I could see her hands: one resting on the concrete, touching his plaque, the other draped in her lap, holding what looked like a framed photo. A water bottle leaned against her leg, and two pill bottles and their lids were strewn on the grass. I couldn't make out anything that presented a danger – well, not to me.

'Yvonne,' I called, moving a little closer.

She didn't move.

'Yvonne,' I called, louder.

This time her head turned in my direction.

'Yvonne, it's Detective Shephard.'

She nodded, and I moved closer still, crouched down in front of her. I picked up the bottles and looked at the labels. In the poor light I could just make out the names 'morphine' and 'diazepam'. Fuck. They were empty. How long had she been here?

I placed the bottles back down and took her hands in mine. They were icy cold, and when I raised my hand to her cheek, it was cold too. Her large eyes followed my actions. I quickly unzipped my rain-coat, pulled it off and slipped it around her shoulders, pulling the hood up over her head.

'I'm going to get you some help,' I said.

'No,' she said, her voice a whisper. 'Please don't. I don't want your help. I don't deserve your help. I want to go out on my own terms. Just leave me to die.'

'You know I can't do that,' I said.

She picked up the photo in her lap, and as she hugged it to her chest I caught a glimpse of a young Freeman family from at least thirty years ago. The movement also revealed something I hadn't spotted earlier. Shit. My heart sank.

'Oh, Yvonne, what have you done?'

I reached out and felt gently around the hilt of the knife that protruded from her belly. However long that blade was, she'd pushed it all the way in. I moved my hand away, watched with horrified fascination as the rain washed the blood from it.

She stared, impassive.

'It's all falling apart,' she said. 'I'm the only one who can end it. I have to pay.'

'What do you mean?'

Rivulets of water were now flowing through my hair and down my face.

'I tried to make it right.' She was garbling her words, the drugs, blood loss, pain, clearly taking effect.

I caught movement out to my right and saw the office door opening, Smithy's shape silhouetted against a glow of golden light. I raised my hand, gesturing him to stop, then raised and lowered my index finger three times. One, one, one. I got a thumbs-up and saw him pull out his phone to make the call.

My attention went back to the woman in front of me. I rested my hand against the side of her arm, rubbing it gently up and down. 'What did you try to make right, Yvonne?'

'The woman. I tried to make it go away. Make it go away. Forever.'

'Which woman are you talking about?'

'Mel Smythe.'

'You saw her?' I asked. She nodded slowly. 'And you tried to make her go away?'

'It was the only way.'

'Why? What did she do?'

Her eyes lifted to mine then. 'She told me.'

'What did she tell you?'

'She saw it.'

'What did she see?'

'She saw, the night he died. She saw it happen.'

Oh Jesus.

'Who did she see? Who did she see do it, Yvonne?'

She was beginning to slump and I reached out to steady her.

'She saw me.'

What the hell? Had I heard correctly? My mind struggled to grapple with the implications of those words.

'Are you telling me that you killed your husband, that it was you – and Mel saw you do it?'

The poor woman shrank even further into herself.

'I didn't mean for him to die.'

'It *was* you? You stabbed Mark Freeman, you pushed him down the stairs?'

'I ... yes ... but he ... he fell.'

Her breathing was starting to get gaspy; she was struggling to string words together.

'It was me, but she was going to say ... he did it. If I ... didn't give the money, she'd ... wait till I was dead, then say it was ... him.'

'Are you talking about Callum?' I asked, gently.

'...Couldn't let that ... happen to my boy.'

Her words were a whisper. I could feel her listing over so manoeuvred my way behind her to sit on the grass and support her as she collapsed back. That was one hell of a blackmail – cynical and evil. The kind that could drive someone to do something desperate.

I cradled this broken woman, trying to die on her own terms by the side of her husband, trying in her own warped way to fix this hell of a mess. My heart went out to her.

'And what did you do, Yvonne?' I asked, my voice a whisper. 'What did you do when she threatened you and your son?'

'I made her go away.'

CHAPTER 50

'You don't have to do this, you know. I can handle it if you want.'

I appreciated Smithy's offer, but given everything that had happened, this was something that needed to come from me.

'Thank you, but no. I've got this.'

The footpath up to this villa had become very familiar, and I would have much preferred to be taking it as the bearer of good news about the case – some resolution, or that word media people liked to use, 'closure', for the family here. Instead, I was bringing layer upon layer of grief.

We climbed out from the shelter of the car and, shoulders hunched against the rain, strode to the porch. My change earlier into dry clothes had done nothing to dispel the chill that seemed to have settled into my bones.

The warm, multi-hued light that emanated through the stained-glass door panels contrasted with the appalling conditions outside, and with the news that was about to shatter the lives of those within.

'Here we go,' I said, and reached out to press the bell. My heart thumped to the drum of the rain.

A familiar yapping accompanied the approach of an amorphous form inside. It wasn't the shape I had been hoping for. The door swung open, and DI Johns filled the threshold. His brows immediately drew together into a look of wariness when he saw who was calling at this hour of the night.

'It's a bit late for a visit, Detectives,' he said, jumping straight on the offensive. 'What do you want?'

'Detective Inspector,' I replied by way of greeting, 'we need to have a word with Felicity. Is she home?'

He placed his hands on his hips, occupying the door frame. 'Why do you need to talk to her?'

The Boss had gone into gatekeeper mode. It didn't surprise me in the least, but today, considering what I'd been through and my subsequent level of fragility, it wasn't helpful.

'We have something really important that we need to talk with her about.'

He looked down his nose at me like I was a bug he'd like to swat away. 'Do you have a warrant?'

This really was not the time for his bullshit. He knew very well we didn't need a warrant for a conversation. He was just being an arsehole. I closed my eyes and gave a weary sigh, before looking back up at him, unable to suppress the quiver of my chin.

'Unfortunately, it's not that kind of a talk.'

He hesitated then, looked over my head at Smithy.

'Just get her, Greg. And I'm afraid you'll need to stick around too,' came the response from behind me.

The Boss pursed his lips then, face grim, and slowly nodded. He would have made enough of these visits in his time to recognise the signs. He turned back into the house and started walking down the hall to find her. He was only part way there when Felicity appeared from the kitchen. She looked past him towards us.

'What's going on?' she asked.

'They need to talk to you – to us,' he said. I couldn't see his face, but his expression must have been enough to make her realise something was up and it wasn't going to be good.

'Oh.' She slowly began to walk towards us. 'I guess you'd better come in then.'

We followed them into the formal lounge, where The Boss sat down on the sofa and guided Felicity to sit beside him. I sat in the armchair opposite, but Smithy remained standing, slightly off to the side, hands held in front of him, head slightly bowed.

There was no easy way to say what I need to say, but previous experience had taught me that in the end everyone appreciated it if you were direct and got to the point. I took a deep breath, steadied myself, and started.

'I'm afraid we have some very bad news for you.' As I spoke The Boss quietly reached out and took his wife's hand. 'I'm so sorry to have to tell you this, Felicity, but late this afternoon your mother died.'

Her mouth dropped open and a look of confusion crossed her face.

'I'm sorry, what? What do you mean?'

'Your mum passed away this afternoon. She was in the grounds of St Paul's Cathedral when she died.'

As the words sank in, I watched the colour drain from the poor woman's face.

'But how? What happened?'

And this was when it would all get even worse.

'It would appear that she took her own life.'

There was a long silence as the enormity of what I had said hit home. Then it was broken by her anguished cry.

'But how can you know? How can you know she did that? Are you sure?'

'I ... I...' This was where I had to fight hard to control my own emotions, control the memories of that scene, the sensations of it still crawling on my skin. Everything was so raw. '...I was there.'

'You saw it happen? You didn't stop her?' By now the crying had started and the words were forced through her juddering breaths.

DI Johns wrapped his arm around her and pulled her in close.

'I was too late to prevent her, she had already...' I was at a loss for words.

'She was still alive when you got to her?' The Boss asked as Felicity sobbed into his shoulder. His voice was leaden, quiet. Gemma had jumped up onto the sofa and was resting her head on her distraught owner's lap.

'Yes, and I was with her when she died.'

'How? How did she?'

'She took an overdose of morphine and diazepam tablets—' Before I could continue, he interrupted.

'But an overdose? You could have got help for that, got her to hospital, got her stomach pumped if you were fast enough.' His words hit home, fanning the flame of guilt I felt for not attempting to resuscitate her, for not trying to save her.

'It was too late. It wasn't just the drugs. She'd also...' I had to pause before I could express it. '...She also stabbed herself in the abdomen. By the time I found her she'd already lost too much blood, was too much in shock. She was too far gone.'

'But how could she have stabbed herself? That doesn't sound right. I couldn't stab myself. Are you sure it was her? Are you sure someone else didn't do it?'

'Yes, I'm sure. It was her. And she told me what she'd done.'

'She was speaking? She could still talk? For fuck's sake. What did she say exactly?'

'She told me she wanted to die on her own terms.'

The Boss shook his head. 'Jesus,' he said, the emotion finally cracking his face, the tears flowing. It was a sight I never thought I'd see – didn't want to see. 'Was there anything else? – Did she say anything more?'

I stalled and looked up at Smithy, who stared back at me, eyes widening.

The Boss caught the interchange between us, and that wary look came back to his face. 'What aren't you telling me, Detective?'

God, what did I say? Was this even the right time? Should I? I looked back at Smithy and he gave a small shrug.

'You might as well let them know, Sam.'

I looked back at the two faces that were now fixed on mine. One who had already been through so much and had had to relive the trauma of her past; one who with all good intent had opened this miserable can of worms.

'I'm so sorry, but before she died, she confessed to the murder of Mel Smythe...' I paused before delivering the final blow. 'And not just that. She also confessed to the murder, twenty-five years ago, of her husband – your dad. Of Mark Freeman.'

Felicity let out a strangled 'No.'
There were no words to express the look on The Boss's face.

CHAPTER 51

My darling Felicity and Callum,

The last few weeks have been hell in so many ways. But I have held on to my secret for long enough.

There is no easy way to say this, but I killed your father. I didn't mean for him to die, I promise. I'd found out he was having an affair, and I was angry and hurt. So that night, the night he died, I pretended to be unwell after the service and went home to lie down. But then I snuck out and went back to the church to challenge him about the affair. And I ended up doing something very, very stupid. Something I have regretted for the rest of my life.

I also killed Mel Smythe. She was an evil woman who was trying to blackmail me. She told me she had been outside the church that night and saw Dad and me struggling on the steps of the church. She said she saw me cause Dad's death. I don't know why she didn't tell the police all those years ago. In many ways I wish she had. She was always a strange woman. Then recently, she somehow found out I was sick. She managed to contact me and threatened that if I didn't give her money she would wait until I was dead and then tell everyone that you, Callum, had killed your father. I still don't know why she would do something so terrible. But I couldn't trust her, and I couldn't let there be any chance that you paid the price for what I had done, Callum. So I killed her. And that I do not regret.

Staring death in the face provides clarity – you see what is truly important.

Please forgive me. I am at peace now.

Tell my beautiful grandchildren I love them.

I am sorry I didn't say goodbye.

I love you both with all my heart.

Mum

xxx

CHAPTER 52

I stared down at the note. For such a light and delicate object, it carried a gravitas that far outweighed its mass. I looked back up at the expectant line of faces on the other side of the table. They seemed to be awaiting my comment.

'And this is definitely Yvonne's handwriting?' I asked.

'Yes, it's definitely Mum's,' he said. His hands were shoved into his jeans pockets and he was swaying from side to side.

A little over twelve hours ago I had been informing a distraught Callum of the death of his mother. And I thought he'd looked bad then. Clearly not much sleep had been had in that household last night. The same could be said for the other two people in the room; they looked like they'd been washed out and wrung through a mangle. Felicity Johns' bloodshot eyes were evidence of the amount of crying that had been going on. The Boss stood beside her, pale, tight-lipped and silent.

'I'm going to have to ask for a sample of her writing for the forensic document examiners,' I said. 'Do you have any cards or letters we can use as a comparison?'

'She liked popping little letters and notes in the post. I'll have some at home.'

'Thanks, Felicity,' I said.

'Me too,' Callum said. 'She did that all the time.'

After the evening I'd had, I'd been looking forward to a relaxed morning, taking Amelia to daycare and a late start at work involving coffee. God knows I needed it. But fate was against me, so after getting the phone call, reorganising the drop-off with Paul and a mad scramble, here I was at nine in the morning standing in Yvonne Freeman's house in the presence of her devastated children.

'Who was the first to arrive – to see the note?'

'That was us,' Felicity replied. 'Greg and I arrived at around eight-thirty, wasn't it?' She looked at The Boss for confirmation and he nodded. 'We'd arranged to meet Callum here so we could talk about arrangements for Mum, get our head around everything, take care of the cat, deal with all that kind of thing.'

There was certainly a lot to have to get to grips with, for all of them.

'And the note was sitting here on the table, like this. No one has touched it?'

'Oh come on, Detective, do you really think I'm that stupid? Of course we didn't bloody touch it,' DI Johns said, his voice a growl. Indignation had drawn him out of his silence. 'As soon as we found it, I rang the station and reported it.'

I could feel the tension ramp up in the room. Emotions were high.

'I was certain you wouldn't have touched anything, but you know I had to ask. Procedure,' I said.

I waited a few beats for The Boss's indignation to deflate a little.

'When I called around yesterday the neighbour said your mother had asked her to look after the cat. As far as you're aware she hasn't been in to feed it? Hasn't disturbed anything?' Said cat was nowhere to be seen.

'No, I don't think so,' Felicity said. 'Lois has my number, so if she'd been in and seen this sitting on the table, she'd have called me straight away.'

Last night, despite feeling shattered, physically and emotionally, my brain was amped and sleep had not come easy. I had spent a fair amount of the night replaying those last moments with Yvonne over and over. Beating myself up about my decision not to try and resuscitate her. Had I made the right call? Was it my call to make? And I couldn't help but wonder if I'd heard her correctly. Or had I misinterpreted Yvonne's deathbed confession? Had it been real or the drug-addled ramblings of a dying woman? Yet here in the cold light of day was confirmation of her testimony, written when she was in full command of her faculties. Written with the intention of being found. For Felicity and Callum it also erased any hope that there had been some kind of warped mistake – that in fact their mother hadn't been responsible for the death of their father, that some other monster had murdered him. That hope had been shattered. Their mother had killed their father. Her confession was sitting indelibly before us, in elegant black ink on cream paper.

CHAPTER 53

The mood back at the station was a weird mixture of jubilance and deflation. There was some of the elation that came with the solving of a case, but it came hand in hand with the knowledge it seriously affected one of our own, no matter he was an arsehole much of the time. There was also the discomfort of having the cases cracked by the confession of a dead woman, rather than by our own systematic investigation. This wasn't where it ended though. We now had to provide the evidence that supported her claims.

One piece of that evidence had been confirmed this morning, and I was having difficulty getting my head around it.

'Can you repeat that, please?'

'Surveillance footage from a private home a hundred metres further up the road shows Yvonne Freeman walking in the direction of Mel Smythe's boarding house at 12.30pm, and then shows her returning at 12.50pm.'

'And you're absolutely sure it's her?' I asked Otto.

'See for yourself.' Once again, a collection of us huddled around Otto's screen to watch security footage. The angle was from high above, looking down past a small front yard and picket fence to the footpath and street beyond, but even so, there was no mistaking Yvonne Freeman as she made her way past, and then, fast-forward, made her way back to what I assumed was her car. I noted she carried a large handbag, which could easily have held the size of knife she'd brought along for the visit. There were no shops in the vicinity of the boarding house. And it wasn't on her way from her home to somewhere important. There was no good reason for her to be there other than to visit Mel Smythe.

'Jesus,' Paul said. 'If those timestamps are accurate, you must have missed her by minutes, Sam.'

The thought had been the first thing to cross my mind. My body gave an involuntary shudder, and I closed my eyes to try and blot out the mental images of the scene I'd discovered in Mel Smythe's room. Her slumped body in the armchair, the blood, the smell, how she had felt warm and heavy as I tried to drag her to the floor, as I tried to bring her back from death.

Paul caught the shudder and placed his hand on my shoulder. 'You okay?' he asked.

'I've been struggling to believe that Yvonne Freeman killed Mel Smythe. That a woman who was small, frail and terminally ill could have the strength and the impetus to stab someone else to death. The sheer violence of it. That would be a monumental act for someone who was young and fit, let alone a woman of her age. So a part of me hadn't believed her confession that she killed either of them. It just seemed implausible. No, impossible.' I indicated towards the screen. 'But here is hard evidence that she was in the vicinity at the time. It's forced me to rethink my whole opinion of the woman, what she was capable of. That she killed Mel Smythe – that she killed them both.'

'That's understandable,' Smithy said. 'And I don't blame you for thinking that way. All of us have probably had similar thoughts running through our heads. And this footage isn't absolute proof, but it does add pieces to the puzzle. It's too early for any results from ESR's forensic examination from the boarding house, but given this video, I suspect it will only confirm her presence at the scene.'

We mulled that over for a while.

'I suppose in a way there's a certain consistency here,' Sonia added. 'In all three deaths, including Mrs Freeman's, there has been some kind of a knife involved – a stabbing.'

She had a point. It was an underlying theme, even if the type and size of the blades varied in the first two instances. We'd have to wait on the postmortem report for the third.

'Mark Freeman's murder still troubles me, though,' I said. 'If she had killed him, the way she went about it was incredibly risky: going home after the service and then sneaking back out to return to the church to do the deed. She could have been spotted at any time or even run into her own children as they returned to the house.'

'Well, she *was* spotted, wasn't she?' Paul said. 'According to what she told you, and what she wrote in the letter, she was seen by Mel Smythe. So, all didn't go to plan. Still doesn't explain why Mel didn't report it at the very outset though – why she kept that crucial piece of information a secret.'

'No, it doesn't. Everything about this whole case seems to come back to people keeping secrets from each other, and from the police, for whatever warped, self-preserving, overly loyal or screwed-up reason. And no one at any point in the first investigation, or in my recent ones, mentioned anything about Mark Freeman having an affair, not even a suspicion. In fact, when I queried the possibility, it was adamantly denied by a number of people.'

'It does provide a motive, though,' Smithy said.

'One as old as the hills,' Otto added.

'Yeah, but motive enough to kill someone on the steps of a church? Surely you'd start by having a grown-up conversation at home,' I said. 'I mean, Paul, if you decided to have a raging affair with Sonia here, I'd talk to you about it first in the privacy of our own home before I cut your balls off.'

Paul winced; the others smiled.

'Maybe she didn't want to have that conversation at home, where the kids could overhear? Decided it would be better somewhere that was neutral territory,' Paul went on.

'St Paul's was hardly neutral territory. It was his domain,' I said.

'True. But think about it: if you found out your husband was having an affair and wanted to challenge him about it, particularly when he was a man of the cloth, wouldn't the church be perfect?' Paul said, arms waving now. 'Drive home the "thou shalt not commit adultery" thing, in the sanctity of his own church. How symbolic would that be?'

'It would be a nice touch. But there's a difference between confronting someone and demanding a conversation, and turning up to the party with a knife. That smacks of premeditation.'

'That's true,' Smithy said. 'Not many people carry around a knife as a matter of course.'

'Sam does,' Paul piped up. I gave him a look.

'You do?' Smithy turned to me.

Actually, I did. Right from childhood I'd always carried a multi-tool pocket knife. My dad had given me my first Swiss Army knife for my tenth birthday, and I'd never looked back. One lived permanently in my handbag in case of emergencies, but I didn't carry it in my pocket, despite the title.

'I carry a multi-tool. You never know when you might need it. But to be fair, I use the pliers far more often than the knife.'

'Okay, so maybe she did regularly carry a knife, in case of emergencies. We'd have to ask her kids,' Smithy said. 'Unfortunately, in this instance, it would appear she used it to stab her husband.'

'But by her own testimony, Yvonne Freeman said she didn't intend to kill him,' Sonia said.

'Then what did she intend to do by stabbing him? Send him a little warning?' I asked. 'Confession or not, the whole thing just seems very strange to me.'

'Unfortunately, we can't ask her that, can we?' Smithy said. 'All we can go on is the fact that before she died this woman confessed to the murders – and not once, but twice. Until we find evidence to the contrary, we have to consider that she's telling the truth. And given the high likelihood that she did murder Mel Smythe, it looks like she did, in fact, as she admitted, kill her husband too. Unpalatable as it feels, the case is closed.'

CHAPTER 54

This case was feeling like a post-curry acid stomach. Despite everyone else's confidence that the cases were solved, that we knew who was responsible, it didn't sit right with me. Like all things that didn't sit right, sometimes you just had to walk it off. So, walk it off I did.

Inevitably, my feet took me back to The Octagon, and the gates of St Paul's Cathedral. I stood there, on the threshold, not quite able to bring myself to cross over into the grounds, to mount those steps. My brain auto-played the tragic scene from last night, and I wrapped my arms around myself trying to ward off both the images and the cold. Too soon. So instead, I moved away to the side and sat on the bench seat at the bottom of Stuart Street. From there I had a view down over The Octagon and its afternoon hustle-bustle, while my back was to the cathedral. But try as I might, I couldn't help but keep checking over my shoulder, succumbing to the prickling feeling on the back of my neck. It was like the grand building was glowering down at me.

I lasted for around two minutes before deciding, nope, this wasn't going to work.

Back on my feet, I started ambling my way up Stuart Street. I was beginning to accept that Yvonne Freeman had most likely killed Mel Smythe, but I still could not reconcile myself with the thought that she'd killed her husband. There were too many things that didn't ring true for me, that just didn't add up.

First there was her out-of-the-blue revelation that her husband had been having an affair. It seemed a strange thing to come out with after all this time and had completely blind-sided her children. There had been no mention of it in the initial investigation, and everyone I had interviewed recently – even Mel Smythe – had attested to the couple's utter devotion to each other. But, to counter those thoughts, if it wasn't true – if he hadn't been having an affair – why would she lie about his infidelity? The claim would forever taint Reverend Freeman's reputation – with his children and his congregation.

Then there was the whole 'leaving the church and sneaking back' thing. That just seemed way too risky and way too complicated to pull off. This wasn't a Hollywood movie, this had been real life, in the midst of a storm in the middle of winter. Sure, saying you had a migraine would mean the family would assume that once home you'd retreated to your room for a lie down, but still. If she had concocted that great plan she would have had to walk home, turn the lights and heaters on, so it looked like she was there, wait hidden in her room until Felicity and Callum were home so she didn't meet them on the way back and to be certain that Mark Freeman was alone at the cathedral, then sneak out of the house unnoticed by the kids, high-tail it down the hill, confront and kill her husband, high-tail it back up the hill to the house, sneak in, dry off, then appear from her room, announcing how worried she was that Freeman wasn't back yet and sending Callum down to check on him. All in the space of, what, an hour?

Lost in my thoughts, I'd trudged up Stuart Street and was almost level with the cathedral carpark entrance when I became aware of a gaggle of boys making their way down the hill towards me. With the obliviousness of teenage boys set free from school for the day, they occupied the whole of the footpath, chatting and joking, weaving and jostling with each other and taking no heed of anyone else. It was clear none of them was moving aside, so I stopped still and braced myself as the tall, gangly wave engulfed me. But like water encountering a boulder in a river, they surged around me and I emerged out the other side, miraculously untouched. I resisted the urge to deliver a passive aggressive 'gee, thanks, guys' and instead muttered 'little fuckers' under my breath as I continued up the hill. I had to remind myself that teenage boys could be clueless, especially in a herd, but then, there was something endearing about their youthful energy and cheerfulness.

At that moment and with that thought, something went clunk in my mind and I stopped dead, turned around and stared after them.

Callum Freeman would have been about the age of those boys the night his father died. The thought that had been hovering at the fringes of my consciousness, the thing that had been bugging me about Yvonne Freeman's confession jumped into focus. She had sent Callum down to the church on that horrendous, stormy night to check on his father. If we were to believe her, that would mean she deliberately sent her teenage child to discover the body of his dad. No way. Who would knowingly do that to their child: set them up for a lifetime of trauma and pain? No one was that callous. In my mind that meant only one thing. She can't have known Mark Freeman was dead.

She'd lied.

She'd confessed to something she didn't do.

Actually, she'd done something way more significant than confessing: she'd sacrificed her life and her reputation – and her husband's reputation too. She was willing to go to her grave having people believe she had committed the unthinkable. And there was only one reason I could think of that would make someone take such extreme measures – make them willing to pay such a huge cost.

'Oh, Yvonne,' I said out loud, eyes welling up with the enormity of it all.

She was protecting someone. The true murderer. And they were someone precious to her heart.

She had killed Mel Smythe to protect them, and she'd confessed to killing her own husband to protect them. There was only one thing that would compel you to do that, and now I had a child of my own, I could understand the lengths you would go to for that kind of love.

Yvonne Freeman lied and sacrificed everything to take it to her grave because she knew people wouldn't dare to question the last words of a dying woman. And she knew we couldn't cross-examine dead people.

Fuck.

I turned and ran back down the hill.

CHAPTER 55

My hand reached out and pressed the doorbell, my heart thudding in my chest. This was the last thing I wanted to be doing.

After what felt an interminable amount of time the door swung open.

'Now what?' The Boss didn't look impressed to see us.

'Detective Inspector,' I said. 'We need to talk with Felicity. Can we come in, please?'

He looked from me to Smithy and back again. 'Don't you think she's been through enough today? Can this wait till tomorrow?'

'I'm afraid it can't. We need to see her now.'

He looked to Smithy for confirmation, like he was the one calling the shots. I hated the way he automatically undermined my authority in any situation. This wasn't the time for gripes though.

'I supposed you'd better come in then. She's down in the kitchen.'

We stepped into the entrance and waited while he shut the door and then led the way through the house.

'This better be important,' he said.

He didn't know the half of it.

Felicity Johns was sitting at the dining-room table, drinking from a mug of tea. She looked up, saw who it was and slowly lowered the mug to the table.

'Oh,' she said, her voice cautious. 'What's happened now?'

Understandable question. It was getting to the point that we were only ever the harbingers of bad news. This occasion was no different. The wee dog, Gemma, must have picked up on the undercurrent as she got out of her basket and moved over to join her ma.

I felt sick to my stomach. After everything that had happened, after all that had been revealed about her past and how she'd been treated, this didn't feel like justice. But it had to be done. There was no point messing around.

'Felicity ... Felicity Johns.' I took a deep breath. 'I'm afraid we are here to arrest you for the murder of Mark Freeman.' Her jaw dropped and her face went pale. 'I will let you know your rights. You have the right to remain silent. You have—'

I didn't get any further before a bellow of 'What?' came from behind me. A hand clamped onto my shoulder and spun me around, and I was confronted by a face incandescent with rage.

'What the fuck do you mean coming in here and making that ridiculous accusation. You have no right to—'

'Greg,' Smithy's voice was quiet and steady. 'You need to unhand Detective Shephard, and you need to calm down.'

The hand didn't budge. Instead, his other hand rose and pointed at Smithy, gesturing as he spoke. 'There is no fucking way Felicity killed her father. For heaven's sake, you have a written confession for his death. What the hell do you think you're playing at?'

I tried to turn my body around to look to Felicity, but the grip on my shoulder tightened to the point of discomfort and held me in place.

Smithy caught my grimace. 'Greg, you really need to take your hand off my officer right now.' His voice had an ominous undertone.

'And you,' DI Johns directed at me again. 'You said you were there, and you heard her say that she did it. You heard Yvonne say it.'

'Greg, don't.' I could hear the tremor in Felicity's voice.

'I'm going to count to three,' said Smithy, 'and if you haven't taken your hand off her, I will remove it for you.'

'What evidence do you have? Tell me, what possible evidence? There was none back then, and there's none now. Because you know what I think? I think this is a stitch-up. You are framing her on purpose.'

'Don't be bloody ridiculous,' I said. 'And let me go.' I lifted my hand and grabbed his wrist, trying to push it away.

'One.'

'Because you've always had it in for me, haven't you? And this is your sick way of getting back at me.' His anger had made him oblivious to the warnings.

'Greg, stop.' Her tremor had elevated to panic.

'Two.'

'You are going to pay for this, Shephard. I will make sure you never work in the force again, you little bitch.' By now his grip was vicelike and pushing my shoulder down.

'Three.'

Smithy moved with surprising speed, chopping into the crook of The Boss's elbow and grabbing the offending hand as it jumped up. I leapt back as fast as I could, before there was any chance of reattachment, but I needn't have worried, because DI Johns had lost all sense of control and had a new target to direct his anger at.

'Get your fucking hands off me.' He threw a punch into Smithy's gut. Smithy's reaction was to push him back against the wall, hard. The picture he rammed into twisted crookedly and cracks spider-webbed across the glass.

Oh, Jesus. Where they were matched in height, Smithy had at least twenty kilograms on The Boss, but The Boss had the brawn of someone who went to the gym and he was fuelled with rage. And as they started to trade blows on each other I knew this had to stop before someone got hurt.

I heard Felicity's scream of 'no, Greg, no,' before I launched in with my own 'cut it out you two, right now.'

That had no effect whatsoever. I could see there was only one thing for it. In a moment when they paused for breath I forced my way between them, my back towards Smithy, hands stretched out, trying to push Johns away. But even as I wedged myself in I realised with horror that a swing had already started its course and my eyes tracked its journey straight for me. Oh Fuck. My face exploded with pain as the fist connected with my jaw. The force whiplashed my head back into Smithy's chest and stars filled my vision. My body felt leaden and I couldn't fight gravity as I slumped to the floor, the taste of blood flooding my mouth. I heard Felicity's scream and the scrape of a chair being pushed out. My eyes raised. Above me the two men were still going at it, trading blows. If I didn't scramble out of there I was likely to get stood on, because God knows they weren't paying any attention to me. I threw my arms around my head in an attempt to protect myself and managed to wriggle some of the way before a pair of arms wrapped themselves around me and pulled me back more.

'Stop it, stop it, stop it!' Felicity yelled, cradling me in her arms. 'Greg, stop it. Don't do this.'

Her pleas fell on deaf ears.

'Greg, don't.'

And finally at a volume and pitch, words no one could ignore.

'Greg, stop it. I did it! It was me. I killed him!' Tears choked her voice.

Both men stopped dead, staring. The silence only broken by their panting.

'What do you mean?'

'They're right. I'm so sorry, but it was me.'

The Boss's expression transformed from one of fury, to disbelief, to stricken.

'No,' he said.

I could feel her head nodding, her chin rubbing against my hair.

'Yes. It was me. I killed my own dad.'

EPILOGUE

There was nothing quite like a relaxed Saturday morning stroll at the beach in the sun. The fact that we were all wrapped up in jackets and hats and the temperature was seven degrees C didn't stop us from enjoying ice cream from the Patti's & Cream truck. It was safer than attempting hot chips, given the number of seagulls hovering around, waiting to dive-bomb us and pilfer the goods. Paul and I walked slowly, arm in arm, to the rhythmic wash of waves against the rocks and sea wall of the St Clair Esplanade. Several paces ahead, Mum and Maggie ambled, chatting away. The only thing missing was a dog. We had to make do with admiring other people's scruffy mutts, of which there were plenty. A little cold never deterred a Dunedinite. I supposed we were an odd kind of a family grouping. Mum had insisted on pushing Amelia in the buggy, and I smiled at the wonky trajectory as she manoeuvred it one-handed, the other being occupied by classic rum and raisin in a waffle cone. The buggy was almost as tall as she was. In contrast, Maggie looked positively Amazonian, if Amazons were into purple vintage woollen coats and crocheted berets. It felt like a perfect moment.

'You know, I think for the first time in my life I actually feel sorry for DI Johns,' Paul said.

The moment evaporated.

'Don't you?' he asked.

I took a second to enjoy the flavour of the salted caramel in my mouth. The cold helped to take away some of the ache in my jaw. The Boss was dealing with the discovery that his wife had killed her father and was in custody, that his mother-in-law, as well as murdering Mel Smythe, had taken her own life in an attempt to shoulder all the blame to protect her daughter, and it had all pretty much stemmed from a teenage pregnancy that his wife hadn't told him about. It had been a tough week in the Johns household, to put it mildly.

'Yeah, I guess I do,' I said. 'And I can't help but feel a little bad, because if he'd never asked me to reopen the Freeman case, then this massive fallout would never have happened.'

'Ah, you funny thing. You're not feeling guilty, are you?' He gave me a squeeze.

'A little.'

'You shouldn't. The seeds of all this were sown a long time ago. Mark Freeman didn't extend the compassion and forgiveness he showed to his congregation to his own family, and ultimately he reaped what he sowed.' It was quite a succinct summary really, if you removed all of the very poor and murderous decisions people made along the way.

'It didn't mean that he should have died for it.'

'I don't think that was ever Felicity's intention.'

Outrage and shock at her father's words and his treatment of her, combined with an impulsive moment of teenage shame and anger had had devastating results – results she had never envisioned.

'It might not have been,' I said, 'but she's still got to live with the consequences now, and so does her family, and The Boss.' It felt very much a case of the sins of the father being visited on the child. 'Do you think they'll discipline DI Johns for the fight – for this?' I indicated to my rather bruised and still swollen face.

'Purple suits you, but not on your jaw. You're lucky it isn't broken.'

'I don't feel that lucky,' I said. There was no escaping the ache.

'You're not going to press charges for assault?'

'I don't want to and I don't think Smithy does either. But it remains to be seen if charges will be laid.'

'They'll take into consideration the circumstances, which were pretty extreme.'

'I hope so,' I said, and I meant it. 'He's going to have enough to deal with supporting Felicity.'

Running into the gaggle of teenage boys walking down Stuart Street that day had made the penny drop that it must have been Felicity who Yvonne was protecting, not Callum. When Mel attempted to blackmail Yvonne over exactly who she had witnessed kill Reverend Freeman that night, Yvonne decided she couldn't risk Mel talking so had taken the extraordinary step of killing her. But what if she had already blabbed? The safest thing Yvonne could do was to make up the story that Mel had used Callum as leverage for the blackmail to illustrate what a despicable woman she was and throw doubt out there if someone else came forward: 'Oh, Mel said it was Felicity' could be countered with 'but Mel told *me* it was Callum.' That would cast more shade on Mel's reliability, and her state of mind, especially as people's opinion of the woman wasn't that flash anyway. Even if Yvonne had harboured suspicions of who might have killed her husband, hearing Mel state it was Felicity must have been a hell of a shock – and heartbreaking. But in a final act of love, she undertook desperate measures to protect her daughter.

Felicity had pleaded guilty to the charge of manslaughter and was due to be sentenced in the next few weeks. My hope was that the sentencing judge would show leniency and take into consideration her age at the time and the circumstances around the event. Both Callum and Aaron had provided statements about that awful night in the cathedral. Surely that would count for something.

To me, one of the saddest elements of this whole awful affair was that Yvonne Freeman's warped attempt at keeping her daughter's secret, and sacrificing herself for her, had failed at the last. After everything she had done – murdering Mel Smythe and then sacrificing her life and reputation for her daughter's sake – it was to no avail. My only consolation was that she never lived to know she had failed and that Felicity would suffer the consequences of her youthful actions.

For Callum and Felicity, they also had to come to terms with the fact their mother could have committed such an awful crime as the killing of Mel Smythe. It still hadn't been confirmed, but the evidence so far was pointing that way. None of us ever wanted to think a loved one was capable of that, no matter what the motive was.

I looked ahead to the stout little figure happily pushing her granddaughter. Did I think my mother was capable of killing someone? Well, that was a moot point.

'You know, I can't help but think none of this would have happened if that family actually talked with each other, trusted each other. If Felicity had gone to her mother first about the pregnancy and talked it through, and just weathered the inevitable shock and accusations. Had just trusted that her mother would have her back. And if they had then gone to her father together, calmer heads would surely have prevailed. There wouldn't have been the fireworks, the recriminations, and the whole bloody tragedy. All that keeping secrets in the misguided belief that they were protecting each other or shielding each other from harm – my God, it just made it all a thousand times worse.'

'Yup,' he said. Succinct.

'Please, don't ever hold out on me on anything important in your life because you worry about what I might think, or that it might hurt me. I'd rather know.'

'You might come to regret that statement when I tell you the unvarnished truth about absolutely everything.'

'Well, you can apply some discretion.'

'Have you ever known me to do that?'

'Good point.' I stopped walking and looked up into his face. 'I am serious though.'

He bent down and kissed my forehead. 'The same applies to you too, young lady. You can tell me anything. You know that, right?'

There were a few things that I had been holding back that needed to be shared. I don't know why it had taken me so long, but it was time. I could honestly say I was finally ready to trust him.

I gave him a smile.

'Yeah, I do.'

ACKNOWLEDGEMENTS

They say it takes a village to raise a child, and, likewise, it takes a community to raise a book baby.

Where would I be without my fabulous publisher and friend Karen Sullivan? Thank you for continuing to support this Kiwi gal on the other side of the world. The Orenda Books team is incredible. Huge thank you to West Camel for your thoughtful editing and for knocking *Prey* into shape, I really value your input and expertise. Thank you to Cole Sullivan, Anne Cater and Danielle Price for getting my book out there and noticed.

Craig Sisterson, you are a star and have done so much for New Zealand literature. You have brought our crime fiction to the world and we are all eternally grateful. Thank you so much for getting my work out there and being so supportive.

When writing crime fiction you always want to make sure you don't stuff up the facts – trust me, your readers let you know. My immense thanks to David Checketts and Dom Flatley for the police and justice-system advice.

I was brought up in the Presbyterian and Methodist Church, so needed help when it came to the intricacies of the Anglican Church. Thank you to the Reverend Jo Baxter Fielding for your help and advice. I am always mindful when it comes to setting a terrible act in a public place loved by so many. Thank you to St Paul's Cathedral. It is a beautiful space in the heart of Dunedin, so do visit it if you are in the city.

I always try to talk with people to get my details right, but all creative licence taken and stuff-ups are completely my own.

Thank you to the Janet Frame Literary Trust for permission to use the quote from Janet's plaque in The Octagon Writers' Walk. The quote is from her poem 'Sunday Afternoon at Two O'clock' (1967).

The writing and reading community is incredible, warm and supportive. It still blows me away that people who aren't relatives or friends buy my books. Thank you so much for enjoying my scribblings and recommending them to others. I am grateful to every one of you.

My family is my rock and I am so thankful for their support and belief. Glenn: hugely appreciate you being king of the BBQ and cooking up a storm while I hid away and wrote my little heart out. To Riley and Corey, your good-hearted jibes and checking in on my procrastination levels were always appreciated.